Child
Left
Behind

Seismic Press

ISBN 978-0-9824928-0-2   (Third Edition 2013)

Comments or requests can be sent to:
seismicpress@gmail.com

The future belongs to those who
believe in the beauty of their dreams.
- Eleanor Roosevelt

Julio C. Arauz

STEVEN MARK PINTO

CHILD
LEFT
BEHIND

First in the Harley Justin Butler Series

SEISMIC PRESS

Nicholl Park, Richmond, Ca. October 15, 2007

Her face was pressed hard to the earth. Blades of fescue grass forced their way through parted lips. She almost got this close as a child. Those endless summers crawling around the backyard, dreamily analyzing insects marching off to fantasy rendezvous. It was her only defense. Now the images began to move faster and no single thought could be cornered, like from the delirium of a high fever but there was no fever. Opening presents at Christmas. Horseback riding on the beach with dad in Acapulco. The thoughts wouldn't stick. Her innocence was her only defense. Under the water, having a breath holding contest with her little brother Juanito. No exit for the air. Consciousness slipping. Suddenly, the pressure was gone and she could breathe again.

She lay still not daring to look left or right. Was he gone? Why hadn't he finished the job? The cool breeze on her buttocks reminded her that she had lost her pants. Her neck was hot. The nylon rope burn stung deeply.

"Oh, sweet pain! I'm still alive," she thought.

Then she heard the footsteps. Glancing through the blades she could make out his outline, baseball bat in hand. She rolled over twice and tried to stand. The first blow hit her lower back, knocking the wind out. She heard his deep breath, then a whooshing sound, then a thud. Cranium open, pink flesh exposed, her soft, brown eyes gazed off onto the eternal sea of darkness.

CHAPTER 1

By the time I realized that I had forgotten to turn off the ring volume, it was too late. The dim light flickering in from the edges of the curtain told me it was still too early to get up. At least, too early for someone who had consumed seven caipirinhas the night before. After three unwanted rings, the standard message and the inevitable beep came a voice all too familiar.

"This is Randy from homicide. Sorry to have to call you at home so early Harley but it's important. Was wondering if I could drop by your office sometime today to discuss the Vargas case? I'd appreciate it if you could call me back as soon as you get this message."

I needed more sleep. That was for sure. Did he need something from the files? What could be so important about the Vargas case that Sgt. Wilson would call me this early in the morning? I wasn't even working that case. Private detectives are often hired by families of crime victims but not directly by the cops except in rare instances when special expertise is needed. The family of the Vargas girl hadn't contacted me. My fatigue quickly overcame my curiosity and I fell back into a deep slumber.

A powerful need to urinate awoke me from a vague dream. This time, I could see bright light seeping in around the edges of the curtains signaling that the day was well under way. I waddled to the bathroom to relieve myself. Turned out my urethra somehow became sewed shut during the night. Light yellow streams of urine spurted out in all directions. My left foot, the wall, the ceramic tiles, all victims of the built up pressure. I wiped up the mess with a washrag from the bath.

"Great way to start the day," I mused to myself.

Visions of the previous night's celebration entered my mind as I gargled a swig of Listerine from the bottle cap. Rosanna Dornelas insisted that she hold a celebration in my honor at Fonda's, a tapas bar in Albany. She had hired me to investigate her ex-husband's finances. A mother of a three year-old, she was having a hard time making ends meet. Her husband Marco suddenly stopped making child support payments claiming he had lost it all on bad business dealings with his partner in Rio.

4

Turned out his textile company's bankruptcy was a sham. 95% of the revenues he received from Brasil Imports, his privately owned corporation, were funneled to an offshore account on the Isle of Mann. Marco was hiding a beachfront property in Ipanema, a fazenda in Parana, and a nightclub in Salvador, Bahia. He was living high on the hog in Brazil while his wife cleaned the homes of the wealthy in Piedmont. Rosanna suspected deceitfulness in the bankruptcy and hired me to track down the money.

I had met her three years ago at the Canto do Brasil, a Brazilian restaurant on Franklin St. in the city. I was with a friend named Klaus, a German national who worked at a local biotech company. He was married to a Brazilian lady who performed in a samba show at the restaurant. Klaus had no trouble getting me to tag along. I had lived in Recife, a city in the Northeast of Brazil working as a teacher years earlier and fell in love with the place. Whether it be a samba show, a concert or a movie, I was a sucker for almost anything Brazilian. We ordered feijoada completa, the Brazilian national dish as an entree and caipirinihas to wash it down. Caipirinhas consist of cachaca, white Brazilian rum made from sugar cane, limejuice, and a heaping of sugar. It doesn't take many of these to modify one's perception of the world.

A couple of Brazilian girls at the next table struck my eye, which in turn inspired me to practice my rusty Portuguese. I was instantly charmed by the one who called herself Rosanna. I introduced myself and was happy to learn that Rosanna was a native of Recife, the same city I had once lived in. If I had had to guess, I would have said that she was a mixture of 40% Amazon Indian, 50% Portuguese royalty with a little African sprinkled in. The way she drew me in with her deep, dark eyes had a hypnotic effect.

I found out that she had just finalized a divorce and was out celebrating. She didn't go into the details and I didn't care. We danced a few times between the tables. Occasionally, Klaus would say something dirty to the girls in German accented Portuguese that made them blush and giggle.

"Eu estou muito feliz te conhecer Harley," (I'm so happy to meet you Harley) Rosanna said with a warm expression.

We talked about Recife, the Brazilian scene in the Bay Area and our failed love lives until the manager said they were closing up for the night. We all exited the Canto do Brasil at the same time. Although I was tempted, I didn't ask her to go home with me. Instead, I slipped her my business card.

"What's a private dick?" she asked in beautifully Brazilian accented English staring at my card. "Are you a gigolo?" she asked smiling from ear to ear.

"Nao, sou investigador particular," (No, I'm a private detective) I responded in Portuguese.

She looked puzzled but then jotted down her telephone number on a napkin and stuck it in my front pocket. We kissed, said our goodbyes, and began walking down opposite directions of Franklin Street on a cool San Franciscan night.

I was certain I would see her again soon but was wrong. The next morning I checked my front shirt pocket for her phone number and it was gone. It must have fallen out somewhere between Franklin St. and my home in El Cerrito. I would have to wait for her to call me. Sadly, that didn't happen until two and a half years later when she needed my services.

It was a warm evening in June. I was boiling pasta when the phone rang.

"Voce lembra de mim?" (Do you remember me?) the warm, feminine voice inquired.

Even though we had only spoken for a few hours two and a half years ago, I immediately recognized Rosanna's voice.

She began speaking in very fluid, though still beautifully Brazilian-accented English. It was clear that she had learned a great deal since we had last met.

"I got a big problem and need your help, Harley. That immoral goat, ex-husband of mine is pretending to be bankrupt to avoid alimony and child support payments. I've heard from friends in Brazil that he is living well and even has a farm in Parana where he throws wild parties every weekend."

I shifted my head down to hold the phone to my ear while transferring the pasta to the strainer in the sink.

"I'm really sorry to hear that. Is there anything I can do to help?" I asked sheepishly.

"You are a private dick, right?" she giggled and then continued.

"You speak Portuguese. You've lived in Brazil. You understand Brazilian culture. Could you help me track down my ex-husband's money? I've had to take a job as a house cleaner in

6

Piedmont just to survive. Eu nao aguento mais." (I can't take it anymore) For some reason she reverted to Portuguese to emphasize how frustrated she was.

"I can pay you some now and the rest when you get results," she negotiated.

We spent the next two hours going over the history of the relationship and in the end I agreed to take the case. It wasn't out of pity or an easy chance to get close to her. She had been cheated plain and simple and I thought I could help.

After she'd been my client for about six months, I began to make serious progress on her case. There were many times when Rosanna would make subtle amorous advances towards me but I always kept a professional distance. I take the private detectives' code of ethics seriously. Having sex with a client is a serious offense.

That said the client detective relationship in this case was very different from what I was used to. I couldn't wait to update her on the progress being made. If she was late with a payment, I didn't care. The case consumed me even though the time I spent on it could have been used helping clients that paid more.

In the end, the results of my detective work paid off. Her ex-husband Marco was now in jail for tax evasion in Brazil and Rosanna was awarded the leftover scraps. When the Brazilian government was through rewarding itself with 3 million dollars, these scraps represented about $400,000 U.S., paid to Rosanna Dornelas resident of Richmond and house cleaner for the rich.

Needless to say, Rosanna was pleased with the results and the celebration at Fonda's was to show her appreciation. Many of her friends were there and Rosanna paid for all. When everyone left, we ordered one more caipirinha and she and I sat next to each other quietly talking. It entered my mind that as of last week, she was no longer my client.

"Voce e legal para um gringo Harley," (You're alright for a gringo), she whispered in my ear.

This was followed by her tongue, which she forced as deep as a tongue could possibly go into my right ear. The sensation was incredible. I could feel her heart beating fast on my arm. The sound of her heavy breathing so close to my ear drum sent shivers down my spine. She then turned to face me and with her deep dark eyes rolling with dream-like pleasure, inserted her wet tongue in my

7

mouth. I had never experienced a more satisfying kiss. The thought occurred to me that this was my first intimate moment with a woman since starting that ADD medication. Was it the drug that was making me hyper-focused on every aspect of her touch? I wasn't sure.

The wool slacks I was wearing did not do a good job of disguising my erection. This did not go unnoticed by Rosanna whose nimble tan fingers began massaging it gently. This may possibly explain the pinched urethra problem I had this morning.

I was about to explode when I noticed the men at the table next to us were staring. Rosanna didn't seem to mind but I thought it was a good time to take it elsewhere. I suggested that we go to my house in El Cerrito but she said she had to pick up her son at 11:00. It was already 11:30. She gave me one more deep kiss.

I walked her to her car. The goodbye hug lasted a good three minutes. Neither one of us wanted to be the first to release. I got into my 1970 Chevy Corvette and took the short drive home to my two-bedroom bungalow style home on Brewster St. in the El Cerrito Hills. After seven caipirinhas, I made sure I drove extra carefully.

I brushed my teeth and looked at myself in the mirror. Besides slightly tired eyes, there was little evidence of last night's party on my face. I looked younger than my 39 years. My curly dishwater blonde hair had yet to show signs of gray. My teeth were crooked but not terribly so. My long chin, an homage to my Irish and Portuguese roots.

"Where was my life going?" I thought to myself.

On the downside, I had already experienced one unhappy marriage to a Japanese woman. On the upside, I had spent several years living abroad; two years in Brazil and 5 years in Japan. Some people never get to see beyond their own backyard.

At UC Berkeley, I had been a math education major with a minor in educational technology. Since I loved to travel, the teaching profession seemed the best route. After graduation, I immediately focused my eyes on Brazil and it wasn't long until I had landed a job teaching the 6th grade at the American School in Recife.

Although I loved Brazil, the job was not always easy. The students were a combination of spoiled rich ex-pat kids mixed in

8

with maladjusted rich Brazilian kids. At the end of the day, I was happy to leave the school behind and head down to the beach.

After my contract was up, I headed back to the Bay Area and got into the substitute teaching circuit. The work was hard but helped pay the rent. While at one of the schools, I noticed a flyer on the wall in the faculty room. It was an announcement from the city of Richmond. They were looking for a goodwill ambassador to send to their sister city in Japan for three months. I interviewed for the position and was chosen.

Although I had never been a Japanophile, I enjoyed the experience in Shimada enough to want to extend my stay after the three months were up. I moved to Tokyo and immediately found a visa sponsor and job at Japan International School teaching high school English. As at the Brazilian school, the students consisted of spoiled rich ex-pat kids except this time with maladjusted Japanese rich kids mixed in. This is where I met my ex-wife Mika.

She was a high school senior at the school but had never been in my class. I sat next to her once on the bullet train on a field trip to Kyoto. We talked about our families, the school, and the differences between American and Japanese cultures. She seemed to have a romantic interest in me but it would not be worth pursuing. I took the teachers' code of ethics seriously. Having sex with a student would be a serious offense and could land one in jail.

A couple of years later, I was at a reggae bar with a friend in the Nishi Azabu district of Tokyo. To my surprise, in walked Mika. It took me a few seconds to recognize her. At school, she was always in uniform. Except for her extroverted, aggressive behavior, there was little to distinguish her from other Japanese high school girls. Now, she was wearing fashionably torn denim and had well-manicured dreadlocks.

The concept of a Japanese Rastafarian, especially one who recently graduated from an international school in Tokyo, was hard to fully comprehend. In fact, it was so absurd I couldn't stop smiling.

"Yow mi sistren, long time nuh see," I said jokingly to break the ice.

She looked puzzled. "Ohisashiburi," (Long time no see), she responded in Japanese.

"How've you been, Mr. Butler? I see you're still in Japan."

9

"Yep. Why don't you call me, Harley? You're a big girl now. Did you enroll in college after JIS?"

"No way! College is a waste of time for girls, you know. Japanese girls go to college just to meet future husbands. No one goes there to study or to pursue a career. I couldn't think of a more foolish way to spend time," she explained.

I knew she was right. It was common knowledge that college in Japan was a mere holding tank. Most of the serious studying is done in high school in preparation for tough university entrance exams. The university you qualify for ultimately paves the way for what company you work for. There is little or no correlation between one's major and one's ultimate career. Whether you were a philosophy or history major, you would end up working as a *salaryman* for Japan Inc.

For girls, the better the university the better the chance of catching a husband who would become a *salaryman* at one of the more prestigious corporations. I respected Mika's decision to rebel from this path. But Rastafarian? Wasn't that taking the rebellion thing a little too far?

That night I took Mika home to my tiny apartment in Hatsudai in the Shibuya ward. We were drunk from way too many Bacardi and cokes. She insisted that we do it doggy style the first time, which I thought was a little unusual. But that was just the beginning. I think we tried about every position imaginable that night. It was as if we were the models for the ukiyoe classic shijuhatte (the 48 ways), a classic Japanese wood-block series from the Edo era illustrating 48 sex positions all with unique names.

We basically lived together for the next several months. She made a living designing displays for department stores and I continued teaching at JIS. She suggested that we get married since we were living together anyway and I submitted. Life was comfortable with Mika but things were about to change.

After the marriage was registered, she immediately quit her job. This disturbed me as she had made no mention of this intention beforehand. She began to stay home and watch cheesy Japanese talk shows from morning to night. It began to drive me crazy. It was clear that our marriage had become Mika's career path. I was her ticket out of Japan Inc. The problem was is that I felt cheated with the deal. She did not disclose these plans beforehand.

I would get home from work and she would be sitting in front of the TV watching Tamori on high volume. Tamori is the king of Japanese talk show TV. I began to despise Japanese pop culture. The sound of the high-pitched canned laughter from the boob tube would irritate me to the bone. I began to think of Mika as a parasite. We stopped having sex. I wanted her out of my life. We divorced after two miserable years.

The only positive thing that came out of these two years was my change of careers. Since childhood, I had a knack for solving mysteries. Had your bike stolen? Go see Harley. Lost your dog? Harley would find it. In high school, it evolved into solving auto theft and discovering whose mom had been cheating with whose dad and vice versa. I had a knack for spotting details that most would ignore.

In spite of this, the idea of becoming a detective never entered my mind. That is until my second year of marriage with Mika. Mika's grandfather had just died and had left half of his estate to Mika's mother (her father had been dead since she was three) and the other half to her older brother. Mika suspected something was terribly wrong.

Although it was tradition in Japan for the eldest son or grandson to inherit the wealth; in life her grandfather was not at all close with her older brother Taro. He was extremely close to Mika though. She visited him every Saturday while we were married and appeared genuinely affectionate towards him. Since Mika's father had died when she was still a small child, Jiji, as she called her grandfather, took over as the male role model in the family.

Mika became extremely gloomy the week he passed away and would spend a lot of time at her mother's house. One night, she came back late to our apartment sobbing uncontrollably. She had a copy of Jiji's will in her hand.

"That akuman (devil) of a brother of mine is up to no good," she exclaimed.

"What are you talking about? Did he come by your mother's today?"

"Yes. He brought this paper with him, which he said was Jiji's will. It states my mother gets half and Taro gets the other half of his entire estate."

"How could that be? He's only seen Taro once in the last five years. Can I see it?" I asked sympathetically.

11

It was on regular A4 size paper and was only three pages long. The first page stated his assets would be split 50/50 between the two. The second and third pages listed what those assets were. Each page had her grandfather's distinct inkan stamped on it and the document appeared official. An inkan is a person's seal or stamp and is used instead of signatures for most important business in Japan. The inkan are usually engraved on the end of a stick of hard wood, bone, or ivory.

I knew Mika's grandfather kept his in a locked safe in the closet in his living room. I saw him take it out once the day he co-signed our lease so we could rent our apartment. In Japan, often it's hard for foreigners to rent apartments without a Japanese co-signer.

"I just know Jiji would have never left me out of his will," sobbed Mika.

"Well, isn't it tradition for the eldest son to?"

"Fuck the eldest son!" she cut me off in the middle of the question.

Even after almost two years of marriage, Mika's directness was so unlike other Japanese that it caught me off guard.

"The answer to your question is yes and no," she elaborated.

"In the old days it was always the eldest son. In modern Japan, as you know society is changing. You have to look at things on a case-by-case basis. Often now inheritances are shared among siblings," she continued.

"I was closer to Jiji than anyone, even my mother. You know that. He didn't even have a relationship with Taro unless you call having a beer together on New Year's Day three years ago a relationship. I smell a rotten fish."

"Let me take a look at that will again," I requested.

She handed me the three-page document and I looked it over carefully. It looked like Jiji's inkan all right. I wondered if it was possible that Taro could have hired someone to try to make a replicate.

"Could you get me a copy of that apartment lease that Jiji co-signed?"

"Why do you want to see that now?" she asked with impatience.

"I want to compare the seal with that of the will's."

She opened the closet that contained our futon on the top shelf, worldly possessions on the bottom and pulled out a file cabinet from the latter. After some fumbling, she found the lease. At first glance, the seals looked identical. They both depicted stylistic characterizations of the character for hiji and kata intertwined. Hijikata was the family name of Jiji.

I grabbed a metric ruler and began taking measurements of the widths and heights of the various strokes in the characters. I still couldn't notice any differences. The two Hijikata characters were very simple. Combined they meant the earth's way. It would have been very easy for Taro to get an inkan maker to try to duplicate Jiji's.

Since we had a scanner hooked up to our computer, I scanned in both a page of the will and the page on the lease that contained his seal. I then isolated both seals and cut and pasted them into two separate Adobe Illustrator files. I juxtaposed both of these images and zoomed in on various parts. At 1000% zoom, I began noticing some subtle variations.

"The will is a forgery," I said confidently.

I proceeded to show Mika the variations I noticed.

Mika studied the screen and said, "Tomorrow we'll take this to the police. You are an amazing man Harley!"

That night I massaged Mika's back not as a lover but as a compassionate friend. She fell asleep quickly. I knew our relationship was over but wanted it to end peacefully. While lying on my futon next to Mika snoring, I made a conscious decision that night. As soon as Jiji's estate business was wrapped up, I would ask her for a divorce.

The next morning we went to the Shubuya-ward police station and showed them what I had discovered. The Japanese police were surprisingly efficient. They agreed with my findings but wanted more evidence. We all went together in a squad car to Jiji's apartment in Aoyama. They made us sit outside while they took fingerprints and made other examinations of the interior. I had told them about the safe that Jiji kept in the living room. Turned out the safe was missing.

A few days later, a search warrant was issued for Taro's apartment. Inside, they found Jiji's safe, the copied inkan, and computer files of the forged will. These all incriminated Taro and it was clear to all that he was guilty of forgery. There was evidence that Taro had unsuccessfully tried to open the combination safe. Only Jiji knew the combination.

Taro was ultimately arrested but was given a light three-month sentence. His mother begged the court for leniency claiming he had a weak mind and wouldn't survive in jail. The company that made the inkan for Taro was fined and ordered to do background checks in the future on anyone ordering a new seal.

When the police cracked the safe open, there was great anticipation in the eyes of Mika and her mom. Inside, they found a will that not only contained Jiji's authentic seal but was also notarized. Mika's jaw dropped when she read the first few lines. Jiji had given his entire estate to Mika, which had to be worth a few million dollars at least. I was thinking to myself that Mika would be able to survive now without my help. It was a happy day for all except Taro.

A few weeks later I asked Mika for a divorce. After a long tearful discussion, she agreed. The whole process was quite simple. There was some paperwork at the ward office for removing my name from the family register and a few other formalities but it was soon over. Mika decided to stay in the apartment and I found another one temporarily.

Jiji's estate was taxed heavily but Mika was still able to keep about a half million U.S. That would keep her going for quite sometime. She offered to help me with the deposit on my new apartment but I refused. I wanted to make a clean break.

Mika only called me once after the divorce. That was the day that Taro committed suicide. He had lost face in the eyes of family and colleagues and took the easy way out. He hung himself from a tree one evening in Yoyogi Park just a month after being released from jail. He left a suicide note apologizing for his actions. Mika didn't seem upset at all. She used an English phrase that she had learned at JIS.

"What goes around, comes around," she pointed out.

We said our goodbyes and that was it. We still exchange holiday cards to this day but are more like distant relatives than former spouses. By solving this case, we both benefited. She didn't need me financially and I was free to go on with my life.

I enjoyed living alone again but began to question if teaching was the right profession for me. I liked the kids at JIS. The administration was friendly. The parents were helpful. I was doing

14

my job just as well as anybody there, I thought. But was teaching the highest and best use of my talents?

What was I good at? I was a problem solver. There was no doubt about that. I remembered one of the cops at the Shibuya ward asked me if I'd ever been a detective. He was impressed at how I spotted the subtle differences in the two seals. That was it. I would research what it would take to become a private detective.

I began my research on the Internet and English bookstores. I found out that there were no official formal qualifications. In California, where I wanted to return and practice, there were licensing requirements, however. None of this turned out to be overwhelming though. A few courses of police science and criminal justice and that was the extent of the education. There was a two-hour examination that one had to pass but that should be a breeze for me.

The biggest obstacle to licensing was that I would need 6,000 hours or three years of actual investigative experience before I could work independently. I wanted to set up my own office but it looked liked I'd have to work for someone else for a while first.

In January of 1998, I wrote a letter of resignation to the director of JIS stating that I would not be returning in April for the start of the new academic year. After work, I began actively looking on-line for private investigator agencies in the San Francisco Bay Area. I read about forensics, criminal law, and how to interrogate successfully. I was confident I could do it well if given the chance and couldn't wait to get started.

I enrolled in a few on-line courses through a respected distance learning organization to get the required courses under my belt. I devoured everything and anything I could about the private investigation business. At the end of March, I left JIS behind and was ready for my new life. Goodbye Tokyo. Hello San Francisco Bay Area.

I had saved about 40 grand in Japan. Soon after returning, I made a down payment on the house in the El Cerrito hills and was ready to begin my search for a private detective agency where I could begin my apprenticeship. Within a month, I found work at an agency called Beat the Cheats in Berkeley. This agency specialized in uncovering infidelities in marriage. Since I was in training, the salary was small but my goal was that future license.

The work was extremely easy for me. A husband or a wife usually wanted evidence that their spouse was cheating. This would improve their chances of a more lucrative settlement when the inevitable divorce was final. We were hired to provide hard evidence. It wasn't hard to get. I'd take videos of spouses entering motel rooms with their lovers. I'd get copies of their cell phone records. Our clients did get their money's worth as we were always there to present hard evidence in divorce court.

After a year, I had had enough of chasing down the infidels. I wanted serious detective work. I found an agency in Oakland called Smith and Sanders Inc. Roger Smith and Bill Sanders were veteran detectives in their 70s. They had been working as a team since the 1950's. I was the first apprentice detective they had ever hired. They were about to retire and wanted someone to pick up the slack as they wound down their final caseloads.

It would have taken 50 years working for Beat the Cheats to learn what I did in just two with Roger and Bill. Although they occasionally would take on a domestic investigation case, the majority of the work was in the criminal arena. Their clients were usually criminal lawyers who needed help finding and interviewing witnesses and procuring forensic evidence. Families would also hire them when they believed their loved ones were wrongly convicted.

Roger and Bill got results and were in demand. They had a ton of connections in the Bay Area. This opened doors for me that would have been normally closed. Voices that seemed reluctant would become cooperative at the mention of Roger and Bill. At the office, they would let me scour over their old files after hours. When they looked at me, I think they saw a picture of their younger selves. I in turn couldn't have asked for better mentors.

Little by little, they allowed me to take on more responsibility. During the second year, I was given my first serious case to work on independently. A family came in the office who thought their son had been murdered by his wife. The physician had listed the cause of his death as heart failure on the death certificate. The wife had the remains cremated two days later. End of story? Not quite.

John Gross was a relatively wealthy American software salesman who met his Russian-born wife Anita about a decade earlier on a business trip to Moscow. They were soon married and made their home in Orinda, an upper middle-class neighborhood in the East Bay. After two years, Anita gave birth to a baby girl. This is when their relationship started going downhill according to John's parents.

They went on to tell a story of several years of an unhappy marriage. Fights over how to raise the child, finances, and house décor were many. Like many unhappy couples though, they stayed together for the sake of the child. His parents believed that this decision ultimately led Anita to poison John.

John's mom said that five years before this her son had a faulty valve in his heart replaced due to a genetic defect. She went on to explain that this was why the physician was so quick to sign the death certificate and why he failed to order an autopsy. Both John's parents were on a golfing trip to Palm Springs at the time and when they returned John had already been cremated. They were completely devastated. Anita had planned to throw his ashes in the bay from the Berkeley Pier but they talked her out of it. Instead, they were placed in an urn. There was a short uncomfortable funeral. The urn was then placed in a vault at Mountain View Cemetery.

The Gross family suspected foul play from the get-go. They discussed their concerns with the authorities but as far as the cops were concerned there was no case. The police took the physicians report at face value. That's when the family sought the help of Smith and Sanders Inc. But even Roger and Bill had their doubts. That's probably why they decided to give me free reign on the case.

Three months later, as a result of my investigative work, Anita was in jail charged with first-degree murder. Most of the evidence I uncovered was circumstantial. I discovered that Anita was having an affair with a man who just happened to be affiliated with the local Russian mafia. I had tape recordings of an interview with one of her best friends who claimed that Anita often mentioned how she wished there was an easy way to get rid of John. I had John's ashes examined by the forensic lab and traces of arsenic were found. The doctor who signed the death certificate was criticized in the media for incompetence.

Not too long after the Gross case, Roger and Bill both decided it was time to retire. They had been contacted by developers who wanted to build an apartment complex where their office stood. Apparently, the offer was too good to pass up. They bought condos in Cabo San Lucas with some of the proceeds and headed south for the easy life. They gave me the greatest parting gift I could imagine. I was to become steward of almost half a century worth of case files. I was in detective seventh heaven. For me, it was like inheriting a wing at the Smithsonian.

Since I had already passed the detective exam and now had the experience needed, it was time to set out on my own. The first step was to find an office. Besides my desk, fax, and computer equipment, I needed enough space for Roger and Bill's filing cabinets plus my own which were starting to increase in size. I wanted a place within a short commute of my home in El Cerrito. I decided to narrow my search to the little town of Albany which is bordered by El Cerrito and Berkeley.

Due to a recent real estate bubble, rents were high. I finally settled on a shared office on the 1500 block of Solano Ave. It consisted of a hallway on the right and two partitioned offices each with their own lockable door. The first office had a brass plaque on the door that read Helen Weinstein *Somato Emotional Release Therapist*. I had no idea what that was and neither did the landlord. He did mention that she only came in sporadically so I would usually have the building to myself. The back office was larger than the front but cost a few hundred dollars more per month.

It was a perfect, convenient location, I thought. Compared to its surrounding neighbors, Albany was a peaceful town. It averaged about one murder every decade. This is impressive when you consider that the cities of Oakland and Richmond average more than 50 times that and they are just a few minutes drive away. The office was nestled between an Italian restaurant and a natural history store called the Bone Room. Within walking distance were at least 30 restaurants, several coffee shops, three pubs, a few scattered antiques shops, mixed in with the usual real estate, attorney, dental and doctor offices. It was a great street to take a relaxing stroll.

I decided to incorporate my one-man detective service to protect my personal assets which is almost a necessity in sue-happy California. I decided on the name Tantei Man Inc. I had first heard the word *tantei* from the Japanese policeman who complimented me on my detective work in Mika's grandfather's case. *Shiritsu Tantei* means private detective in Japanese. It really didn't matter much

18

what my company's name would be as 99% of my clients would come from references from the Smith and Sanders' connection. I just needed a name to conduct business. Tantei Man was as good as any.

During the next few years, I built a solid reputation as a results oriented, hard working detective. It got to the point where I could almost pick and choose my clients. At first, I depended on the Smith and Sanders' association but now I was getting more and more work from friends and relatives of previous, satisfied clients. Word of mouth and goodwill are the foundations of a successful business.

As a policy, I would never give out my home phone number to any client. I had made only one exception to that rule and that was with Rosanna. The last thing I wanted was nervous clients calling me in the middle of dinner or late at night. The local police departments and detectives had my home number and the only reason I gave it to them was for emergencies. That turned out to be a mistake as they would call me at home with all sorts of requests for information about past cases of Roger and Bill's. That was the one downside to inheriting their files. A lot of local history was in those drawers.

As I turned on the coffee bean grinder, I began wondering how those files would help Sgt. Wilson with the Vargas case. All I knew about the Vargas case was from what I read in the newspaper and that wasn't much. It happened a few weeks ago. A 17-year-old Mexican girl was found brutally murdered and possibly sexually assaulted in Nicholl Park in Richmond. It didn't even make the front page. Murders of minorities in Richmond had become so commonplace that they had been demoted to third page news. Usually gang related, people had just become too accustomed to reading about them. I decided to wait until I got to my office before calling Sgt. Wilson back.

I boiled an egg and washed it down with coffee. After scanning through the local paper, I looked out at the view of the San Francisco Bay. Although my house was small, the views were fantastic. I had a clear unimpeded view of the bay, the Golden Gate and Bay Bridges, and the San Francisco skyline.

I shaved, brushed my teeth again, and took my daily dose of Concerta. Considering the quantity of drinks I had consumed, I didn't feel that bad. My throat was dry and the whites of my eyes were a little red but I was ready to head to the office to catch up on my work. Images of Rosanna danced in my head as I searched for my car keys. I couldn't wait to see her again.

I found the keys under a newspaper on the kitchen counter. I set the alarm and then headed out the kitchen door to the garage where my Corvette waited. My house was just a few seconds drive to Arlington Blvd, a road that traverses the East Bay hills from Richmond to Berkeley. I normally used it all the way to the Thousand Oaks Blvd. where I would head down local streets until I got close enough to Solano Ave. to walk to my office.

There were two simple brass plaques on the front door. The one on the upper-left corner read Helen Weinstein *Somato Emotional Release Therapist* and the one on the upper-right read Tantei Man *Private Detective Agency.* As the landlord had promised, Ms. Weinstein was hardly ever there. In fact, we had only crossed paths once. We had exchanged pleasantries and that was it. I still didn't know what a somato emotional release therapist was.

I entered the front door and walked down the short hall to my back office. On the wall that bordered Weinstein's office were Roger and Bill's file cabinets. I had a large wooden executive desk facing the eastern wall. On top of the desk, set my computer, printer, scanner, and fax machine. I had a Balinese wooden name plaque on the desk that read Harley Justin Butler – *Private Detective.* It was a gift from a client who had taken a trip to Indonesia. Against the back wall, stood my file cabinets. The only natural light came from a two-foot wide skylight on the 10-foot high ceiling.

As usual, the answering machine's red light was blinking. There were seven messages. A few were from potential clients asking me to call back, one was from Rosanna who blew me a kiss, and the last was from Sgt. Wilson asking if I'd have time to meet with him today about the Vargas case. I was thinking it was time to hire and train a secretary to help weed-out the not worthwhile cases and take care of some of the paperwork.

I looked up Sgt. Randy Wilson's phone number in my organizer and dialed it. A secretary who acted like she knew me said he was out but she'd page him and have him call me back. I returned a few of the calls and arranged a meeting with a potential client. I was about to step out for some fresh air when the phone rang.

"Hey Harley. How are you doing old buddy?" he asked me like a long lost friend.

I had met and worked with Sgt. Randy Wilson many times before and we got along well. I considered him a friend and a trustworthy contact.

"Just fine, Randy. What gives?"

"We need your expertise old buddy."

"Yeah right. What could that be?" I joked. It was clear that he wanted something.

"You mentioned the Vargas case. How could I help you there? The victim had only been in the country for a short time so I doubt there's anything in Roger and Bill's files that would be helpful to you."

"Don't need anything from the files Harley. Like I said, I need your expertise."

I pondered this for a second and asked. "Well, what is it, Rand? Spit it out."

"In a nutshell, we need you to go undercover."

"Not my cup of tea, old boy. I got enough on my plate at the moment. What's this about anyway?"

"It'll take awhile to explain. How about I bring a sushi box from Yusan's over and we'll discuss it. No obligation, all right?"

The Yusan restaurant on San Pablo Ave. made the best sushi in the Bay Area and I was getting hungry.

"Okay. I'll hear you out but I can't promise you anything."

"Great. I'll be over in about 45 minutes with two deluxe sushi boxes."

I hung up with my curiosity still unsatisfied but at least I'd have lunch taken care of.

It was about 2:30 when Sgt. Wilson knocked on my door with two beautiful sushi boxes. He was wearing blue jeans, a long-sleeved white shirt, and an Oakland A's cap. I cleared a spot for him on the other side of my desk. We didn't waste anytime getting started and gobbled down one piece after the other. When we were about half done, his face became serious.

"We're beginning to think the Vargas murder was not gang related. In fact, we think she may have been murdered somewhere else and her body dumped at Nicholl Park. Alma Vargas was a straight A honor student who according to her parents and friends had goals of attending a top university. The only thing out of the ordinary we've uncovered is that she was fighting for school reform."

Sgt. Wilson was a short, thin man whose baritone voice didn't match his physique. He could have been described as a miniature version of Clark Gable if it wasn't for the 1/4 in. wide scar that ran diagonally across his forehead. He was a seasoned street cop who rose up the ranks to detective through a combination of perseverance, intelligence, and hard work. I liked and respected him because unlike some cops, he seemed genuinely concerned with improving the quality of life in the community he served. He went on with his story.

"Turns out she was ruffling the feathers of the administration of the school as well as folks at the district office. I'd hate to think someone in charge of our schools would be responsible for her death but we need to look at all angles. By all accounts she was a very popular student at LBJ High and popular for the right reasons."

He had my interest. I was always a sucker for an underdog story and students at LBJ High were definitely underdogs. I knew that the student body was mainly made up of low-income African Americans mixed in with fresh across the border Mexicans and recent Southeast Asian immigrants. There were plenty of page three stories about problems and incidents at LBJ High in the Contra Costa Times.

"I know resources at the Richmond P.D. are limited, Randy. I also know a kid getting killed in Richmond is sad, especially someone with her potential. But hell, at least three kids get killed there every month. So where are we going with this?"

"We are under a lot of pressure from the Destinos Latinos group. They're out babbling to the press that if the Vargas girl would have been Caucasian, the case would have already been solved." He swallowed a piece of maguro sushi and continued. "I don't think that is necessarily true but the negative press is hurting the department's image. We've got an important bond measure coming up next November and need all the support we can get. We've made it a top priority to try to solve this case and that's why I'm here Harley."

"Who are Destinos Latinos?" I asked.

"It's a national nonprofit organization consisting of Hispanic entrepreneurs and business people. Their stated mission is to improve the quality of life of Latinos living in the United States. They are involved in mentoring programs for youth and provide scholarships for college. I think they are a positive force in the community but can be a real pain in the ass when they want to be," Randy explained.

"What made them so interested in this case?"

"The Vargas girl was mentored by the organization. They got her out of English as a Second Language classes and made sure she took college prep courses. Her teachers said that she spoke English fluently the day she arrived and her vocabulary was as big as or bigger than her American classmates. Apparently, she learned it from simply reading books and watching American TV programs. She got straight A's and took advance placement courses. When she became a senior, she applied for a scholarship from Destinos Latinos. They offer three fully paid scholarships a year to exceptional Hispanic students. According to their spokesperson, Alma was on track to be one of the successful candidates and was interested in attending Stanford if accepted. A journalism professor at Stanford was willing to sponsor her visa. She was a poster child and success story for Destinos Latinos."

"How long had she been in the country?" I asked.

"Her whole family including Alma illegally immigrated here about a year and a half ago from the city of Hidalgo del Parral in the state of Chihuahua. Somehow, they successfully crossed the border during the night near El Paso and then worked their way up to Richmond where relatives were there to greet them. Alma's parents didn't even want her to attend school but she was determined. Her cousin hooked her up with Destinos Latinos and they helped her enroll at LBJ High and get into the right courses. She impressed them and they went the extra mile in helping her."

"You said earlier she was fighting for school reform. What did you mean by that?"

Randy took a swig of Diet Coke and scratched his head. "You name it, she was fighting for it. She wanted smaller class sizes, more course offerings, better discipline, better equipment, and easier access to counselors just to name a few. Basically, she thought LBJ High students should have the same quality of education as those in neighboring communities of Albany and Piedmont. After all, this was public education."

"Do you have any leads on who might have killed her?"

He pulled on his left ear and responded. "Nothing substantial. We don't think the murder was gang related, nor do we think it was random."

"Any idea what she was doing in Nicholl Park so early in the morning? The body was found by park maintenance workers around 7:00 a.m. if I remember correctly."

"We think she was taken there or tricked into going there by the killer. At this point, we are uncertain. We still haven't determined if she was killed in the park or somewhere else and the body dumped there. The coroner set the time of death at between 5:00 and 6:30 a.m. The autopsy revealed significant traces of Restoril and alcohol."

"Her parents must have known what time she left the house that morning?" I asked.

"The last time Sr. and Sra. Vargas talked to Alma was right after school the previous day. She said she was going to a friend's house to work on a homework project and would be home for dinner around 7:00 p.m. She never came home. We still don't know who that friend was or if she was telling the truth about the homework project. Her parents were afraid to call the police for help because of their illegal status."

"Did she have a boyfriend?"

"Yes. He's a senior at LBJ High named Ricardo Oliveira. Like Alma, he is straight A student. He had a verifiable alibi for that afternoon and evening though. After school, he went with friends to the El Cerrito Plaza to go shopping. He stayed there until 6:30 p.m. when his mother picked him up. According to his mother and sister, he did not leave the house that night. So far, I believe him. He appeared to be genuinely devastated by Alma's death. Curiously, he is the only Brazilian at the school."

"Does he have any idea who she may have met?

"No. He mentioned a few of her girl friends by name. We interviewed them and they all said they had no idea who Alma met or where she could have gone. We have a long way to go on this case my friend. That's why I'm here."

"Okay. Enlighten me, old buddy. How can I be of service?"

"We want you to take a teaching job at LBJ High," he said straightforwardly.

The absurdity of his suggestion nearly knocked me out of my chair. "First you bring sushi. Now you're providing the entertainment. What do I owe you?"

"Think about it Harley. You're one of the best private investigators in the Bay Area. You're the only detective I know certified to teach in public schools. We want to get you on the inside talking to people. You'll only have to do it until the case is solved or by the end of the school year, whichever comes first."

I was still in shock. "I don't think I can help you Randy. I got a business to run here. It sounds like an interesting case and if I can help you any other way, I'd be glad to but -" He cut me off.

"I understand this would be a major sacrifice for you Harley and we are willing to compensate you for that. The department is willing to pay you its highest sub-contracting rate. You will earn a teacher's salary based on the district's salary schedule. On top of that, you will earn a $20,000 bonus if the case is solved. The department is dead serious about solving this case."

I pondered his offer and replied. "LBJ High is a tough school. Your monetary offer sounds great but the thought of-" He cut me off again.

"There is a Computer Application's position available as of yesterday. It was being taught by a long-term sub who was offered a position in another district. I just found this out from the head of security at the school, Mr. Prince. Classes will be small as there are only 24 computers in a class and labor law states that you can't have more students than workstations."

"So how did you arrange this Randy? I mean parents won't be happy if they find out a detective with ulterior motives is teaching their kids."

"No one would know. We wouldn't want the principal, the superintendent, the board of education, or anyone else in the district to compromise our investigation. You'll have to apply for the position and be hired. I know you have good credentials Harley. That's why I came to you."

"What if they hire someone else?" I asked.

"Then we'll have to try something else," he shot back.

"For right now, time is of the essence. Let me know if you'll do it within 24 hours. No hard feelings, if you're not interested."

We shook hands and I told him I'd think about it. I thanked him for the sushi as he headed out the front door. I sat there in front of my computer screen contemplating his offer. I weighed the advantages versus the disadvantages. I would have to cut down on almost all private detective work while involved with this investigation. I'd have to get into a teaching routine which means getting up early, planning lessons, and evaluating students' work. There would be the stress of working with difficult teens. On the upside, I'd make a lot of money. Perhaps enough to pay off my mortgage. When it was over, I'd be on easy street for a while.

There was also the intrigue of the Alma Vargas murder to consider. A young girl from Mexico with great potential possibly killed because she was trying to make life better for herself and her peers. Cases with this much meaning don't come around that often. But there was also no guarantee I'd be able to solve it.

I took a hike up to Indian Rock in nearby Berkeley, hoping that the fresh air and sweeping view of the San Francisco Bay would clear my mind. I looked out at the sunset and tried to imagine Alma as a 15 year-old girl in Mexico dreaming of a better life. I could see her running across the border with her family under the cover of night dodging border patrol agents. I formed an image in my mind of her trying to make the best of her educational opportunities and setting goals for college. I then saw darkness as those dreams were extinguished.

I decided at that moment that I would go along with Sgt. Wilson's plan. I would interview for the teaching job. I would try to find Alma's killer. It wasn't the money driving my decision though. I became a detective to right wrongs. If I didn't take this case, I knew I'd regret it in the future. If what Randy said about Alma was true, then this was a case worth taking.

As soon as I got to my office I called Randy. I advised him of my decision and he thanked me. I told him that I would need total access to all files on the case including the autopsy report. He agreed but reminded me that I hadn't been hired yet and that getting my job application materials in order should be the priority for tonight and tomorrow.

I updated my resume but there was a problem. How would I account for my several years of private detective work? I decided to simply leave it out. If they asked me what I'd been doing during that time, I'd say I was a private computer consultant which was not

26

totally untrue. I was often called by friends and relatives to troubleshoot computer problems. I knew that was stretching the truth but there was a higher moral force at work here.

I downloaded the application packet from the district web site and filled out all the application materials. I made copies of all recommendations written by administrators from my teaching days. I then faxed everything I had to Principal Ramos at LBJ High and the personnel department at the district office. I decided I would follow-up with a phone call tomorrow morning.

I drove home thinking about how one's life can change so drastically in just one day. Last night I was celebrating a successful conclusion to an investigation. My life was going well, I thought. I helped people solve problems. I enjoyed my work. I thought I had something special going with Rosanna. Why did I decide to risk this peace for something as yet unknown? I still couldn't answer completely.

CHAPTER 2

I woke up at 6:30 Friday morning to the loud sound of static mariachi music coming from my alarm radio. It was stuck between two stations and couldn't decide which one it wanted to play. I heard a fuzzy version of Vincente Fernandez's Mexico Lindo y Querido followed by a crackly, monotone male voice babbling about the price of soybean futures. It provided just the right level of annoyance to inspire me to get out of bed and shut it off.

Just like my doctor had predicted I would, I was feeling more focused. I made some toast and jam and got the coffee brewing. After that, I washed down my daily dose of Concerta with a cup of water. I had only been taking it for a month now and wasn't sure if I should continue. It all got started when I went to my doctor with a severely swollen eye, a result of walking into the side-view mirror of a pick-up truck. I was on a late afternoon stroll and was thinking about a case when it happened.

He asked me a set of questions that I later found out were used to confirm adult ADD. I told him that my mind would often drift off on its own journey even in mid-conversation. The tendency to go off on tangents that were sometimes unrelated to the topic being discussed was normal life for me. It didn't always happen. Some people like Randy could hold my undivided attention but they were exceptions. There were times where I had a tendency to go into deep thought to the point where I'd almost completely tune out the external world. This would cause some people to think that I was ignoring them. On walks, I'd occasionally bump into objects like that side-view mirror or even people. The doctor seemed absolutely confident that I had had ADD since childhood and that it had simply gone undiagnosed. He said that I should try Concerta for three months as an experiment and if it worked, I could stick with it. At this point, I was unsure if it was doing me any good.

I telephoned LBJ High and asked for Principal Ramos. The secretary seemed impatient as I explained who I was and that I had faxed a resume the night before. She didn't seem to know what I was talking about until I mentioned that I wanted to apply for the Computer Application's position. When I told her I wanted to arrange for an interview with the principal as soon as conveniently possible, she put me on hold for 15 minutes. When she finally came back, she said that Mr. Ramos would be able to see me at 11:00.

I took a quick shower, shaved, and brushed my teeth. I found a pair of navy blue slacks, a white shirt, and a Jerry Garcia tie. I began preparing my mind for the interview. I had experience with tough interviewers and I knew it was wise to try to anticipate their questions. Why should we hire you over person B? That was one question I had heard more than once and any interviewee worth his salt should be ready for it. I felt I was. It wasn't the interview I feared though. I feared the unknown.

Was I about to make a stupid mistake? LBJ High's students are probably about as difficult as students could be. More than half never graduate. There's a sad joke going around the East Bay that LBJ stood for Life Before Jail. Although I had experience as a detective dealing with people from the mean streets, my teaching experience had been in private schools teaching the kids of the well-to-do. Would I be overwhelmed at LBJ High? Could I keep control of the students?

The fact was I hadn't been hired yet. I would take this a step at a time. I phoned Rosanna to tell her of my plans and asked her to keep them confidential. I trusted her. She laughed and asked me if I was sure I knew what I was doing. Rosanna lived in a small house in the Richmond Annex, a different part of Richmond from where the students at LBJ High were drawn.

In parts of the East Bay, as in many parts of the country, a major freeway was the man-made barrier separating the classes. On the east side of Interstate 80, were the relatively affluent communities of Albany, El Cerrito, and Richmond View. The Richmond Annex was like a first step into these areas. It was on the east side of the freeway but just barely. Rosanna lived in a small studio on San Luis St., a street that ran parallel and right next to the freeway. Even with all windows closed, one could hear the hum of the passing cars from inside.

The majority of students at LBJ High came from an area called the Iron Triangle. The Iron Triangle is a place cut off from the rest of Richmond by intersecting railroad tracks and the highway. Its residents are the poorest of the poor. The neighborhood is a mixture of fresh across the border Mexicans mixed in with desolate African American families. The crime rate and infant mortality are high. Most windows are covered with steel bars. Nobody from the outside goes in unless they really have to or are lost. Turf gangs rule the streets. Murders are commonplace and topped 50 last year. It's bizarre to think that if one were to drive a mere five minutes, you could be in a town like Albany which averages less than one murder a decade.

At 10:30, I jumped into my car and drove north to Barrett Ave. that would take me down from the hills. As I passed 23rd Street, I thought about how it could have been the main drag of a city in Mexico. There was a taqueria on almost every corner and most all shops and businesses had Spanish names. A few blocks later stood LBJ High which took up an entire block. A mural painted on the side read Home of the Riveters. The school colors were dark silver and white. The silver color represents iron in homage to the town's industrial heritage. The name Riveters came from the fact that the school was opened during WWII when the former Kaiser shipyards played a big part in the war effort. Men were on the frontlines and some of the wives who stayed behind helped out at Kaiser by working as riveters. The school mascot was a muscular lady wearing a bandana holding a pipe wrench in her hand.

The school was originally called Richmond Industrial High but changed its name to LBJ High in 1965. It was not too long after President Johnson gave his Great Society Speech that he took a tour of poor schools throughout the country. Somehow Richmond Industrial High got on the itinerary. He made an inspiring speech in the school gymnasium. A few months later, someone on the school board proposed a name change citing that Richmond Industrial High had a bleak sound to it. The logical alternative at the time was LBJ High. 10 years later, the old school was torn down because it couldn't meet the stricter earthquake codes and a new windowless high school was built.

The teachers' parking lot was entered through a side street. I parked my Corvette next to a beat up old Ford Pinto. My Corvette was well protected with the latest alarm system. I knew if it wasn't, it wouldn't last long in this neighborhood. I walked over to the cyclone gate entrance but it was padlocked. I imagined they did that to keep strangers out and students in. On the north side of the parking lot, there was an opening leading to Barrett Avenue. I walked around to the front entrance. On the left side of the entrance was an iron, life-size statue of LBJ covered with graffiti. Its tablet

30

read, "There are those timid souls who say this battle cannot be won; that we are condemned to a soulless wealth. I do not agree. We have the power to shape the civilization that we want. But we need your will, your labor, your hearts, if we are to build that kind of society." I believe that was a quote from his Great Society speech.

I entered through the front entrance and made a sharp left to enter the main office. There was a secretary talking casually on the phone. I tried to make eye contact with her but she would have none of it. She hung up the phone and began shuffling through papers.

"Excuse me. I have an interview with Mr. Ramos." I said in a loud voice.

"He's in a meeting. Have a seat. It'll be a while." she responded, barely acknowledging my presence. She was a heavy-set African American woman that appeared to be in her 40s. Her hair was elaborately braided. The name plate on her desk read Virginia Perkins.

I sat against the wall next to the trophy case. The trophies were from years past. I noticed that the most recent was from a basketball championship in 2003 but most of the others were from the 70s and 80s. On the wall, above the principal's door were the photos of the ex-principals. From 1995 to 2005, there was a new principal every year. Mr. Ramos was in his second year which might have some positive meaning, I thought.

An angry woman came in who appeared to be in distress. She said her daughter had just been suspended for talking back to Mr. Prince, the site supervisor. She demanded to see the principal immediately. Ms. Perkins sighed and picked up her walkie-talkie.

"We have a red 15. Can you come to the office Mr. Prince?"

"I'm on my way," he responded.

I imagined that red 15 must have been code for out-of-control parent. Mr. Prince came in and tried to escort the lady off campus. When she insisted on seeing the principal, he grabbed her arm and told her it's time to go.

"Don't touch me, you son of a bitch!" she screamed. "I'll be back!" she warned as she slammed the door and walked out.

Mr. Prince smiled at Ms. Perkins and said, "Just another day in paradise."

31

It was obvious that Mr. Prince was used to this kind of incident. He was a heavy-set African-American man who looked to be about 6'6". His fleshy, baby face made me think of the Pillsbury Doughboy. It took a certain kind of person with an iron will to work security at a school like LBJ, I thought. Most people simply could not handle the stress.

At around 11:30, the door to Mr. Ramos's office swung open. A well-dressed man with a briefcase left briskly and headed out the main entrance. I stuck my head in and made my presence known. "I'm here for the interview," I said.

"I wasn't aware of any interview this morning," he shot back.

"I faxed my resume yesterday and was told by the receptionist to come in at 11:00."

I looked over at Ms. Perkins and said, "Did anyone give Mr. Ramos my resume?"

"Just a minute," she said and walked into another room. She came back with a stack of papers and began shuffling through them. "Are you Harley Butler?" she asked.

"Yes. I thought I had made an appointment."

She walked over and handed me the resume and cover letter I had faxed. It appeared that no one had even looked at them. She peered into Mr. Ramos's office and said, "He's interested in the Computer Application's position."

Mr. Ramos told me to take a seat across from him. He took a few seconds to glance at my resume, then looked up and asked, "So you want to teach at LBJ High? When can you start?"

I was taken aback by his question. Less than a minute ago, I was thinking I'd have to reschedule because my resume hadn't even been checked out yet. Seconds later, I'm being offered the position. Perhaps this could have made the Guinness Record Book for the world's shortest interview.

"I can start right away," I answered. "I've already submitted all the paperwork to the district office. All I need is my TB shot and I'll get that today."

"Can you start tomorrow? The class has been taught by daily subs since the long-term sub left us. The students need consistency."

"Yeah, I can start right away. Can you give me a quick tour of the department?" I wanted to see the classroom and some of the students. It still wasn't too late to change my mind if I didn't like what I saw.

"Sure," he replied. "Follow me." We walked down a hallway until we arrived at room 207. The door was locked. He opened it with a master key. The substitute looked up at us from behind the teacher's desk and smiled. There were 26 work stations of which about 20 were occupied. It was surprisingly quiet. It appeared that the students were not working on any task in particular. Some were playing games. Some were playing streaming video and listening with headphones. Others were checking e-mail and instant messaging.

"What class is this?" I asked Mr. Ramos.

"It's the Computer Application's class. You'll have three of these and two graphic design classes."

It was obvious that the sub was simply babysitting the students. The thought entered my mind that they would be resentful of me for spoiling the party. Even though my goal was to solve a crime, I intended to take my teaching responsibilities seriously. I would have classroom rules and demand students stay on task.

Mr. Ramos grabbed my arm gently and said, "Let me introduce you to the tech guy Mr. Chirac. He's the head of the technology department." He pulled out his master key and opened room 208, the room next door. Inside, students were doing pretty much the same thing they were doing in room 207 except the speakers were on. A rap song was blaring out from one of the work stations. There was no sign of a teacher in class.

"He must be out fixing someone's computer," he explained. At that point the lunch bell rang and the hallway was suddenly filled with students. It was noisy as hell.

We walked back to the office. He gave me a copy of the bell schedule, welcomed me aboard and said I could start tomorrow fulltime. He advised me to arrive early and try to meet with Mr. Chirac before 1st period. He said he'd phone personnel immediately to let them know I'd been hired. I shook his hand and thanked him feeling almost guilty at how easy it was to pull it off.

I drove down to the district personnel office to finalize the paperwork. I was fingerprinted, photographed, and got to choose a health plan. They said I could start on Step 3 of the salary schedule until my international experience was documented. That would be a bit of a hassle but worthwhile as the salary difference between Step

33

3 and Step 7 was significant. They gave me a form to take to a medical center to get a TB skin test. The clinic was only a few blocks away on McDonald Ave. I would have to wait 48 hours for the result but was done for the day. Mission accomplished.

When I got back home, I phoned Sgt. Wilson to let him know I got the job. He was pleased. He said he would provide me with all the files relating to the case including the autopsy report tomorrow. The department had already developed quite a few profile sheets on many of the teachers, staff, and students at LBJ High and that they would come in handy for me as I started my snooping. I thanked him for that.

At about 7:00, Rosanna came over with her son and we had dinner together. She congratulated and hugged me. When she left we made a promise to hook up over the weekend. I put a quick lesson plan together and then hit the sack at about 11:00. I couldn't get to sleep wondering what tomorrow would bring.

CHAPTER 3

I woke up at 6:00 sharp after a restless night, took a quick shower to wake up and picked out some semi-formal clothes. I wanted to look professional but not overdressed. I boiled an egg, my usual low-carb breakfast, and scanned the paper. I was glad it was Friday for a couple of reasons. I would have time to reflect on the Vargas case before getting too involved with the new job. Secondly, I'd get to spend some quality time with Rosanna.

I swallowed down my daily dose of Concerta with the last swig of coffee. I tried to think hard on how the drug was affecting me. For the past month I had been around people who had held my interest so I couldn't be sure if I was drifting off more or less during personal interaction. I hadn't bumped into anything lately but that could have been pure luck. I had no idea how it was affecting me sexually. It sure didn't stop my erection the other night at Fonda's. The one thing I did notice was a change in my dreams. Somehow they seemed less vivid. I used to wake up with strong memories of the previous night's dream images. Now, it was as if I wasn't dreaming at all.

I called Sgt. Wilson and left a message for him to call me back. I asked if he would be available after work for dinner and a beer together at Brennan's in Berkeley. I looked out my living room window at the view. Besides the great view of bridges, I could see highway 80 and a little beyond that, the shadows of the Iron Triangle.

At 7:15, I jumped into my car and headed towards LBJ High. It took me about 12 minutes from start to finish. The gate to the hallway that was padlocked yesterday was now open. I walked down the hall towards room 207 and 208. The school was two stories high in some places. This made the hallways unusually dark on the first floor where the computer classes were held. I found the physical environment to be a bit on the depressing side.

The door to room 208 was wide open. I popped my head in and said, " Are you Mr. Chirac?"

"Yes. You must be Mr. Butler? I'm glad you're here." he smiled and invited me in. The man sitting at the desk appeared to be in his late 50s. He had thin gray hair and a handlebar mustache. He looked just like the guy on the Get out of Jail Free card from the Monopoly game.

35

"How can I help you get started?" he asked.

"I'd like my class schedule and my own key to room 207 for starters."

He wrote out my schedule in pencil and explained as he went along. I would teach Computer Applications periods 1, 3, and 4. During 2nd period, all teachers taught a scripted program called Corrective Reading for 40 minutes. After period 4, there would be a 35-minute recess for lunch. Period 5 would be my prep period and in periods 6 and 7, I would teach Adobe Illustrator classes. The classes were 49 minutes long. The school day ended at 3:15 except on minimum and rally days when it would end at 2:00. Today was a rally day. He then showed me the textbooks available for each class.

"Let me introduce you to the head secretary Ms. Perkins," he offered. "We'll see if she can dig up an extra key for room 207.

"I met her briefly yesterday. She seems to have her hands full," I said.

"Don't we all," he noted.

Ms. Perkins was able to find a key for room 207 on a key ring that looked to have about 100 keys on it. She had me sign out for it. It was now 8:15. Mr. Chirac showed me where to pick up my attendance scantrons. I was feeling nervous with anticipation. Classes would begin at 8:25 after a five-minute passing bell.

We walked back to our classrooms. Students were talking loudly in the halls. Mr. Chirac said that if I needed anything he'd be right next-door. His relaxed and nonchalant manner had a calming effect.

As I said before, the classroom had 26 workstations. There were four rows with four computers each on the left side and five rows with two computers each on the right. There was a large space of about 10 feet in width between the left and right sections. The computers all faced a big white screen at the back of the class. The teacher's desk was set behind in such a way that I would be able to see what all students were doing from this one location. I thought the layout was well thought out.

The passing bell rang. I had decided to take a gradual approach to getting control of my students. I knew that coming in as a marine drill sergeant would poison the atmosphere. I sat behind my desk and watched as the students strolled in. There was obviously no seating chart as students seemed to sit wherever they wanted. It looked like the Hispanic population held a small majority at LBJ High and this was reflected by the students coming in. Interestingly, 10 years ago the student population at LBJ High was around 90% African American. Intense immigration from Mexico and El Salvador over the past decade had dramatically changed the ethnic makeup of the Iron Triangle.

The bell to start class rang. I was surprised that only nine students had shown up even though 22 were listed on the attendance scans. They sat down and immediately started their computers as if I wasn't there. I decided to wait about five minutes before introducing myself. During that time, another 5 students casually walked in. I walked up to the front of the class.

"Good morning everyone. My name is Mr. Butler and I'll be in charge of this class from now on. I understand that you have been taught by temporary subs for the past few weeks. Today, everybody starts with a clean slate. You will be graded by me and me only."

"Just relax and get paid," a male student sitting in the back blurted out.

"I intend to do just that but first I want to get you started on today's activity." I had learned from my earlier experience teaching that losing one's cool never paid off, even if a class was getting out of control.

"You mean I'm not going to get credit for the work I've already done," a female student complained.

"Yes and no," I replied. "I got a better deal for you. Right now, as far I am concerned, everybody in the class has an A. From here on out, you have a choice. Maintain that A or lose it. You can earn from 0 to 4 points a day. I will bring a syllabus tomorrow with the details on how to earn or lose points. We will have a seating chart and classroom rules. Being late is one way to lose points."

A few students continued to surf the web while I was speaking. I knew I couldn't expect miracles the first day so I didn't call them on it. I handed out the activity I had prepared to break the ice. It was a simple survey with questions about hobbies and interests. I paired them off and had them interview each other and take notes. The idea was to have them introduce their partner using the notes.

When I paired one of the male students with someone nearby he complained. "This is bogus! What's the fucking point?"

"I want to get to know you," I responded honestly.

He shrugged his shoulders but cooperated. The students began asking each other questions: "Who's your favorite musician? What are your dreams for the future? What do you do in your free time?" Perhaps because they were used to receiving no direction in class, they were secretly happy. I noticed a couple of Hispanic females were having trouble with the questions. I helped them out the best I could. If you speak Portuguese, you can communicate with Spanish speakers to an extent.

After about 20 minutes, I told them to stop. I continued with my directions. "Take the highlights of your interview and summarize them into one short paragraph about your partner. You'll have 7 minutes to do this." They began writing away. Again, I helped the two Hispanic girls who were having trouble. A few minutes later, I advised the class that time was up. "As I call on you, I want you to stand up and introduce your partner to the class. Any volunteers?"

An African American girl named Katrina raised her hand. "I'll do it," she exclaimed. "That's what I like to see. That's how you'll earn four points," I said. "Now, using your paragraph, stand up and introduce your partner to the class."

Katrina and her partner stood up. Katrina, tall and slender, contrasted oddly with her partner who was short and obese. She began her introduction. "This is my friend Nytasia. She lives in Richmond and takes the bus to school. She doesn't have a favorite author or book. Her favorite artist is E-40. He's mine too. She has no dreams for the future." Since they did a fine job, I started the applause.

Students took turns until only the two Hispanic girls who could not speak English were left. I didn't want to embarrass them so I asked if anyone was capable of translating. Surprisingly, the student who told me to relax and get paid volunteered. He was wearing a white t-shirt that had an enlarged photo of Alma Vargas ironed on. Above the image of Alma, was her name printed in large black letters followed by RIP. Below her image, the phrase Corazón de Estudiante (Heart of Student) arched around a hand drawn heart. Asiel Vasquez strutted over to where the two girls were sitting.

I advised them to read two or three sentences and then to pause for Asiel's translation. He did an excellent job of translating. Turned out both of the girls were from the state of Chihuahua in Mexico and had only been in Richmond for a few months. They

38

were crazy about some Mexican rock group I had never heard of. Their dream for the future was to get married and have kids. I praised Asiel for doing such a good job. I mentioned to the class that some people make good money doing what Asiel just did. They are called interpreters. I promised to show them next week how to do job searches on the Internet.

The one commonality I noticed among all of the students was the lack of goals. None of them mentioned wanting to be in a higher-level profession like doctor or engineer. The majority simply didn't have any dreams. It was as if they had accepted their ghetto destiny as some sort of divine design. I thought that if I could at least get them to see themselves as having more potential, to see beyond their iron-barred fishbowl, my short stay at LBJ High would have more value than simply solving a murder.

The bell rang and the students left. Soon others were straggling in. The class was called Corrective Reading and was taught by all teachers during period 2. It was a program designed for schools where students were not reading at grade level. There was no planning required for this class. The teachers' book was scripted and one simply followed the instructions. I decided to skip the book and instead did the same activity I did with period 1. This way I could find out a little about who my students were. At least the ones who showed up. This was a shortened period so I had to speed up the process.

The day went on without any major incidents. The students did seem to get more rambunctious as the day went on and some were very rude but I managed to maintain control in all classes. I was lucky that my prep period was scheduled right after lunch. This would give me a combined 85 minutes to prepare, evaluate, and think.

For lunch, I drove over to the Home Depot on San Pablo Ave. as I needed to buy a washer for my leaky bathroom faucet. I bought a sandwich and a coffee from a little food stand in front of the store and sat on a chair in the autumn sun watching the customers come and go. There were Hispanic men, young and old, lined up on San Pablo Ave. and in the parking lot. They were waiting for work, for someone who needed some grunt labor for a low price. It looked like a scene from Steinbeck's Grapes of Wrath, except these were Mexicans, not Okies. As I watched them, I

39

wondered if any of these men, most-likely illegal aliens, had any kids who attended LBJ High.

By law, children of illegal immigrants have a right to an education. In 1994, Proposition 187 was sent to the voters with the support of then governor, Republican Pete Wilson. This referendum was designed to deny basic social services including public education to illegal aliens. It passed by a large majority playing on the xenophobic fears of people. Its constitutionality was immediately challenged in the courts and was eventually killed under Governor Gray Davis.

I was sure that quite a few of my Hispanic students were illegal. Alma Vargas certainly was. It was my opinion though, that if a child is already in this country, it's better to have them in school than out. It's common knowledge that it cost more to incarcerate than educate. We did need a competent border control. That was for sure. Without it, we'd become the third world that others were trying to flee. But once they made that arduous, dangerous journey and ended up in a place like the Iron Triangle of Richmond, it was better to include rather than exclude. Exclusion ultimately leads to desperation and that's when crime shows its ugly face.

I finished my sandwich and drove back to LBJ High for my last two classes. I had decided to lay low for the first two weeks. I wanted the students and staff to get used to my presence before asking too many questions about the Alma Vargas case. Didn't want to blow my cover. In my seventh period Graphic Design class, I noticed the name Ricardo Oliveira on the attendance scan. That had to be the Brazilian boyfriend of Alma. He was one of the many absences that period.

The bell rang at 3:15 right after the rally. School was over. Thank God it's Friday. By 3:25, most students had already left and it was getting quiet. I spoke to Mr. Chirac about my day. He said he was glad to have me on board. It appeared that he was the man about campus. Besides maintaining the school's network, he said he was constantly being called out of class to troubleshoot a multitude of problems. He used to teach only two classes and had the rest of the day to troubleshoot. Due to budget cuts, the administration increased his class load to five. The trouble was everyone was still expecting him to fix his or her computer problems. He was forced to leave his students unattended, while he went about solving the technology problems of the school. He told me he was getting burned out from the situation. I promised to help in anyway I could.

I drove back home and immediately took a nap. People say teachers get a lot of time off. What they don't usually tell you is that it is one of the most energy draining professions out there. I normally didn't take naps but I sure needed one now. I woke up at 6:00 p.m. and the message light on my answering machine was blinking. The first message was from Rosanna. On the next one, I heard Sgt. Wilson's voice.

"Thanks for the invite Harley. Brennan's sounds good. How about 7:30? I'll bring all the files I promised and the autopsy report. Hope you survived the day in one piece," he said laughing. "Call me back to confirm."

I took a quick shower to wake up. I was feeling good and my mind was focused. The nap worked. I called Randy back and left a message for him to meet me at Brennan's. I watched the CBS news for about 15 minutes and then decided to drive down to my office to pick up the mail. I could access my telephone messages remotely but wanted to check on the office. There were several letters addressed to Tantei Man but most were from vendors hawking the latest spy equipment. I tossed them in the can. The answering machine was blinking as usual. There were three messages from potential clients but I would have to blow them off. I decided to record a new message for my answering message to save time in returned calls: *Thank you for considering Tantei Man for your detective services. Due to an unusual large number of caseloads, we are unable to take on any new clients at present. We see this situation as temporary and look forward to serving you in the future.*

I began to think about how long it would take to solve the Vargas case. It was now the second week of November. One thing was for sure. I'd be making a lot more money than usual with the double salary. I did feel that my reputation as a detective was at stake. Would this plan work or end up being a waste of departmental resources? I'd have to take it day by day.

When I looked at my watch it was 7:30. I was running late. I jumped into my Vette and drove down to Brennan's. Brennan's was one of the oldest restaurants in Berkeley. I used to dine there with my parents when I was a kid. It is situated on the corner of 4th St. and University Ave. under an overpass in an industrial part of town that was experiencing a rebirth. I pulled into the parking lot and walked in through the back entrance. It was a large restaurant with a rectangular bar in the center. The walls were wood-paneled on the bottom and painted a dark industrial, textured green on top. It was an old style worker's cafeteria and not ashamed of that fact. The rectangular bar was full but there were plenty of empty tables. I saw Randy sitting beneath a blown-up photo of John Brennan, the restaurant's founder. The photo was of John with one of his prize heifers.

As you enter Brennan's, the first thing you notice is the sound. The large openness of the building creates a lot of paths for sound to travel and at some point it seems to all blend together, creating an ambient hum. One would be aware that people were talking but actual words were indistinguishable. This would be perfect to have a private conversation with Randy, I thought.

I walked over to where he was sitting and said jokingly, "Thanks for saving me a seat." There were empty tables all around him. "Let's eat first and talk shop later," I suggested.

He agreed. We walked over to the food line which had only one person in it. The menu was listed in chalk on a blackboard. We grabbed our trays and contemplated the menu. He ordered the barbecued beef brisket and mashed potatoes and I chose the corn beef and cabbage, a dish I used to enjoy there in childhood. As we were paying, I noticed a neon sign to the right of the front entrance that read Brennan's Irish Coffee in bright, red and green. Like a Pavlov dog, I obediently ordered one from the bar and asked Randy if he wanted one. He did so I ordered another.

We carried the trays back to our table and immediately went to town on our meals. The food, though not capable of winning any gourmet awards, hit the spot just right. I was starving. The mixture of Irish whisky and coffee was beginning to put me in a good mood. Randy walked to the bar and came back with a couple of Lagunitas on draft.

"Okay, old buddy. How was your day?" he asked.

"It went well. The students behaved a lot better than I expected."

"Any dangerous incidents?"

"You know Randy, I think most people have a misconception about high school students from low income areas because of the media. Movies like Dangerous Minds and Coach

42

Carter portray these kids as scary looking gang-bangers for dramatic effect. When you see these kids up close, they are not scary at all though. Cynical and jaded, yes. But scary, no."

"Looks like you found your calling Harley."

"Not quite Rand. When I got home this afternoon, I was beat. I fell right to sleep. I usually never take naps. I look at this experience as a one time adventure, like joining the Peace Corps for a year."

"Did you make any connections?"

"Got to know my students a little bit. Mr. Chirac likes to talk. He'll probably be useful as we go forward. Alma's Brazilian boyfriend is in my period 7 class but he was absent."

I went on to explain my strategy of laying low for the first couple of weeks as I was still very much an outsider at LBJ High. "Did you bring the files?" I asked.

"Got the whole works right here in my briefcase. We've developed quite a few profiles on students and staff of interest. The autopsy report is intriguing. As I mentioned earlier, high levels of the drug Restoril and alcohol, apparently tequila, were found in her system. Restoril belongs to a class of drugs known as benzodiazepines. The coroner said the drug acts as a sedative in low doses but in higher doses can produce a hypnotic effect. Mix in alcohol and you have a dangerous, mind altering cocktail."

"Do you have any evidence that she experimented with drugs?"

"Her boyfriend Ricardo mentioned that they had once tried marijuana together but she didn't like it. In fact, he said when he used it again, she almost broke-up with him. Her diary confirmed this."

"Do you have the diary?" I asked.

"Her parents were reluctant to give it up. A spokesperson from Destinos Latinos went to their house and explained how it would be of value to the investigation and that it would be returned to them as soon it was examined. Translations of the pages of the diary are included with the files I'm giving you."

"Thanks. That could be useful."

I ordered the next round of Lagunitas and we continued our conversation. I decided to change the subject. It was Friday night after all. We don't have to take work everywhere. I thought.

43

"How's your love life going?" I asked. Randy had confided in me months ago after his divorce that he would never marry again. He had come home from work in the middle of the day unexpectedly and caught his wife in bed with another man. He kept his cool and didn't shoot the guy even though he was armed. He filed for divorce and for custody of their two kids but his wife had the better lawyer. She got custody and a generous part of Randy's paycheck. I knew he was hurt deeply by this. A lesser man would have turned cynical but not Randy. He put his all into his work and helping the community he served.

"Not much happening on the love life front," he responded.

I proceeded to tell him about Rosanna while he looked at me with envious eyes. Other than the thick scar on his face, he was a very handsome, albeit a short man. Men of his integrity were in short supply as far I was concerned and I knew he'd be a great find for someone someday. "I'll ask Rosanna if she has any friends interested in going out with a good cop. You got to get on with your life my friend and what better way then with a girl from Ipanema."

"Let me know when you set that up," he said.

It was time to head home. He opened his briefcase and handed me several large brown envelopes.

"We'll keep you updated as new information comes in. Destinos Latinos is still making a stink about this. We've had 46 murders so far in Richmond this year. The files for all these take up only two drawers. Alma's file already takes up more than half of one. According to everyone we've spoken to, she was a special girl in more ways than one. This is one of those cases that is crying out to be solved. The problem is our leads aren't getting us anywhere." We shook hands and departed.

When I arrived home, I immediately called Rosanna to set up Saturday's date. She had arranged for her son, Joãozinho, to spend the night at a friend's house. We would have the night to ourselves. She said she'd drop by my house at 6:00. I suggested that we dine at Skate's on the Bay.

I watched TV for a while and then went to lie down on my bed. Due to the nap I had taken earlier, I wasn't that sleepy. I decided to browse through the files. Randy and other detectives had interviewed several staff members and quite a few students. Their notes were summarized. I looked at the first sheet.

44

Name: Jerry Cheasty Date of Birth: June 13, 1964

The notes were handwritten in sloppy cursive: Math teacher, came from Minnesota three years ago, used to be gay but through a Christian group claims to have become ungay through prayer. Met wife, a former lesbian at group meetings. Wife is a teacher in another district. Alma attended his geometry and calculus class.

The idea of someone praying not to be gay seemed sad to me. I had been around long enough to know that gayness was something you were born with. That Mr. Cheasty is setting himself up for a life of misery, I thought. I read a few more.

Name: Adam Bergman Date of Birth: February 12, 1962 Notes: Social Studies teacher, very close with Principal Ramos, helps out with administration, skydives in his free time, Alma attended his American Government class.

Name: Jake Duckworth Date of Birth: March 28, 1974 Notes: Economics and History teacher, upset with current administration, thorn in Principal's side, doesn't attend teacher meetings, Alma attended his US History class, coaches debate team, Alma's favorite teacher.

Name: Judy Rosales Date of Birth: October 15, 1980 Notes: English teacher, born in the Philippines. Came to USA as baby, naturalized US citizen, has a boyfriend on the front lines in Iraq, Alma attended her English class.

Name: Manuel Ramos Date of Birth: April 30, 1969 Notes: Second year as Principal of school, was a teacher at another high school before that, local success story, came into the country illegally with parents when he was 10 years old from Chihuahua, product of local schools, well-liked by district administration.

I read several more and then pulled out the autopsy report. The cause of death was listed as blunt trauma to the head. There were photos of her head which was split open and her backside that had a large contusion. The coroner theorized that the victim had probably been knocked down by the first blow and then finished off by the second.

She had a blood alcohol level of .20 which is clearly drunk and a high level of the drug benzodiazepine commonly known as Restoril in her system. If I could figure out why she had gone out on a binge like this, I'd be closer to solving the case. There was the possibility that she may not have taken the drug or consumed the

45

alcohol of her own free will though. I was at point 0. Even good high school students get wild sometimes. Had she just been unlucky and partied with the wrong people?

I pulled out a smaller envelope that contained several photos of Alma and her friends. She was truly a magnificent beauty with long brown, wavy hair and a very healthy body shape. In all pictures, her brown eyes radiated confidence and had a way of drawing you in. It was sickening to think that the flesh in those autopsy photos was that of the same Alma.

I put the files away and tried to think of more pleasant thoughts before sleeping. Tomorrow night at this time Rosanna would probably be in this bed with me. That was a nice thought. I got an erection just thinking about it.

I slept until 9:00. I had no memory of any dream. Must be the effects of the Concerta, I thought. I made some coffee and looked over my class textbooks. I was already quite familiar with the applications I had to teach. It was just a matter of setting up a project for the students. As a student, I used to hate teachers who would lecture half or all the period. To me, that was time wasted. I could only keep focused and interested for a few minutes. My class would be student oriented and project-based, I decided.

Around 11:30, I drove down to the Albany YMCA on Kains Ave. to work out. I try to get in three good workouts a week. I ran on the treadmill and did my usual routine on the weight machines. I had a little curry and nan at an Indian restaurant called Cafe Raj and decided to take a walk up Solano Ave. towards my office. I checked my mail and answering machine and then walked back to my car. It was a lovely sunny day. The sun was accustomed to setting around 5:30 during this time of autumn. I called Rosanna to see if she could make it a little bit earlier so we could watch the sunset from our table at Skate's. She thought that was a great idea and said she would come right over.

Back at my house, I read the entirety of Alma's diary in speed reading style. I'd go back to it later. Nothing jumped out at me as crucial to the case but that didn't mean something meaningful wasn't hidden between the lines. I did a little yard work and then went inside to wait for Rosanna. She arrived a few minutes later in an older model Toyota Corolla. We embraced and went inside. She knew that I was teaching at LB J High but I had to make it clear to her that she needed to keep this fact completely confidential. She

46

said she understood the situation and that I could trust her. It wasn't her I was worried about though. I knew it was possible that someone at the school could recognize me as the detective from Tantei Man but I would stick to my story; that I needed a career change. It was far from the truth but blowing my cover could compromise the investigation.

As she sat on the sofa, the late afternoon sun illuminated her face. "Nice view," she said looking out on the bay. She had smooth, almost Asiatic quality skin that had a perfect light brown tone. Her large black eyes radiated warmth and beauty. She had the ideal Brazilian female body; small firm breasts, fairly thin waist, and a healthy sized butt. She walked over to the living room window. "Come here, Harley," she requested gently. I walked over to stand by the window. We turned to face each other. Her eyes became serious with passion. We began to kiss.

She tugged at the bottom of my sweatshirt and had me raise my arms. I helped her get it off the rest of the way. She stuck her tongue in my ear which magnified her heavy breathing. She then began to slide her tongue over my chest and belly. I was frozen in pleasure. She was now on her knees.

"It doesn't get any better than this," I thought to myself as she continued doing things for several minutes.

She looked up at me with her dreamy, black eyes and let out a laugh. "That was so fast," she said.

She was right. Before the medication, my mind would drift off during sex. This allowed me to delay the climax and last longer. Was I now going to be a premature ejaculator? I wasn't sure.

I embraced her again. I had always felt completely at ease with Rosanna. Any sexual tension, if there was any, was now gone for me. I could see this was going to be a relaxing evening. We took my car to Skate's on the Bay and requested a window seat. We ordered a bottle of 2003 Matanzas Creek sauvignon blanc and some smoked chipotle prawns as an appetizer. As the sun set on the bay, we talked about everything imaginable. Her English was beautiful. Our entrees arrived and we ate and drank slowly as the sky gradually darkened.

I asked her if she had ever heard of Ricardo Oliveira. I knew the Brazilian community in the East Bay was getting larger and more spread out but I thought that since she lived in the Annex, she may have heard of him or his family. She thought about it for a few moments and said,

"I don't know the family personally but I've heard of them. I think the Oliveiras manage a pizzeria on 25th St. near the City Hall. Their son was going out with that Mexican girl who got murdered."

"That's right. Her name was Alma Vargas. She's the reason I'm undercover, you know. Ricardo is in one of my classes at LBJ High. Haven't met him yet though"

"That poor thing. Must have been traumatic for him. I've heard he's in a baixa astral. How do you say that.... baixa astral in English?" she asked.

"You'd say he was in low spirits."

"Yeah, that sounds right. Life is fragile and bad people are in our midst. That's why pure souls like us have to stick together, Harley."

I agreed. "You said the Oliveiras ran a pizzeria near 25th St. That's not too far from Nicholl Park where the girl's body was found. You don't think he would be capable of?" She cut me off.

"All I know is what I hear. I've heard he is a gentle easygoing boy who wants to become a dentist. People say he's heart broken and becoming a little withdrawn. That's not very Brazilian like. You never know but unless he is a great actor, I doubt if he had anything to do with it."

"You're probably right. Anyway, let's talk about more pleasant things," I said.

"Like dessert," she laughed. "Cheese cake sounds good."

After leaving Skate's, we went for a walk out on the Berkeley Pier. It started to get cold especially for Rosanna who had spent most of here life living not too far from the equator. We got back to my house around 9:00. I put on an old Alcione CD. We danced, played, laughed, and made love until the wee hours of the morning. I wished I could have framed that evening in eternity.

The next morning, we had breakfast and took a walk hand in hand through the neighborhood. She was even more beautiful in the morning light. I liked the fact that she didn't wear makeup. Of course, she didn't need to. She told me that she had been an accountant in Recife before she got married. I asked her if she wanted to work with me someday as an office partner. She liked that idea.

This was the first night we had ever slept together but it didn't feel like it. I had the strange feeling that we had somehow always been together. Maybe that's the way it is when someone finds their soul mate, a feeling of arriving home. When we got back to the house, she told me she had to go pick up Joãozinho. We agreed to do something together later.

That afternoon we went to the Berkeley Marina. It was a windy day by the bay. I bought a kite for Joãozinho even though he was a little young for one. He seemed to like holding the handle and watching it fly. I told Rosanna about the Concerta I was taking.

"You Americans have a pill for everything," she exclaimed.

I told her about my ADD problem and she just laughed.

"You're a dreamer, Harley, an artist in motion. Don't let those doctors plant a seed in your mind. Sure, you're distracted but that's because you're so in tune to the whole. Others narrow down reality, for convenience. You take it all in at once. That's a gift, not a sickness. Anyway, in my opinion, it was a crime to prescribe that poison to you. I think you should flush it down the toilet."

She made a lot of sense to me. I did have a strange feeling that something was missing, a kind of emptiness that I couldn't quite put my finger on. Anyway, it felt good to have someone like Rosanna looking out for my best interest.

We had dinner together at Spenger's Fresh Fish Grotto, which sits kitty-corner from Brennan's on the other side of the overpass on 4th St. After dinner, she drove me home. She said she had a great time and wanted to meet more often. I did not have problem with that. When she drove away, I somehow felt lonely. That's the problem with falling in love. You know exactly what you are missing.

I spent the rest of the night working on my syllabus that I had promised to give the students on Monday. It included a brief course description, the class rules, and grading policy. I went to bed with images of Rosanna, the Alma Vargas case, and the day ahead dancing in my mind. In spite of that fact, I did not dream.

49

CHAPTER 4

The next two weeks went smoothly at school. I established order and structure in the classroom and got to know a few of the teachers and staff. I made a point of not asking questions about Alma and was confident no one suspected that I was undercover. I got to know most of my students including Alma's boyfriend Ricardo Oliveira. He was happy to have a teacher who knew about Brazil but seemed depressed and withdrawn as one could imagine.

Whenever I met a new teacher or support staff I would check the files that evening and match the face with the profile if there was any. I was taking it all in and getting the big picture. I found most of the teachers to be professional in demeanor. I found some of the support staff to be inept but not extremely so. The physical environment of the school was depressing though. The hallways were dark and there was no natural light in the classrooms. As I had suspected, most students were reading and writing far below grade level. How did this happen? The answer is complex but the lack of a familial support network was the biggest culprit as far I could see.

Wednesday was a minimum day for students but teachers were required to attend a staff development meeting in the library. This would be my first staff meeting at LBJ High. The agenda topic was how to approach the No Child Left Behind (NCLB) sanctions. LBJ High had been identified as a school that was failing based on statewide-standardized test results in math and language arts. I found out that NCLB was set up so that penalties would gradually increase if these scores did not improve by a certain amount. LBJ High was going into its 6th year as an NCLB school. This meant that the school would be forced to provide supplemental services and take some form of required corrective action. The choices for potential corrective action were provided on a bulleted list on a handout that teachers picked up as they signed in for the meeting.

❖ replace school staff relevant to the failure
❖ institute and implement a new curriculum
❖ significantly decrease management authority in the school
❖ appoint outside experts to advise the school
❖ extend school year or school day
❖ restructure internal organization of the school

50

The teachers signed in, picked up the handouts and headed to circular tables spread out around the library. I sat down at a table with Mr. Chirac and the art teacher. Joe Martelaro was 60 years old and had been teaching art at the school since 1973. Joe had been a staff member way longer than anyone else. He was about 5'8" and slender in build. Physically he looked closer to 70 than 60 with a well-weathered face. His physical presence contrasted oddly with his youthful and spirited personality. There was only one other teacher with a significant history at LBJH and that was Mr. Bergman, one of the social studies teachers who had been there since 1993.

Principal Ramos was there as were the two assistant principals, Mr. Calloway and Ms. Anderson. Mr. Ramos stood up to start the meeting.

"In spite of all the hard work you are doing, we can't escape the consequences of President Bush's No Child Left Behind legislation. As you know, our test scores were just a little short and now we need to make some hard choices. At your tables, I'd like you to discuss the potential corrective actions and come to a consensus on which one would be the best fit for LBH High. I know this is not a pleasant task but the only other alternative is to have someone make the choice for us. At 3:00, we'll reconvene."

There was silence and looks of resignation on the teachers' faces. Ms. Wexler, the English as a Second Language (ESL) teacher, stood up and spoke.

"So this is the price we pay for wanting to help disadvantaged youth. Staff development time should be used to work on how to better serve our students, not to deal with bureaucracy created by this moron of a president of ours."

Jane Wexler was in her mid-50s and became a teacher later in life. There was something in her voice and way of speaking that reminded me of Judge Judy. It was clear she wasn't afraid to speak her mind.

"This is the dilemma we are faced with. The fed orders the state. The state orders the district. The district orders the principal. I have to order the teachers. It may not be the way we want it but that's the way it is," Mr. Ramos responded. He walked abruptly out of the library.

"I'm glad I'm retiring at the end of the year," said Mr. Martelaro glancing down at the handout. "This No Child Left

Behind bullshit is a crime. Bush wants to penalize the poor schools for low-test scores but doesn't want to pay for the social programs that these kids really need. Look at this list. There is not one thing on it that will benefit our students."

"I haven't been here long enough to form any strong opinions on the NCLB sanctions. Frankly, I don't know much about it. All I know is that I heard the phrase *no child left behind* used in sound bites during the last two presidential elections. I hope you guys can fill me in," I said.

"Let's go over each one of these potential corrective actions. That'll give you a better understanding. Harley, can you take notes?" said Mr. Chirac.

"Sure," I replied.

Mr. Martelaro led the discussion. "Okay. Let's look at the first one. Replace school staff relevant to the failure. There are already systems in place to remove incompetent teachers. Teachers are evaluated every year until they are permanent and after that every other year. I'll tell you what these sanctions are going to do. They are going to scare bright young promising teachers from working in schools with poor kids. Who in their right mind would want to put up with this extra bullshit?"

Mr. Chirac nodded in agreement and I took notes.

He read the next one. "Institute and implement a new curriculum. I have no problem with a new curriculum but how's that going to get our kids off crack, stop them from having babies, get their fathers out of jail. NCLB doesn't address these issues. We've tried so many new curriculums here, I could wallpaper this school with them. It's total bullshit."

He went on. "Significantly decrease management authority in the school. We're understaffed as it is. There are no better people to manage this school than the people who already know our kids. We keep getting new principals and assistant principals every year. We all suffer as they go through their learning curves."

"Isn't this Mr. Ramos's second year?" I asked.

"We were all surprised that he was asked back. The district has been playing musical principals for the last decade. It could be a good sign. We'll have to wait and see," responded Mr. Chirac.

"The fact that he was asked back seems like a positive sign," I shyly noted.

"You never know," replied Mr. Martelaro. He went on with the list. "Appoint outside experts to advise the school. This is the heart of the NCLB nonsense. Do you have any idea how many consultants are getting rich from this legislation? People who can't teach become consultants. They pull already overworked teachers out of their classrooms to teach them what they already know. Then they pay the consultant 5 times a teacher's salary to do this. Sound like a scam? It is. We have a guy here right now, Mr. Burke, who is making a killing from NCLB. He's paid 150 bucks an hour to teach us about fucking Bloom's taxonomy. Shit, that's the first thing you learn in any school of education. This dipshit draws us out of our classes for his workshops so substitutes have to be paid. It's a complete waste of money."

I took notes vigorously. He continued. "Extend school year or school day. Won't make a difference because it doesn't address the real issues facing the kids. Most of us are here until 5:00 anyway."

"One more to go. Restructure internal organization of the school," Mr. Chirac yawned and added. "This school gets restructured every time we get a new principal. We've already volunteered to teach an extra period for no extra pay with that Corrective Reading program. Sure let them restructure to their heart's content. I'll vote for this one. It's the most vague."

Mr. Martelaro laughed. "I'll tell you the truth here. The real hope for this school got bludgeoned to death in Nicholl Park last month." He looked at me. You've already heard about Alma Vargas, haven't you?"

"Just what I've read in the paper," I lied.

"She was sure something. A student like her only comes around once in a generation."

"Really? What was so special about her?" I asked.

"Everything," responded Mr. Martelaro. "Not only was she a straight A student but she was demanding to be challenged. She requested extra work from her teachers and that they adhere to high standards. She pointed out flaws in the school's facilities and invited the press to come and take photos. She somehow got a copy of the class schedule from Acalanes High School, an upper-middleclass school in Lafayette and asked why LBJ High class listings were so pathetic in comparison. She looked at our school like a dirty little secret that needed to be revealed. Along the way, she earned the respect of a lot of teachers and students but pissed off quite a few too."

"It's even more impressive when you consider that she was officially illegal in the country," said Mr. Chirac.

"Do you guys have a theory on who killed her?" I asked.

"Superintendent Jennifer LeCroc," said Mr. Martelaro laughing.

"She definitely had a motive," added Mr. Chirac smiling. "She didn't visit our school once in the 05-06 school year, even though her office was less than a half a mile away. Because Alma filed all those official grievances, she was forced to come here a lot more often than she wanted. The negative press the school district was getting visibly disturbed her. She addressed us at a faculty meeting in September and said something I found bizarre. It went something like this:"

We open our doors and schools to immigrant children. One of these children wants us to do more. She's not happy with what we are providing. Maybe we should just hand out 10 thousand dollar checks at the border. I don't know. We live in an upside down world.

"There was an uncomfortable silence in the room and a few teachers walked out in the middle of her speech. Alma wasn't asking for handouts. She just wanted to help fix a dysfunctional system. I find it sickening that the person in charge of education in the largest school district in the East Bay didn't have the vision to see the beauty of that. We all know that a public education is not the great social equalizer it once was. But Christ, she was trying to fix it at a grassroots level what all these consultants and legislators have failed at for years." Mr. Martelaro was visibly upset.

"Did either of you have Alma in your class?" I asked.

"I did," replied Mr. Martelaro. "The art work she created was amazing."

"Do you mind if I take a look at it? I love art."

"Not at all. After this pathetic meeting, I'll take you over to the art room."

At that point, Mr. Ramos walked in. "I hope you've had time to come to some sort of consensus in your groups. Who wants to volunteer to go first?"

Mr. Cheasty, the formerly gay math teacher raised his hand aggressively. "Our group felt that hiring outside experts to advise

54

our school would be the best route or at least the less painful. No one can say we don't need help, can they?"

Ms. Wexler quickly stood up. "We can help ourselves. You might want to give up control of our destiny so easily but I don't think anybody else does. We are professionals. We don't need pseudo-professionals who don't know our kids telling us how to teach them."

A few other teachers made comments until Mr. Ramos took control of the floor. There were about 10 groups. Most groups chose the restructuring option. I found myself completely focused on what everyone was saying even though the content was often insipid and repetitive. I began to get a headache. I imagined that if I had not been taking Concerta, I would have simply drifted off. But no, I was focused on every detail of every comment.

Mr. Martelaro spoke for our group. He was quick and to the point. The last group included Jake Duckworth, Alma's favorite teacher. Mr. Chirac whispered that this was the first meeting he had attended in months. When he stood up, the room suddenly became unusually quiet.

"Our group has decided not to cooperate in honor of Alma Vargas. Even though she was young, she saw the hypocrisy of the No Child Left Behind legislation in a way that most of us cannot fathom. Mr. Ramos, I know you are being pressured by the district to come up with some sort of corrective action. I sympathize with you there. But right now, we are at a crossroads in this country. The middle and upper-middle class have chosen exclusive neighborhoods and private schools for their kids and don't want to pay for the disadvantaged youth anymore. NCLB was designed to penalize these poor schools further even though it masquerades as a school reform measure. Let's meet to talk about how to really help our kids. We should be talking about how to finance and implement after school mentor programs and high quality group homes that can make a difference. But no, we have to spend our precious time reacting to this legislation sponsored by this totally detached president of ours. Mr. Ramos, you can choose to go along with NCLB or you can choose to become a real leader. Real leadership takes guts."

At that, Mr. Duckworth walked out of the room to a round of applause.

"Jake just expressed what a lot of us were afraid to," said Mr. Chirac. Jake Duckworth was a history teacher in his early 30s and was Alma's favorite teacher according to my files. He was handsome, well-built, athletic man who looked to be about 6'3". I found out he had grown up in Oakland and was a dedicated surfer. He was planning to participate in the upcoming Maverick's Surf Contest in Half Moon Bay. I was intrigued by his rebellious yet intelligent nature and the fact that he was close to Alma. I had to find a way to talk to him.

Mr. Ramos's face had turned red. He called for the good of the order. Ms. Hemmerich, one of the social studies teachers stood up and said.

"We need to come to a consensus on if blue slips are going to be the only valid hall pass. I keep getting students coming to my class with passes written on everything from notebook paper to gum wrappers."

According to my files, Mary Hemmerich was a recent Bay Area transplant from Idaho. She had a reputation as a competent, no nonsense instructor. She had intense, bullfrog like eyes that made you want to turn away when she looked at you. For the next 20 minutes, the teachers discussed the merits of everyone being on the same page when it came to hall passes. My headache worsened as I focused on the uninteresting yet somehow important dialogue.

Finally, Ms. Wexler, who was the school's union rep stood up. "Look, it's 4:50. We're only required to be here until 4:30. It's time to wrap it up. Those who want to stick around and talk about hall passes, feel free." She called for the good of the order and the meeting was finally adjourned.

"Teachers like the sound of their own voices. If Ms. Wexler hadn't cut in, they would have babbled on ad nauseam," Mr. Martelaro explained as we walked towards his classroom. His room was in the 900 building portables at the edge of school near the football field. His classroom consisted of six large, solid wooden tables that had locker sets embedded beneath them. Like his face, the tables were weathered and full of character. Stools were placed upside down on top. He walked over to a storage closet and came out with three large canvases that appeared to be about 6 feet high and 4 feet wide.

"These are some of Alma's acrylic works," he said. He placed the first one on the table so that its width was 6 feet. She had divided the canvas into three equal sections with translucent gold lines about three inches thick. In the first section, was an image of what appeared to be a family of four crouched around a bush. The mother had her finger over her mouth as to if to say hush to the little boy who was crying. Off in the distance, there is an SUV with a uniformed man, most likely a border patrol agent, standing next to it looking through binoculars in the direction of the four. Her sense of perspective was excellent. The middle section was subdivided into three sections from top to bottom. In the top, was a depiction of a man, apparently the father from the first section, doing landscape work at a beautiful house. In the middle section, the mother was depicted on her knees scrubbing a floor. In the bottom part, the young girl was depicted raising her hand in a classroom with a big smile on her face. In the final section on the right, a woman is depicted on the phone sitting behind a desk with the presidential seal of the USA on the wall behind. A plaque on the desk read President Vargas.

"She sure had a sense of humor and talent to spare," he said smiling. "She picked up on two-point perspective just like that and had un uncanny sensibility in the use of color. I'm going to see if I can get these in the permanent collection of the Richmond Art Museum."

He set up the next two paintings. The first one was a disturbing depiction of a hallway scene at a school. It showed a mix of African American and Hispanic students walking down a hallway with blank, empty expressions. They were dressed in the usual attire of gang-bangers, baggy pants, t-shirts, and bandanas. Some had headphones on. No one carried books or binders.

"This is a powerful painting," I noted.

"You're telling me. She not only picked up on the technical aspects of painting quickly, she immediately recognized the medium's potential for self-expression. Alma was taken aback by the apathy and self degrading behavior of a lot of her peers and I think that's where this painting came from."

"Did she have a lot of friends?" I asked.

"She had a group of close friends that seemed to be growing. She was unusual in the sense that unlike other good students who just kept to a small group, she tried to have an impact on her classmates who were failing. Some of them gave her a hard time but that didn't stop her from trying."

"Do you think she could have been killed by one of these failing students."

"I have no idea. That's a possibility I'm sure."

"You were joking about Superintendent Jennifer LeCroc killing her, weren't you?"

"Of course. But heck, with this district anything's possible. All I know is that we lost a bright light the day she died."

"Have you heard any rumors on why she was killed?" I felt safe now asking questions.

"Just one. I've heard talk among students that it may have been a case of mistaken identity. A student told me that she had heard that Alma was mistaken for a girlfriend of one the sureños and kidnapped and killed by the norteños, a rival gang. I reported this to the police but it turned out the story didn't hold water."

I was familiar with these two groups. As their name partly implied, sureños were gang-bangers from southern California and Mexico while norteños were from the north. The gang members at LBJH were mostly sureños while at the other high schools in El Sobrante and Pinole, they were mostly norteños.

He showed me the last painting. It was a depiction of a young man with no shirt and blue jeans lying on a bed, looking directly at the viewer. I recognized this young man immediately as Ricardo Oliveira. "Has he seen this?" I asked.

"Sure. He modeled for it. Alma called this one her masterpiece but I think the others are more powerful."

I thanked him for showing me her work and then headed towards the teachers' parking lot. When I got home, I took an Advil for my headache, had a small frozen dinner, and called Rosanna. I told her about how I was able to focus, even on the most insipid dialogues and that the ADD medicine seemed to be working, though I did have a pretty severe headache.

"That's wonderful Harley, if that's what you want. I'll take the distracted, unmedicated Harley any day of the week though. Go tell your doctor that your girlfriend wants you off the Concerta," she said.

"I'm considering taking your advice. Not sure if my headache was from the medicine, the job, or both. The truth is I don't really see the point of being completely focused on what everyone says when 90% of all said is either uninteresting or irrelevant. I'm beginning to think my so-called ADD is a natural defense mechanism to protect me from mediocrity. I'll call my doctor tomorrow about getting off it."

"Why don't you just stop right now? Your doctor just might try to confuse you," she said.

"When he prescribed it, he made a point of telling me not to stop it on my own. He said that could cause adverse reactions."

"Adverse reactions to the profits of the pharmaceutical company he is pimping?" she laughed. "Anyway, I'm missing you like crazy. When can I see you?"

"How about this weekend?"

"Great idea. I'd like to make dinner for you on Sunday. Make a plan to spend the night at my place," she suggested.

"Sounds like a date. I'll be counting the hours. Tchauzinho."

I decided to reread some of the translations of Alma's diary in bed. It appeared she started her journal the day she left her hometown of Hidalgo del Parral.

Hidalgo del Parral - March 23, 2006

Tomorrow is the day. We will take a bus to Juarez early in the morning. Papa has made arrangements to meet the coyote there. The instructions for me and little brother Juanito are simple. "Don't ask questions. Don't cry. Obey our every command." This is a sad day for me. I know we are poor and our opportunities are few but my friends, my life, and my world are here and tomorrow they will be only memories. I'm scared that something bad will happen but will try to be strong for my family.

Juarez - March 25, 2006

After a long, bumpy bus ride we arrived in Juarez. We walked for two hours on a hot noisy street. We were thirsty and hungry but did not complain. Finally, we arrived at an old apartment building and papa went inside. Mama bought us paletas to quench our thirst. After an hour, Papa came out and we followed him back up a flight of stairs to the seventh floor. The living room was full of people. There was a small TV on the floor and several men of all ages were sitting around it drinking beer and watching a soccer game. I did not like this place and felt scared but kept it a

secret. There were three bedrooms in the apartment and we went
into the middle one. There were old dirty blankets spread all over
and three other families sitting on the floor. There was a 15-year-
old girl named Ruth from Camargo with her family of five. I had no
idea how we would all sleep in this room. Ruth asked me if I wanted
to go for a walk. Mama said I could if I took Juanito with us. We
walked around the neighborhood until we found a game arcade. We
had no money to play so we watched other kids. Ruth told me she
didn't trust the Coyote. He charged her father less than the other
families and this made her suspicious. I told her not to worry. I
later regretted telling her that. Back at the apartment, Mama
brought several tamales that she bought at a stand. They were not
as good as Mama makes but we were hungry. We sat around and
talked with the other families for a long time. When we finally got
ready to sleep, we discovered that there was not enough room for
everyone so a few volunteered to sleep in the hallway. The
apartment was noisy with conversations and people snoring. I truly
hated this place and was glad I'd only have to spend one night here. I
awoke soon after falling to sleep to the sound of two men arguing. It
was Ruth's father and the coyote. Ruth's father was saying please
don't do this, when I get to the other side I promise to send you
more money. The coyote told her father to shut up. He then called
out to Ruth to wake up and come with him. I could see she was
trembling with fear. Her father hugged her and said please forgive
me. I couldn't sleep thinking about what was happening to Ruth and
fearing that someone would come for me. After what seemed an
eternity, I heard doors opening and Ruth walked back into the
bedroom. I made a space for her next to me and tried to comfort
her. She was sobbing like a small child. I knew she had been
violated but didn't ask her about the details. I told her things would
get better on the other side. In the morning, Mama brought back
bread and juice. It's now around noon and I am sick and tired of
this place. Ruth is looking depressed. I hope she can have a good
life. She is a nice girl. Tonight is the night we cross. Wish us luck.

Las Cruces, New Mexico – March 27, 2006

You guessed it. We made it to Gringolandia. It was not
easy though. Around one o'clock in the morning about 30 of us
including Ruth's family crawled into a tunnel. We had to squat to

walk and the journey took several hours. When we emerged, we were in America. Our clothes were completely covered with mud. After walking for 20 minutes, we all took off our clothes at the same time and abandoned them. We had extras in the sacks. It was a funny scene but no one laughed. Right before dawn, we heard the sound of an engine. A big jeep pulled up and parked. Papa whispered for us to hide in the bushes and lay low. The branches were rough and scratched our skin. Juanito began to cry but suddenly stopped. Through the brush, I saw a man in uniform using binoculars pointed in our direction. Would we be caught and put in jail? My heart was beating fast. We heard a door slam and the sound of the engine again. I could feel the vibration of the earth as the jeep approached closer. I heard men speaking English but couldn't make out what they were saying. Through a tiny gap in the branches, I dared to look out. About 100 meters away, I could see that Ruth and her family were being handcuffed. A van arrived about 15 minutes later and took them away. I felt so sorry for Ruth. She gave her innocence for nothing. When it was clear, we continued on our journey. We were thirsty and our water supply was gone. The sun had completely risen by the time we arrived at a paved road. Papa seemed to know where he was by a number on a sign. We found some bushes to hide behind near the road and waited. Juanito and I did not ask why. We could hear the sound of cars going by. Finally, an old green van slowed down near the number sign. Papa said let's go fast. We ran towards the van and jumped in through the back door. There were several people in the van and it was hot inside. Papa paid the driver some money. We drove for about an hour. Along the way, the van stopped to let people out at different locations. We were let out on a quiet street with some warehouses. Papa said we would not have to wait long. I asked him if it was okay to ask questions now. He hugged me and said yes, yes, yes! I asked him what we would do now. He said his cousin Francisco would be here soon. We were still very thirsty. Sure enough, in about 15 minutes Francisco pulled up in an old American car. It had faded, white paint mixed in with rust. The plaque on the side read Cutlass. He had water and food, which we readily accepted. Francisco said he would take highway 25 to Las Cruces and we would stay in a motel there. We knew the further we were from the border, the safer we would be but we still needed rest. In Las Cruces, we found a motel called the Sleep Inn. That's a *funny name. Uncle Francisco paid. There are two beds in the room and it is very comfortable. We took showers, cleaned our clothes, ate and drank. I just asked Papa if I could take a walk and he said no. I feel like I'm living in a dream. Finally he let me and Juanito use the swimming pool. It was so refreshing. We splashed and played for about an hour. Finally, we had a breath holding contest under water that I won easily. Right now, I am more happy than sad but am getting very sleepy. Compared to where we slept yesterday, this is paradise. What a day! What will tomorrow bring?*

Blythe, California – March 28, 2006

We left Las Cruces after breakfast and headed towards Highway 10. Uncle Francisco said that this is the highway that would take us to California. I don't remember the names of all the towns we passed through except the big ones, Phoenix and Tucson in Arizona. Right after we passed the border of California, the Golden State, the car overheated and we had to pull over. I was scared that we would be caught but we got lucky. A Mexican American family from Bakersfield saw us and pushed us to a gas station in a town called Blythe. The man at the gas station was nice and fixed the car very quickly. My father paid for the new water pump, whatever that is. Right now, we just finished eating at a Denny's restaurant and are getting ready for the rest of the journey. Francisco said that we would drive all night.

Richmond, California – March 31, 2006

We have moved into Francisco's house in a city called Richmond. It's not too far from San Francisco. We live on Alfreda St. which is close to 23rd St., the main avenue. I don't have to worry too much about communicating with Americans because almost everyone around here speaks Spanish, except the Blacks and Asians. This is not the same America I saw on TV and in the movies. I have three cousins: Maria (seven years old), Nadia (10), and Felipe (15). They have already been in America two years and attend school every day. I was curious how an illegal resident could attend school and Felipe said every child in the country legal or not, has a right to an education. Felipe is a soccer star at

62

Richmond High School and sometimes his name gets printed in the local newspaper on the sport's page.

Richmond – May 3, 2006

I haven't written in this journal for a while mainly because there hasn't been much to write about. I stay home and help around the house during the day with Mama and Aunt Rosa. Papa and Francisco leave early every morning to look for work, Sometimes they go to a place called Home Depot and sometimes they go to a place in Berkeley called Truitt and White Lumber. They stand on the corner until someone stops and offers them a job. They usually get some hard labor job and make about 50 dollars a day. Some days they do better, other days they are not picked up at all. Still we are much better off than when we were in Mexico and Papa is even saving money for his own car. Mama is looking for house cleaning work and she wants me to help her. I want to go to school but Mama and Papa think that's a bad idea. They say I will just waste my time in school but I know I won't. America is the land of opportunity, right? We risked our lives to come here, we should do everything we can to succeed. Papa and Mama can't see beyond their hard-working world but I want to work hard for a new life. I still think about poor Ruth and what happened to her. She lost everything for nothing. I must do well in her honor.

May 25, 2006

I am excited. Felipe took me to the offices of an organization called Destinos Latinos. They have a small office at the Dias Plaza in San Pablo, not too far from here. They help Latino kids get enrolled in school and make plans for the future. I want to start school in late August when the American school year begins. I need to have my transcripts sent from Hidalgo del Parral, translated to English, and then sent to the school district. Then I need to register with the district. I hope I can convince Mama and Papa that this is the right thing to do.

May 27, 2006

I have a headache. I was arguing with Papa all night about going to school. He worries about being deported and thinks an education won't do much for me. I told him that I wanted to make him proud and he said he already was. He told me to forget it but I won't. I will persist until he gives in.

May 28, 2006

Another night, another fight. Last night, I threatened to run away if I couldn't attend school. Papa said he wasn't going to let me get them sent back to Mexico. I am depressed but I have an idea. I will try to get Papa and Mama to come with me to the Destinos Latinos office.

May 30, 2006

Today is Sunday and everyone is in the house. I talked Felipe into helping me try to persuade my parents. They flatly refused to come with me to Destinos Latinos. If I can't bring my parents to Destinos Latinos, then I will need to bring Destinos Latinos to my parents. I will visit them again tomorrow.

May 31, 2006

Today, I am optimistic. I visited Mr. Franco at Destinos Latinos and explained my situation. He said he was impressed by my desire for an education and would do anything in his power to see that I get enrolled in school. I asked him to drop by our house Wednesday evening around 7:00. I'm worried that Papa will explode when he finds out. To avoid another stressful night, I will keep it a secret until just before he arrives. I hope I will be forgiven.

June 2, 2006

Just a few minutes before Mr. Franco arrived, I told my parents that we would have a visitor. Felipe helped by saying that Destinos Latinos were good people and they only wanted to help us. Papa was angry but before a big argument could start, there was a knock on the door. Mr. Franco was very gracious and listened to my parents concerns with respect and interest. He told them that a school was the best place for Juanito and me and could actually help in eventually obtaining legal status. He told them about the process of enrolling in school and listed all the steps we would need to take. When Mr. Franco left, Papa took a deep breath, looked me in the eyes, and said this: "If an education is what you want, I will sign you up. Remember, time is money, so do your very best." I hugged him as hard as I could and cried. He promised to take me to the district office soon to sign up.

June 4, 2006

I had to wait a few days but on Friday Mr. Franco came by our house and drove us to the district office. I could tell that Papa was nervous but Mr. Franco told him to relax. There were a lot of papers to fill out and documents we would need but we were going forward. The district official said that we would not know the school we would attend until a week before school started in late August but that based on our address, I would most likely attend LBJ High and Juanito would attend Downer Elementary School. I can't wait to start but we have the whole summer in front of us. Mr. Franco mentioned an Adult School in Richmond where I could study English over the summer. I studied English on my own in Mexico by listening to music and playing American movies with Spanish subtitles over and over until it stuck but I still want to get better. I can speak English much better than Felipe and he's been here for a few years.

I put down the diary and began to think about the lack of progress I was making. It was time to move forward but what could I do. I was focused on the details of the case but my mind had apparently lost the ability to roam, those seemingly random flights into tangent that since childhood had led me to the concealed truths. I stared at the ceiling for five minutes but all I noticed was the textured paint. I thought about the case but I couldn't get beyond the details. I was like a jet airplane on the runway that had lost its ability to take off.

CHAPTER 5

As soon as I awoke on Thursday morning, I tried to remember my dreams but drew a complete blank. I got on the phone and left a message on my doctor's answering machine. I told him I was considering taking myself off Concerta but wanted his opinion first. I had a quick breakfast, took a Concerta, and then headed out for another day at LBJ High.

At the end of period 7, I asked Ricardo Oliveira to stick around for a while and help out with some computers that had broken down. Unlike most of the students, his interest in computers went beyond surfing the web, e-mail, and game playing. He wanted to learn what made them tick and spent lots of time after school in Mr. Chirac's classroom helping out with the multitude of technical problems that presented during the school day. I asked him if he would help install a couple of hard drives in computers in our room that had gone bad.

When everyone had left, we disconnected the two sick machines and pulled out the faulty hard drives. I decided it was time to start talking to him about Alma. We had the Brazilian connection thing going and I felt comfortable getting personal.

"You know, I'm really sorry about your loss. I didn't know Alma but everyone I've met who knew her thought the world of her. If there's anything I can do to help you get through this, let me know."

"Morte é foda!" (Death Sucks!) he softly said in Portuguese. "People keep telling me I'll get over it. That time heals all. I don't believe it for a minute. Nothing good comes from the death of a bright light like Alma. Sure, my life will go on. But what about the quality of my life? She was the air I breathed. Now, there is just emptiness. I don't think there is anything anyone can do to help."

There was an awkward silence as I tried to think of what to say. Basically I agreed with his death sucks philosophy. As an adult though, I tempered it with a we are all doomed anyway, let's make the most of it slant in spite of the sadness. Still I knew that everyone had to deal with the death of a loved one in their own unique way. I had to choose my words carefully as to not sound phony.

"Death sucks big time," I said. "All we can do is try to live our life in a way that our loved one would be proud. Think about how Alma would have wanted you to live."

His eyes filled with tears and soon he was sobbing. I put my arm around his shoulder. "She would have wanted me to keep up the fight to fix this place. She would have wanted justice for her death." He put his hands on both temples as if his head was going to explode.

"Why don't you start a club in her honor?" I suggested. "I would be happy to sponsor it. You could figure out all the best ways to honor her memory."

He looked at me still holding his head in his hands. "That would be good. That would be good," he said twice catching his breath.

"Well, let's finish installing these hard drives. We can talk about this tomorrow."

I pulled the two new hard drives out of their wrapping and handed one to Ricardo. We quickly inserted them in the drive bays and attached the cables. We closed the casing, set the computers into their locked down position, and powered them up for a test run. All systems go.

"Thanks for the help Ricardo. I got to tell you that young people like you and Alma give me a lot of hope for the future. Let's do right by her."

His eyes were still watery. I gave him the traditional Brazilian abraço (hug), bid farewell, and watched him as he took off down the hall. I straightened out my classroom and prepared a lesson for the following day.

On the way home, I dropped by my Tantei Man office to pick up the mail. Everything looked pretty much like I'd left it except for a little dust accumulation. Even though the answering message I recorded stated that I couldn't take on new cases for a while, there were several urgent requests for me to call back. I decided to ignore them. Hopefully, my absence wouldn't have a long term effect on my future business but it was too late to change anything now.

My stomach was empty so I walked a few blocks down the street to Gordo's for a burrito. I took a window seat and munched on my burrito while watching the people walk down Solano Avenue. It was drizzling outside but no one carried an umbrella.

67

"Hey Harley, long time no see," a voice from behind me said.

I set my burrito down and turned around. It was Gary Sealy, the mayor of Albany.

"Well, how are things at city hall?" I asked.

"You know how boring those City council meetings can be. We got a bunch of lefties trying to stop the cell phone companies from getting permits to install antennas next to their houses. Believe that? These same morons are trying to prevent the Robinson project from happening on the shoreline and the Safeway condo project."

"Albany is a small, safe town. A lot of people want to keep it that way," I responded.

"These same people seem to forget that revenues make the world go around," he exclaimed. I didn't feel like getting into a political debate about quality of life vs. increasing local revenues so I just nodded my head. I had met Mayor Sealy at several chamber of commerce meetings over the past few years while trying to promote Tantei Man. He was of short stature but what he lacked in height he made up for in width. He was a local mover and shaker, not above cronyism, and a staunch card carrying Republican. He was getting a lot of local press these days due to his support of the controversial Robinson project. Robinson Inc. was a group of developers from Southern California who wanted to build a strip mall on the shoreline in what was currently the parking lot of the race track. If successful, this project would permanently alter the skyline view of thousands of East Bay residents. Goodbye Golden Gate Bridge. Hello Barnes and Noble. Mayor Sealy got in the long line and said goodbye.

I wrapped up the rest of my burrito and left. While I was walking back to my car, I thought about how different the issues in Albany and Richmond were in spite of their proximity. Here in Albany, hundreds of people could mobilize quickly to fight a cell phone company from getting a permit to install antennas. Right down the road in Richmond, kids were getting murdered at an alarming rate, and nobody seemed to get out of their chair.

When I got home, the first thing I did was check my answering machine. There were messages from Randy and Rosanna but none from my doctor. I called Randy back and gave him a progress report. He told me not to be discouraged; that he had faith

68

in my skills. I called Rosanna and we chatted for about two hours. She asked me if I wanted to go with her to La Peña, a Latin culture club, on Friday to have dinner. She said she would bring along her friend Kátia and asked me to bring a friend if I wanted. I immediately thought of Randy. I called Randy and he agreed to come along. Friday night was set.

I reheated the rest of my burrito and washed it down with a glass of guava juice. After watching some TV, I headed to bed to pick up where I left off in Alma's diary.

June 21, 2006

The summer in Richmond is nothing like the summer in Chihuahua. Some days are warm but a lot of days are cool. In Mexico, I'd be burning up right now but I'm very comfortable here. My life has been pretty uneventful the past few weeks. Mama got a job as a house cleaner and Papa leaves early every morning to stand in front of Home Depot. I mostly stay in the house taking care of the annoying Juanito but today I attended my first English class at the adult school. The adult school is in a pre-fabricated building at the edge of the LBJ High school campus. There were about 30 students, mostly Mexicans but there were a few boys from Yemen and a few girls from Laos. I know absolutely nothing about these places. The teacher's name was Mr. Sanders. He handed out some paperwork and modeled how to introduce oneself. It was fun but I didn't learn anything. I ended up helping some of the other students. I was hoping for a more advanced class but Mr. Sanders says this is the only one offered in the summer. Anyway, it's nice to get out and meet people. LBJ High is about a 15 minute walk from our house.

July 12, 2006

Papa didn't get home until after dinner tonight. He had a big smile on his face when he walked through the door. He said he made $200 for the day. That's much better than the $30 to $60 that he usually gets. Juanito and I had a big laugh when we heard him speak English for the first time. He said, "another day, another dollar" which I guess is an American expression. Papa changed his mind about wanting to buy a new car. He is afraid he'll have

69

trouble with the police. He catches a ride with Uncle Francisco and helps pay for the gas.

July 15, 2006

A new student enrolled in the English class today. His name is Ricardo Oliveira and he is from Brazil. He is extremely handsome and smart. I was getting bored with the class but with Ricardo there, I shall continue to go. He asks lots of questions to the teacher and is not shy. After class, I walked over to his family's restaurant and they offered us some pizza. His parents were very friendly and warm. Ricardo said he could speak Portunol (a mixture of Spanish and Portuguese) but we ended up speaking English most of the time. I can't wait until tomorrow to see him again.

July 25, 2006

Last night, I had a date with Ricardo. We went to a shopping center called the Hilltop Mall. I had to beg Papa to let me go. One of Ricardo's Brazilian friends named Junior drove us there. We walked around looking at all the things we couldn't afford to buy. When Ricardo grabbed my hand my heart melted. We sat on a bench in front of Macy's talking for an hour. When he kissed me, I thought I'd pass out. I will dream of him again tonight.

July 30, 2006

Today was the last day of English classes for the summer. Ricardo and I were by far the best students and the best speakers of English. Most of the other students went back to Spanish the second they left the classroom. Mr. Sander's final advice was to use the English language daily. He said if you don't use it, you'll lose it. So far, it looks like only me and Ricardo are using it. I will remember that class forever, not because of the English I learned but because that is where I met the love of my life. I am thankful that Mama and Papa like Ricardo and his parents seem to like me. Perhaps it is because we are both so charming. Ja! Ja! Ja! High School begins in a few weeks and I pray that Ricardo and I are placed in the same school.

August 20, 2006

Today, we got our school placement letters, just four days before school begins. I was beginning to think they forgot about us. Just like the lady at the district predicted, I was placed at LBJ High and Juanito at Downer Elementary School. I called Ricardo immediately and found out that he too was placed at LBJ High. This is a happy day! We will celebrate this weekend.

Before leaving for work on Friday, I left another message for my doctor about stopping Concerta. I decided that if he didn't call me back by tonight, today's dose would be the last. I would go cold turkey.

At LBJ High, it was a rally day and students were completely crazy. It was as if everyone was on speed. As I stood in front of my classroom watching the students walk by, I thought of Alma's painting of the students with the blank stares. There was a certain kind of collective insanity out there rooted in hopelessness and manifesting itself in inarticulate hollering back and forth. Civility was as foreign to these students as Belgium. Garbage would be tossed to the ground even if a trash can was a few feet way. There was no social, civil, or national conscience at LBJ High that was apparent. There were a few students like Ricardo that offered hope but the majority truly represented a significant decline of civilization. Perhaps by following Alma's path, I could find some hope in this madness.

I did have a good rapport with my students. After a month though, the job was beginning to wear on me and I began to seriously question my decision. It was clear that a lot of these students were not ready for the real world, unless you consider the Big House the real world. Quite a few routinely came late or didn't show up at all. I was constantly confiscating candy or picking up wrappers that students would discard on the floor. The average student had an attention span of about 10 seconds and would go off task if not reminded constantly. In spite of my strict "no eating in class" policy, candy wrappers and crumbs could be found all over the place. The janitors had only cleaned my room once since I'd been there. When I asked why the answer was budget cuts. There was a girl in my first period class who was obviously a crack head.

Mercedes would come into class stoned talking to herself and would do her best to agitate others. When I asked her other instructors how she performed in their classes, the reply was simply "that's just the way she is".

I definitely needed to move forward but wasn't sure how. Was it the Concerta or was it the unorthodox manner I was conducting this investigation that was causing my investigative impotence? I couldn't be sure. The Alma Vargas memorial club may be the key to moving forward but I would need Ricardo's help. Anyway, the old saying, "thank God it's Friday" had special meaning for me today.

In spite of a well-designed lesson plan, the students were not cooperative. Most played games or surfed the internet and avoided their projects. The rally schedule meant most classes were short. That turned out to be a blessing as I was losing my patience. Since I had started, I had not yet referred one student to one of the Assistant Principals for discipline. I was tempted many times to fill out those referral forms today though until I reminded myself that the AP's were too busy breaking up fights around campus. By 2:15 when the last bell rang, I was exhausted. I chatted with Ricardo and set up a time to discuss the Alma Memorial Club next week.

It was now time to go to the rally in the gym. Entering, I walked right into a wall of noise but it wasn't the sound of school spirit. A skinny black girl named Deena tried to get the attention of the masses sitting precariously in the four filled-to-capacity bleachers. Although the sound system was working fine, her voice crashed into the wall of noise and was obliterated. Mr. Prince, the site supervisor, took the microphone and said in a voice approaching a shout. "If you don't shut up, you will be given a Saturday school. If you don't show up for Saturday school, you will be suspended." He somehow managed to get the attention of the masses and then handed the microphone back to Deena.

The show went on in spite of the noise. I couldn't make much sense out of the program but it consisted of several dance routines set to rap music. At 3:15, it was all over and I had a pretty bad headache. I walked straight to my car instead of returning to my classroom and drove home.

Once home, I took an Advil and crawled into bed for a nap. I awoke around 6:00 feeling a little better and checked my answering machine. No calls from my doctor. My Concerta days

72

were officially over. There were messages from both Rosanna and Randy confirming the night's plans. I took a shower and then made a cup of Earl Grey tea. The plan was to meet at La Peña at 7:30 and have dinner before the show.

I arrived there a little early. La Peña is easy to recognize as the facade of the building is covered with a large colorful mural depicting scenes from South America. Inside, it is divided into three sections. There is a restaurant on the north side called Cafe de La Peña, a small concert hall on the south, and a small bar in the center. Since I was the first to arrive, I went directly to the bar and ordered a caipirinha. A ballad I recognized was playing on the sound system. It was a Mercedes Sosa song, Inconciente Colectivo (Collective Unconscious). After a few minutes, Randy arrived and I ordered a caipirinha for him. It was his first ever.

7:30 came and went but no Rosanna and Kátia. This didn't surprise me as I knew from experience that Brazilian time was the opposite of Swiss. We ordered a couple of more drinks and Randy, the consummate professional, brought up the case. "You know Harley, there's a lot of random violence in the Iron Triangle. Look at somebody the wrong way and you're dead. I'm almost certain that's not the case with Alma though."

"I agree. The Restoril and high levels of alcohol in her system just don't mesh with the kind of person she was. I know good kids, even honor students get wild and do things adults don't expect but Alma wasn't your typical honor student. I'm leaning to the theory that she was drugged, sexually assaulted, killed somewhere and then dumped in the park. I need to get to the who and why of the motive and that isn't easy."

"There's always the chance she was stalked and abducted for simple sexual motives. If that's the case, your work at LBJ may be in vain but until we find out, you've got to go forward buddy. Destinos Latinos call us everyday asking for an update."

The Gilberto Gil song Refazenda was now playing but I stayed focused on the conversation. The Concerta was still in my system, I thought.

"The autopsy report mentioned fibers on her clothes. Have you found out if they match any carpet or surface area in her parent's house?" I asked.

"All but a few of the fibers have been accounted for. Remember, she'd been at school the whole day before so she could

73

have picked them up in a number of places. Anyway, we're still working on that."

I was about to ask him about those few unaccounted for fibers when in strolled Rosanna and Kátia fashionably late. Kátia was from São Paulo and of Italian descent. She had sandy blonde hair, blue eyes, a very nice figure and was about 5 feet tall. This was a blessing as Randy was only a few inches taller. We made our introductions with the traditional kiss on each cheek. There were a few guys at the bar who looked at us with envious eyes as we walked over to the restaurant section.

The next few hours were spent enjoying conversation, eating a variety of Chilean dishes, and sipping caipirinhas. Kátia spoke English well but with a stronger accent than Rosanna. Randy was all smiles. He asked the girls questions about Brazil with sincere curiosity. He looked like a child in a candy store. It was the first time I'd seen him go so long without mentioning work.

Rosanna and I decided to take a walk to get some fresh air. We began to kiss and embrace but slowed down knowing that we couldn't sleep together for another two days.

"I can't wait until Sunday, meu amorzinho (my love). We'll spend the day together. I'll make you dinner and you can spend the night. Then we'll have breakfast and I'll send you off to work."

"Sounds like a married couple, doesn't it?" I noted.

"Difference being that we're happy," she laughed.

Rosanna's dark eyes had a hypnotic effect on me. As soon as our eyes connect, I'm drawn in deeper and deeper. It's like I'm being led down a path to some sort of enlightenment. When the bond is broken, I feel like someone who once knew nirvana but was now just an ordinary man. My attraction to her was obviously more than sexual but I couldn't quite put my finger on the essence of it. She was conveniently beautiful but the attraction was much more than that. The other evening when she dropped by it was like she was sending me a message. Let's get the worldly things out of the way quickly so we can take it to the next level. The climax is not the end. It is the beginning. That blow-job experience did not make me think of her in a cheap way. Unlike me, I could see that she was in complete control of her being and confident. I respected that.

I pondered about how her husband Marco must had been a shallow man not to have recognized her special grace but then I

74

thought about chemistry. Rosanna and I were obviously connected. After talking to her for about a half an hour that first night we met in San Francisco, I felt that she had somehow always been there in my life. But if we were predestined, why did I lose her phone number that night and why didn't she call me until she needed my services two and a half years later? I decided to ask her why she waited so long.

"You and I both know Harley we connected that night. That was very real. It's strange but I knew that we would meet again and would be together. I had just completed an ugly divorce and there was a lot of negative energy hovering over my aura. That energy needed to be expunged. I didn't want to corrupt the purity of our connection. I thought about you often over those years though and have a confession to make. When I hired you, I was hoping it would bring us together. Please forgive my deception."

Her explanation made complete sense. We walked arm and arm back to La Peña. Along the way, we passed a club called the Starry Plough and peeked inside the door. There was a poetry slam going on. Some African American guy was on the stage rapping out a poem he called War at Home.

I don't see your eyes
But I hear your lock switch
You don't hear my cries
But you think about my cock bitch
Your war in Iraq makes
your eyes twitch But
there's war at home Yes,
a war at home
And every ghetto kid from New York to L.A. been drafted
Since the day of our birth we've all been shafted There's
a war at home
Yes, a war at home

Rosanna grabbed me by my arm as if she was annoyed and we continued our walk back. I asked her what she thought of the poem.

"É pura merda! (It's complete shit) You've been shafted since birth. Yeah. Yeah. Yeah. White America will not allow you to rise. Yeah. Yeah. Yeah. I came to America with great sympathy for the American black man. In Brazil, I had read about the Klu Klux Klan and was under the impression that white America was hopelessly racist. My experience since living here has shown me something different. Yes, I have seen a little of the white racism that I expected. I know it still exists. What I also see is that the popular culture is feeding a victimization myth. Just watch any of the hip hop stations. The message is loud and clear. We're victims but somehow manage to be arrogant, jewelry rattling, misogynists. Then this merda is marketed like Coca Cola to the mindless masses. Just like the former slave masters, the popular culture like rap is keeping the black man down. I'm sorry but I haven't heard any meaningful rap lately."

Rosanna was sure opinionated. I thought of rap as simply a medium of expression, limited only by the talents of the rapper. But recently, I too had noticed that some of the lyricism had become fairly superficial in nature. Maybe it was because the medium itself had been around for so long now that the sound was becoming monotonous, tired and repetitive. Was I getting old? I don't think so. I was never one to swallow everything the pop culture fed me, even as a kid.

We peeked in the window of the restaurant section and saw Randy and Kátia laughing and chatting away. We sat back down at the table and finished off the remaining appetizers. We decided to skip the show and stay in the restaurant. At 11:00, Rosanna had to leave to pick up Joãzinho from the babysitters. Randy and Kátia exchanged phone numbers and promised to meet again soon. Rosanna reminded me about Sunday and then they both walked out the door. As we eased our way back to the bar, some guy at a nearby table gave us a "how could you let them go home alone" look.

"This was the most fun I've had in a long time, Harley. I've never met anyone so easy to talk to. How do you do it buddy?"

"Well once you go Brazilian there's no turning back," I joked.

"I mean I haven't been out with anyone but my ex-wife in years. I thought I'd be tongue-tied but these girls just knew how to make you relax. So natural and personable."

"They can be a pain in the ass when they want to be. Generally speaking, Brazilians are more affectionate than Americans. They call it calor humano, human warmth. It's the day to day hugs and kisses and genuine affection shared between friends. It keeps you sane and helps you sleep at night. I think I slept deeper and more profoundly when I lived in Brazil."

"Wow! You make it sound like a religious experience."

"In a way it was. I've traveled the world and no other country hooked me in the same way. Sometimes I'd meet other foreigners in my travels who became obsessed with everything Brazilian. It doesn't happen to everybody but to quite a few it does."

"Not sure I want to convert just yet old buddy but I did like Kátia. Let's do this again sometime soon."

"I'm sure we can make that happen. You know, Rosanna is the only one close to me who knows I'm undercover at LBJ High. I just couldn't keep it a secret from her."

"As long as you can trust her Harley, I know you went out on a limb for us by going undercover as a teacher. I know that was a lot to ask. I just want to acknowledge how grateful we are. The department has complete confidence in you."

"I hope I don't let them down," I said sheepishly.

We ordered coffee and talked for about an hour with the intent of bringing our blood alcohol levels down before driving home. Back at the house, I hit the sack immediately. My head was spinning but somehow I managed to fall asleep quickly. It had been a long day.

I woke up about 9:00 a.m. with a slight headache even though I hadn't drunk enough alcohol the night before to cause a hangover. At least, I didn't think so. I made some coffee to see if caffeine withdrawal might be the culprit and did feel a little better after a cup of strong java. I had my usual boiled egg for breakfast while reading the morning paper. On page three there was a lengthy article about unsolved murders in the East Bay over the past three years. It was sad to see Alma's picture next to gang-bangers who had probably died in petty retaliations. The article didn't offer anything new about the case and simply stated that her body was found bludgeoned to death in Nicholl Park.

After breakfast, by habit I grabbed the bottle of Concerta and took a capsule out. I was about to put it on my tongue when I remembered the promise to myself to stop. I flushed the remaining medicine down the toilet. As I watched the water swirl and last pill disappear from sight, I wondered if the bacterial life living in the sewer would now be more focused.

My headache worsened. I got on the computer and did a search using the keywords Concerta and withdrawal. At drugs.com the information was clear. Do not stop taking the medication without first consulting your doctor. Side effects of sudden withdrawal could include but are not limited to severe depression, unusual behavior, and tiredness or weakness. I wondered what they meant by unusual behavior. I felt comforted by the fact that death wasn't mentioned as a side effect. Since my doctor hadn't called me back, I imagined that the withdrawal couldn't be that bad. Anyway, Dr. Rosanna had given me the go ahead and she answers to a higher calling.

I decided to take it easy Saturday. I pulled weeds in the garden and noticed that there were a few empty areas that could use some sort of plant or flower. I drove down to the Berkeley Horticultural Nursery on Hopkins Street to go plant shopping. For me, visiting a well-designed nursery like Berkeley Horticultural was like going to the Louvre. I could spend hours looking at the plants in all the different sections. The color contrasts, smells, and textures could keep me interested for a long time. Since it was late fall, I settled on some daffodil bulbs that could provide some color come spring. I took them home and planted them carefully in the soil in front of my house.

After lunch, I began thinking about Alma. Seeing her face in the morning paper had put me in a blue mood. I imagine that most people just scanned the article thinking very little about the real lives of these people. She was obviously so much more than just another dead ghetto kid. I needed to find out as much as I could about her. I picked up her diary, sat down on my lazy-boy chair and started to read.

September 13, 2006

I don't know whether to laugh or cry. This is not how I imagined high school in America would be. LBJ High is old and in bad condition. Some rooms are so hot you can't concentrate. The bathrooms have no towels or toilet paper and are filthy. The classrooms have no windows. The walls are old and faded and there's lots of trash on the ground. Is this a school or a prison? Many students don't respect their teachers. Some teachers don't expect much from their students. It will be easy to get good marks but will I learn anything? Ricardo advises me to go for the good marks and to self-educate. He is the light in this otherwise grim, dark place.

October 22, 2006

I've had no time to write in my journal recently. Things have been getting better at LBJ High. About a month ago, I asked my counselor if I could get transferred out of my ELD (English Language Development) class and into an advanced placement English. They said they'd call me in to discuss it but they never did. I was placed in a class with students who can hardly speak English at all. I had become Ms. Wexler's helper. That was okay but what about my education? During the second week of school I took something called a CELDT test that is supposed to check my English ability. It was such a simple test that I would have been shocked if I had missed one question. I complained to Mr. Franco at Destinos Latinos and he came to meet with my counselors. The counselors didn't look too happy to see him but the next day I was classified as FEP (Fluent English Proficient). I then found out that LBJ High doesn't have an advanced placement English class. Shit! I was placed in Ms. Rosales's regular English class. She's nice but the students are sometimes out of control. Ricardo and I aren't in any classes together which may be for the best. I know if he were near me I couldn't concentrate.

November 12, 2006

The 1ˢᵗ quarter ended two weeks ago but I finally got my report card today. Unlike Mexico where they use a number system, the gringos use an A through F system with an A being the best. Guess what I got? Straight A's of course. Funny thing is I don't feel so proud, as the coursework has been too easy so far. I demand to be challenged! Ja! Ja! Ja! The other day a teacher named Mr. Duckworth made an announcement on the school intercom that he was sponsoring a debate club. Both Ricardo and I attended the

79

informational meeting after school. Mr. Duckworth explained that we would study something called rhetoric and learn how to win an argument. Both Ricardo and I thought it would be great for our English. In late spring, we would compete with students from other schools in a debate on some topic to be chosen later. I have found my challenge. Now, we have something to look forward to at LBJ High. Mr. Duckworth is smart and good-looking. I wish he was my teacher. Maybe next year.

December 4, 2006

Last night Ricardo and I went to the movies at the Century 16 theatres. We saw Lord of the Rings. The film was beautiful. Believe it or not, we have not experimented with sex yet, at least until last night. After the movie, we did some things in his truck but I am still a virgin. No, I'm not a bad girl. I just love him so much.

December 25, 2006

Ho! Ho! Ho! Merry Christmas! Last night Ricardo and I went to see some Christmas display in El Cerrito that everyone was talking about. After that, we went back to his house. His parents were celebrating at a friend's apartment so Ricardo had the house to himself. Yes, I am no longer a virgin. I felt no pain, only pure pleasure and love. I'm glad he used a condom. Today we opened presents early and had a big breakfast. I want to see Ricardo but he has to stay with his family and I have to stay with mine. We'll have plenty of chances to meet over the rest of the winter break.

January 3, 2007

The winter break went by way too fast. I got to see my love several times though. He took me ice skating at the Berkley Ice Rink last night but I hated it. I couldn't go more than 20 meters without falling. Ricardo was very patient with me. He said it takes time to learn. Today my ankles were aching. Maybe we Mexicans are not made for the ice but why does this crazy Brazilian like it? Today, at the debate club meeting, we received this year's debate topic: "Should public high schools in California require uniforms?" I didn't think it was the most exciting topic but Mr. Duckworth insisted that learning to debate was the goal and any topic would do. For the debate, we would have to take a stand either for or against wearing uniforms in school. We learned that the best way to win a debate is to understand completely both sides of an argument. Know your enemy better than he knows himself, Mr. Duckworth constantly reminds us.

January 24, 2007

In the debate club today, Mr. Duckworth talked to us about the power of the ordinary person. He gave a PowerPoint presentation on several ordinary people who did extraordinary things. He talked about how Erin Brockovich, a single mother, brought down a power company accused of polluting a city's water. He explained how Cesar Chavez improved the lives of thousands of migrant farm workers through determined activism. He showed a video clip of Martin Luther King's I have a dream speech and talked about the American civil rights movement. He then asked us to brainstorm what all these people had in common. Some of the things we came up with were: wanted to right wrongs, didn't give up, believed strongly in their ideas, inspired others, and determination. A little later he asked us to come up with a list of things that we thought were wrong with our school. The list we came up with was endless. We mentioned everything from toilets that didn't flush to not enough advanced placement classes. He then told us to organize our list from what we thought was most to least important. This part was harder. In the end, we settled on better facilities but more advanced placement classes came in at a close second.

My headache worsened so I set the diary down. I put some ice in an old sock and placed it on my head. I made a cup of black Earl Grey, caffeinated tea and clicked on the TV. Using the remote, I turned the channel to Judge Judy. She was trying to determine whether to award a female plaintiff $500 in lost wages due to a bad hairdo performed by a defendant's salon. The plaintiff claimed the hairdo was so bad that she was embarrassed to go to work for a week. Rather than wait for the decision, I switched the channel to Oprah. She was interviewing a group of Republican Christians who claimed to had been gay at one time but turned straight through

81

prayer and church support. I immediately thought of Mr. Cheasty. I found out that he was Alma's teacher both last year and during the first quarter when she was killed. He had a reputation as a hard working and conscientious professional. I made a mental note to make contact with him.

My headache wouldn't go away. As soon as I pulled the ice off, the pain returned. It wasn't severe but a constant, annoying mild throb that started in the upper forehead. I put the ice back on and continued to watch TV like a bored suburban housewife until midnight, getting up every now and then to change the ice when it melted. I had a restless night, tossing and turning. My thoughts were random and unfocused. My only solace was that it had to be a temporary condition.

CHAPTER 6

In the morning, my headache seemed to worsen. I was tempted to pop a Concerta thinking that withdrawal could be causing my misery but remembered that I had flushed them down the toilet. I ground some Peet's coffee beans and made a nice, strong cup of java to have with my standard boiled egg. A little later, I decided to take a walk to see if fresh air would help. I crossed Arlington Blvd. and passed through the small but pleasant Arlington Park. A group of cub scouts was having an archery contest. I sat in the grass and watched as their attempts wildly missed the target. The air was autumn crisp. I took deep, slow deliberate breaths that helped me feel a little better but not much.

I walked up a path that led to a boy scout lodge called Camp Herms. Little cub scouts were running all over the place carrying wooden cars of all shapes and colors. A banner in front of the old building read 2007 Pinewood Derby. I continued up a trail that led up the hillside behind the lodge. After about 30 minutes of exploring, I headed back to the house. My headache was still pretty bad. I took a couple of Advil and went back to bed. Again I tossed and turned and slept on and off. I looked at the clock and it was 3:30. I decided to call Rosanna to cancel.

"I really want to see you but I got a pretty, severe headache and I'm afraid I'll be bad company," I explained.

"Harley, it's the withdrawal symptoms of those stupid drugs. See what those doctor pimps did to you?"

"You may be right but it's too late now. I have to go through with this."

"Get your bunda (ass) over here right now. I'm going to cook you a meal and make you feel better," she ordered.

"Okay. I'll do my best," I said.

I was thinking that I'd have to call in sick for Monday. I couldn't imagine spending a day at LBJ High with this sort of headache. Anyway, I could call the subfinders hotline from Rosanna's house early Monday morning if I still felt bad. I took a shower and let the hot water massage the top of my head and upper forehead. The pain seemed to subside with the water pressure but would resume as soon as it stopped. I got dressed, gathered everything I'd need for Monday and put it in my briefcase. I headed out the door to the garage and jumped into my Corvette. My headache seemed to be worsening.

I arrived at Rosanna's house on San Luis St. in the Richmond Annex in about 15 minutes. As she hugged me and let me in, I could smell a mixture of herbs and spices. Joãozinho was on the floor playing with little toy cars.

"Whatever you're cooking sure smells good," I complimented.

"Peixe com leite de coco" (fish with coconut milk) "I picked up some fresh codfish at Spenger's this afternoon. It's made with a lot of Brazilian secret ingredients cooked just right," she said with a wide smile.

She was wearing one of those white laced dresses from Bahia that went down to just above her knees. It contrasted beautifully with her light brown skin.

"You wait here with Joãozinho and I'll prepare the cure."

With that she danced on air through a short hallway back to the kitchen. Her front room was comfortable. There were a few bean bag pillows on the floor but no chairs or sofas. A small end table sat isolated in the corner with a small art nouveau style lamp. Next to the lamp was a paperback entitled O Dom da Morte (The Gift of Death) by Jacques Derrida. The walls displayed different examples of Brazilian artesenato spread out with just the right amount of negative space. There was no TV. Out the front window, I could see the concrete sound barrier that protected from some but not all of the sound from Highway 80. I sat down in front of one of the bean bags and rested my aching, throbbing head. I could hear the enthusiastic voice of Elba Ramalho coming from the CD player in the kitchen down the hall. Joãozinho made the sound of an engine and rolled his toy car across my forehead. It had the unintended effect of relieving some of the pain. For the next hour, I just rested there, looking at the wall and listening to the sounds of Rosanna's music mixed in with the ambient hum from the highway. My nose absorbed the smells of whatever those secret ingredients were. None of these things seemed to help my head though. It was hurting worse than ever. I was about to doze off when Rosanna waltzed in.

"Come on boys. Time for dinner."

We followed her down the short hallway and entered the small kitchen. There was a tiny, indented dining nook on the side

84

surrounded by windows which looked out onto the side fence. There were three tall wooden chairs. I sat across from Joãozinho and Rosanna sat with her back to the window.

"Are you feeling any better Harley?"

"To be honest, no - but thanks for inviting me. Even with a severe headache you look marvelous."

"Flattery will get you nowhere," she joked.

I forced a smile. She sure had learned a lot of English expressions, I thought to myself.

"Então, vai fundo! (Dig in!)," she commanded.

With that, we began passing the plates around. The fish was lightly covered with coconut milk and some green and red spices that I couldn't make out. There was a lovely salad and a dish full of palmitos that we passed around. The codfish melted in my mouth. The palmitos provided the perfect textural contrast to the soft fish. She opened a large bottle of Brahma beer, a well-known Brazilian brand and filled our glasses. I was about to refuse when I remembered that nothing else had helped my headache. Maybe beer was the secret. In spite of the pain, I did have an appetite. I gobbled up my first helping and began sipping the beer. Joãozinho finished his meal quickly and left the kitchen. Rosanna encouraged me to get more and I obliged. She then asked me to unbutton my pants. I remembered that nice custom from Brazil. It was done as a way of loosening up the waist line that was expected to expand during the course of a meal. I popped the top button. Sure enough, this made me feel at home.

"You don't look well, Harley. Your eyes are bloodshot and you have rings under them. Why don't you go to bed right after dinner? I'll stay up with Joãozinho for a while and come to bed later."

I agreed to her nice suggestion. We ate more and talked about whatever came up. I asked her about the book on death I saw on the table in the living room.

"You mean "O Dom da Morte?" she asked to confirm.

"Is that a mystery novel?" I asked.

She laughed. "No, it is required reading for a philosophy class I'm taking at the community college. I was lucky to find a Portuguese translation as it is pretty heavy stuff, not exactly easy reading. Jacque Derrida is the father of deconstruction and in this book he explores death. It's very interesting."

85

"Excuse my naiveté but what's deconstruction?" I asked.

"I don't want to make your headache worse Harley. It's very hard to explain. Even Derrida resisted trying to explain the meaning of deconstruction. It has something to do with trying to understand the implicit and unspoken ideas behind one's thoughts and beliefs. As a detective, I imagine you use it all the time unconsciously."

If I had been clear-headed, I would have loved to have spent more time chatting with her. As it was, my head began to throb like mad as if it was going to explode. I apologized to Rosanna for being such boring company, thanked her for dinner, and asked if I could lie down for a while. She led me down the hall to her bedroom. Inside, was a comfortable queen-sized bed. She gave me a kiss on the forehead and promised to return after getting Joãozinho to bed. I stripped to my underwear and sunk my head into one of her soft pillows. Like her dress, the bed and pillow covers were made from intricate white linen.

What was I doing here? Should I get up and go home? My head throbbed. I didn't want to keep Rosanna awake all night with my moaning and groaning but what could I do? I was here now and she would be in this bed shortly. I put my hands around my temples and began to squeeze to relieve the pain. It was as if there was a heart beating in my upper forehead that wouldn't be content until it broke through my skull. I began to change positions restlessly. Every minute felt like 15. It looked like I would be in for a long night. I could hear the sound of the shower running in the bathroom. I remembered how the water pressure relieved the pain and thought maybe I'd ask Rosanna if I could take one. On second thought, what was the point? The pain would come back as soon as I removed the pressure. I couldn't stay in the shower forever.

After what seemed like an eternity, Rosanna walked into the room smiling. She had a white towel wrapped around her body and her hair was still wet. Combed straight and curling inwards at the bottom, she resembled one of those flapper girls from the 1920s. She inserted a CD into the Bose player on the dresser.

"Maybe a little bossa nova will be good for your head," she suggested. "I often play this song before sleeping. It helps me dream."

Caetano Veloso's sensual version of the song Avarandado by João Gilberto began spreading through the audio spaces of her bedroom.

"Thanks for having me over. I just don't want to burden you with my pain. I wished I was feeling better but if I were home, I'd just be alone with this throbbing head. Even with this intense pain, it's nice to be with you."

She smiled.

"It will pass and then you'll be glad you stopped taking those meds."

"Is Joãozinho asleep?" I asked.

"Yeah. He always sleeps quickly. One of the perks of being an active boy. I'm sure the system will try to medicate him once he gets in school but I'll never allow it."

The pain in my head did not subside. It was as intense as ever. I was in absolute misery. Rosanna walked around the bed and lit candles on both end tables. She then let the towel drop to the ground. I was not at all interested in sex in this condition and was secretly hoping she wasn't going in that direction.

She stood there nude at the end of bed and just looked at me. The soft glow of the candlelight on her face made her look almost saintly. Her head tilted and her eyes gazed towards me with a maternal look that reminded me of one those renaissance paintings of the Virgin Mary. It was impossible for me to tell what she was thinking but her look had a hypnotic effect. The song on the CD player just ended so she turned off the power and then returned to the same location, maintaining the same saintly expression. I laid on my back with my head resting on one of the two soft pillows covered with the intricate white, lace work. I looked directly into her mysterious dark eyes wondering what she was going to do next. Her face continued to glow as if the candlelight seemed to know exactly where it was. Suddenly she spoke.

"Tell me where it hurts, Harley."

Her voice seemed other-worldly.

"On the upper-forehead and the top of my head," I responded timidly.

"I want you to stay where you are. I will make you feel better. You have to believe that I can do that. Do you believe it?"

"I do," I said weakly and still in pain.

87

She walked over to the side of the bed and then knelt down beside me. The mattress made a creaking sound. She placed her palm about a half an inch above my forehead and began to move it slowly back and forth, up and down. I could feel the heat coming from her hand even though she did not make any actual physical contact. It was as if her palm was somehow slowly sucking the pain outwards.

"That helps," I said.

"Shhh. Don't say a word the rest of the night," she calmly ordered.

She then began to lick my forehead, digging her tongue into my skin with pressure up and down, left and right. Just like her palm, her tongue seemed to be forcing the pain outwards. She began to breathe heavily and asked me to slide forward a little bit. I obliged. I thought she wanted my penis when she squatted over my chest, one knee on either side of my torso. Instead, she turned completely around until all I could see was her back. She backed up slowly until she was right above my head. Just like from her palms, I could feel the heat even though she had not made physical contact with my forehead. Suddenly, I could see intense light coming down in rays out of her vagina. It was the kind of light you'd see illuminating the face of Jesus in those old paintings. The light struck my forehead and seemed to remove all the weight from my head. Finally, she made physical contact with my forehead and although I could not see the light externally anymore, it remained behind my eyelids as an afterthought, as intense and golden as ever.

The pain was gone. My entire head seemed to be gone for that matter. Although I could feel her weight, it was more like a dance than any sensation of pressure. Her vagina was wet and my forehead began to gradually moisten. I could feel her lips going up and down, left and right. My hair began to moisten too. Her vagina seemed to be opening wider. She focused her movements on the area where my forehead met my hair on the top of my head. I could hear her moaning but wasn't sure if it was from pleasure or pain. Her vagina opened wider and wider. It was now covering both temples and still expanding. I felt stuck for a moment. Suddenly my ears and eyes were covered but I could still see that magnificent golden light. I could also still hear the soft hum of cars passing by on Highway 80. Strangely, the muffled hum had a comforting effect. Next, my nose was covered but instead of blocking my ability to smell, my olfactory sense seemed to be as acute as ever. But it wasn't the inside of a vagina I smelled. It was the smell of spring. Not like any spring I had experienced recently, more like a childhood, innocent spring. Her vagina was now swallowing me at a rapid pace. As it covered my mouth, I worried about suffocating but instead the exact opposite happened. Fresh spring air, entered my lungs. I took a deep satisfying breath. The air tasted like it did when I was a child and the world was new. Eventually, my entire body was engulfed by Rosanna's warm vagina but instead of feeling trapped, I felt liberated and reborn. The pain in my head was clearly gone!

I opened my eyes and looked straight up. The sky was an intense blue. I decided to sit up and look around. I was sitting in the middle of a valley surrounded by rolling, green hills covered with mature oak trees. Where was I? If I had to guess, I would have to say it was somewhere in the Napa Valley. The place looked familiar but I couldn't identify exactly where it was. I decided to walk around and explore. As I stood up, I noticed my feet were not touching the ground but hovering a few inches above. I began to move around by the power of my thoughts. I noticed a comfortable looking place under an oak tree on a nearby hill and my body began to travel in that direction. There was an immense feeling of peacefulness and wonder surrounding the whole location. I noticed a small paved road down below and soon began traveling down it. A little while later, I entered a small town with well-maintained, old two story houses surrounded by picket fences on both sides of the street. Sitting in a rocking chair, on one of the wrap-around porches, I could see my late Grandma Butler waving to me with a pure smile on her face. The color of the homes was intense and fresh. I liked this place. It felt comfortable. Grandma Butler stood up and began pointing down the street as if to tell me to go in that direction. I ended up in front of a mid-sized white church. The front door was ajar so I floated in. The church was empty except for a young girl in prayer kneeling in front of the altar. The sunlight from the one circular window in the front of the church cast a small but bright circular light on the back of her head. She had long brown wavy hair and was praying in Spanish. I stood there and watched for a while. I couldn't make out the words she was saying but it was obviously a prayer. I decided to gravitate towards the altar little by little. When I was about five feet away, the girl slowly turned her head around.

"Gracias, Harley. You are a good man."

It was Alma Vargas and she was more beautiful than any photo could possibly portray. I was at a lost for words so I just looked at her in amazement. She turned back around and whispered, "En el nombre del Padre, del Hijo, y del Espirito Santo. There was minute of silent prayer and then she spoke again.

"La persona de mi confianza me traicionó. A pesar de eso, mis sueños no han muerto, tú sabes?"

Spanish is close enough to Portuguese for me to have understood that she said a person of trust had betrayed her and that in spite of that her dreams would live on. She then spoke in English.

"Harley, your work has been blessed."

She then walked right past me, smiled and headed towards the door.

"Alma, don't go," I pleaded. "Tell me who betrayed you."

She slipped through the door not speaking or looking back. I hovered towards the outside but there was no sign of her. She had completely vanished.

"Breakfast is ready. Time to face the world," said Rosanna tickling me. "You didn't last long last night. How are you feeling?"

I rolled off the bed and stood up slightly disoriented. My head felt light and free. There was no denying it. I was okay.

"Just fine! Boy, what a night," I exclaimed.

"What you mean? You barely budged. Why don't you take a shower and meet us in the kitchen," she suggested.

I thought it a little strange that she hadn't asked me about my headache. Did she know it was completely gone? Did it matter? I hadn't felt this good in a long time. It was as if I had a tune-up on all five or was it six senses. I took a shower and the water felt great. I could see and hear better. Was this how I felt before Concerta? I wasn't sure. Anyway, I had made it through the night and then some.

After getting dressed, I met Rosanna and Joãozinho at the kitchen table. It looked like breakfast would be papaya and croissants.

"Looks great," I complimented. Where'd you pick the papayas?"

"The Monterey Market," she laughed.

She poured some coffee and I added some cream. Out the window, it looked like it was shaping up to be a sunny autumn day. She asked me if I was enjoying the new job. I said I was but one year would be enough. I asked her if she would like to help me out at Tantei Man.

"You know, I'm not the secretary type Harley. Maybe I could become a detective like you." She looked at me for approval.

"You know that's not a bad idea. If you're serious, I can show you what it'll take to get a license. The hardest part is meeting the real world experience requirement. You can get that with me at Tantei."

"Are you sure you want a partner? You know what they say about mixing love and work," she smiled.

"The reality is I have my own way of working. I always thought a partner would cramp my style, get in the way if you will. I'd make an exception for you though. I've got a feeling you'd enhance my skills."

She giggled. "Let's talk about this later. I want to do something positive with my life and help people the way you helped me. Good karma, you know?"

Joãozinho asked me if we could go kite flying. I told him I'd love to but had to work. He then scrambled away from the table and headed towards his room. I thanked Rosanna for having me over and apologized for being boring company. There would be no need to call subfinders, I thought. I felt great. I gave her a hug, picked up my briefcase, and headed out the door.

I drove parallel along the highway until I crossed Carlson Blvd. and went up the freeway onramp. McDonald Ave. exit was a short one mile away. I'd be at LBJ High in no time. It was Monday. I was going to teach at a tough school but I felt good about it. The sky was clear and so was my mind.

I pulled into the parking lot, said hi to the graffiti covered statue of Lyndon, and headed to room 207. It was still early and not too many teachers had arrived yet. Even Mr. Chirac, the early bird, was nowhere to be seen. I organized my lesson for the day, straightened up all the chairs, and prepared the overhead projector. Unlike most mornings, I had time to spare. Last night's dream entered my mind. Yes, I had dreamed. Either that or Rosanna had an awfully big and interesting vagina. The strange thing was it felt real. The colors vivid. I knew Alma from photos but now I felt like

91

I knew her in 3D living form. She said that someone she had trusted betrayed her. Well, that bit of information wouldn't be much help. I kind of figured that. If I were to believe a dream, I could eliminate the possibility that her murder was random. I couldn't though. She also said that my work was blessed. I'll always accept a blessing. Even if it comes in a dream.

While waiting for the students to arrive, I made a pact with myself. I would work more aggressively on the Vargas case. After all, I was now a regular, familiar, card carrying staff member at LBJ High. I could nose around about Alma and no one should get suspicious. I had a good rapport with her boyfriend Ricardo and would sponsor the Alma Vargas Memorial Club. That should give me free reign.

Mr. Chirac arrived and stuck his "get out of jail free" face in the door. He asked me about my weekend. I lied and told him it was okay. He needlessly reminded me that the masses would be arriving shortly. The passing bell rang and students came slowly strolling in. 1st period was always the quietest class. Probably because the students were still sleepy. I had pretty much accepted the fact that not much progress if any would be made on the case during class. That would have to happen before or after school and during my 5th period prep time. I would try to make my classes enjoyable and rewarding for both the students and myself. This was not always easy as the students were not always cooperative. Still I had to try. A strong work ethic was part of both my Portuguese and Irish roots.

Period 3 was when the Pledge of Allegiance was read as well as the rest of the school announcements. When the voice said please stand, as usual none of the students stood. When I asked the students why they didn't, they just shrugged and said "what's the point?" There was obviously not a lot of American patriotism at LBJ High. It was clear that most if not all of the students were not even listening. The announcements ended with the usual, "have a good day at LBJ High, home of the Riveters." At least I would take that advice. There was about 30 seconds of silence when a voice I recognized burst through the intercom.

"Good morning. This is Mr. Ramos. Sorry for the interruption. This is a reminder to all teachers that there will be a staff meeting after school in the library at 3:30."

There was another minute of silence and then another voice, loud and authoritative blasted through the intercom. This voice seemed to get the students' attention.

"Attention students! This is Mr. Prince! Listen carefully! If I catch anyone – I mean anyone wearing pajamas to school – you will be summarily sent home and automatically suspended. Did I make myself clear?"

"What's the big fucking deal about wearing pajamas to school?" said Nytasia loudly.

I had noticed a few students wearing pajamas around campus and didn't think much of it. Kids make all sorts of fashion statements. Baggy pants. Baseball caps with the tag still on worn sideways. But pajamas? What kind of statement did that make? I was too lazy to get dressed this morning. I was running late and had no time to get dressed. Maybe I was just getting old but the whole pajama fad was beyond me.

During lunch, I decided to visit the outspoken Mr. Duckworth. I rarely saw him around campus and he hardly ever showed his face in the faculty room. He had mentored Alma and could have valuable information. Our new Alma Vargas Memorial Club was the perfect excuse to disturb his lunch. Duckworth's class was out in the 900 building, a group of portables at the far southeast end of campus. His door was locked so I gave it a knock. He opened it and gave me a what the hell do you want look.

"Sorry to interrupt your lunch but was wondering if I could come in and talk to you a little bit about Alma Vargas. I'm sponsoring a club in her honor."

He rolled his eyes, gave me a second look-over, and invited me in.

"What makes a new teacher so interested in a dead student he's never met?" He looked at me suspiciously.

"I have her boyfriend Ricardo in one of my classes and from what he and others tell me, she was a real positive force on this campus."

He looked at me impatiently but I continued. "From what I understand, she was ruffling the feathers of the administration folks down at the district headquarters. She wanted the kids in Richmond to have the same opportunity as those in Piedmont and believed education was the great equalizer. I've heard that you were sort of a mentor to her and that she loved your debate club." Of course, I couldn't tell him that I had read her diary. He appeared to withdraw in thought and there was an awkward 15 seconds of silence.

"You're not a spy for Assistant Superintendent LeCroc, are you?"

I laughed nervously. "Why would LeCroc hire a spy? That's crazy, don't you think?"

"Not if you're raking in a salary well into the six figures and you see someone as a threat to that. Alma exposed to the outside world a lot of the incompetence at this school and the district administration. She caused people to start to question the ineptness of the district office. Letters were written to the editor by people complaining that heads should roll downtown. This is phenomenal when you consider the short time she'd been in this country. She was stirring up the pot and was a threat to the powers that be. They looked at me as the driving force behind Alma but they were mistaken on that front. She was her own person."

"I can see why you might be suspicious of me," I said with a smile. "I bet there are some people downtown who'd like to see you move on."

"God bless the union!" He slapped his palm on his desk to emphasize. "If encouraging students' critical thinking skills was against the rules, I'd be long gone. Anyway, I got to be extra careful these days so they don't try to fire me on some technicality. I'm sure they're looking for something."

"Let me tell you straight out that you can trust me. Even though I'm new here, I'd like to think of myself as someone who has the students' best interest in mind." I felt like telling him who I really was but couldn't. It was too early. He had information about Alma that could be useful and I had to somehow get through his rough shell.

"Let's use the Alma Vargas Memorial Club to keep her activism alive and inspire the students," I continued.

"You sound like you have potential as a teacher. Sorry about the spy thing." He held out his hand and I shook it. "When Alma was killed I got depressed and cynical. She's just someone that can't be replaced. The week after she died was the hardest. I was thinking of calling it quits, grabbing my surfboard, and just running away from it all. But I knew Alma would have been disappointed in me if I had. It's not too often around here that a student can influence a teacher that way. Alma truly understood the hypocrisy of public education in the United States."

"What do you mean by that?" I asked.

He looked at me restlessly. "Some people still naively believe that education is the great equalizer in this country. In reality, it never has been. There was hope in the late 60s and early 70s that we were moving in that direction but somehow over the past two decades that vision of equality has been lost and now it is more lost than ever. Within our district boundaries, anyone who can afford it, sends their kids to private schools. Otherwise, they move to an area like Albany or Piedmont where the real estate is expensive, financially excluding the riff-raff that they wished didn't exist. There's really no difference between these public schools and private schools. In one the family pays a tuition, in the other they pay through the nose in property taxes. I live in Albany and am approached almost once a month from an organization called School Care for donations. I tell them to fuck off every chance I get. You see, even in these well-to-do areas, public funding is not enough for everything needed to run a well-rounded school. So what do they do? They subsidize their child's education through donations and local parcel taxes which in my eyes makes it no longer a public school but some sort of hybrid."

"You can't really blame people for wanting the best education for their children," I challenged.

"No you can't!" He pounded his palm on the desk again. "But you can blame people for ignoring the big picture! By subsidizing these public schools with donations they are keeping the kids in Richmond down. How's that you ask? Well, let's take Albany and Piedmont for example. Let's say that there was a law against people donating money to school causes in these cities. Imagine no more local school parcel taxes allowed. Soon parents will start noticing that the schools are being under-funded. Programs would eventually be cut. Facilities would slowly start to fall apart. At that point, families would have to start taking action. They would be faced with tough decisions like supporting a statewide tax for public education. Perhaps even a revamping of the sacred way property taxes are assessed, forever altered by Howard Jarvis with his Prop 13 in the 70s. Now, their school activism will have to support not just their own kids but all the kids in California, including the poor folk right here in Richmond. These people would never vote in a system like that though. They have no problem supporting their own children but look at kids right on the other side of Highway 80 as being from some far away country and feel no responsibility at all towards them. They rationalize their lack of compassion with thoughts like the kids in the ghetto will just destroy what they get anyway. The sad part is this. These people have the power and the education to make change. The families around here have to worry about where their next meal is going to come from."

"So what do we do?" I asked.

"I have some ideas but most people think they are crazy so I keep them to myself and a few special students. Alma was one of them."

"I'm listening," I prodded. "I'd love to hear what you had to say."

"The bells going to ring in a few minutes so I'll be short. In a nutshell, we need to scare the folks on the other side of highway 80 out of their complacency. Holding protest signs in support of education reform in front of LBJ High will get us nowhere. We need to bring the community on this side of highway to that side and let them hear our voices. Imagine the reaction if 500 black and Hispanic kids and their parents marched around the private school Prospect Sierra in El Cerrito. The parents would shit their pants. The next day, they could make noise in front of the Head-Royce School in the rich part of Oakland. In short, since we can't rely on the compassion of the people in these communities, we need to tap their fear. We need to let them know that the bubble they created for themselves can easily be popped. Want to stop this from happening again? Support our schools too!"

The bell rang and it was time to get back to class. I thanked him for a fascinating discussion and asked if we could continue it some other time. He promised to help out with the Alma Vargas Memorial Club and that was my goal. Mission accomplished. I thought his ideas were way out there but valid. I could see why the students liked him. He spoke his mind articulately and forcefully, had sharp critical thinking skills and his ideas were well thought out and powerful. A perfect debate coach, I thought.

It was more than halfway through the work day and I was still feeling lively and energetic. It was now my prep period. Since I had already prepared for my lessons, I decided to go out for a quick bite to eat. I usually brought a lunch but for obvious reasons did not have one today. I headed a few blocks down McDonald Ave. to Casper's for a hot dog. As I drove past 23rd St, I thought about the old Doggie Diner that used to be on the corner. Its giant concrete 200 lb. fiberglass wiener-dog head would beckon hungry residents like a religious icon. In its place now was a McDonald's parking lot. That's the way it is with locals. You remember how things used to be and are living witness to the fact that change is not always for the better. Schools had sure gone downhill in the area over the past 20 years. On the other hand, a lot of social progress has taken place during that time. I guess the world can evolve and devolve at the same time.

At Casper's, a joint that hasn't changed much from the old days, I ordered a classic steamed dog with everything but relish. My mind was on Mr. Duckworth's spiel about educational inequities. At the same time, I thought about Alma and how she was fighting for LBJ High to have the same course offerings as nearby richer schools. It was now crystal clear who planted those seeds. When the lady behind the counter said my order was ready, I must have completely ignored her.

"Sir, your hot dog is ready. Do you want it or not? Sir?"

That last sir got my attention. It appeared my beloved ADD was coming back slowly. I apologized for being distracted, paid for my hot dog, and set down at the counter. I still felt refreshed and energetic. As I ate, I could see the Richmond Police station across the street and wondered what Randy was doing at the moment. He would be expecting some progress soon. After all, the department was forking out big bucks for this investigation. What did I have at this point? Nothing really. I needed to fit in at the school before I could start snooping around. Now, I was ready. All I knew was the obvious. Alma was found brutally murdered with traces of Restoril and alcohol in her system. Alma was an illegal alien. She was a star student not afraid to the stir the pot. She had a Brazilian boyfriend who loved her. She inspired some and annoyed others. But who could have killed her? Who had the motive? Any guess would be pure conjecture at this point.

I glanced at my watch and was surprised to see that it was 1:30. The passing bell would have already rung. I rushed out to my car and sped back to school. By the time I got back, the halls were already empty except for the line of my students standing outside room 207.

"You're late Mr. Butler!" yelled Michelle Saechao smiling.

"Got stuck in traffic," I lied. Michelle was one of the more on task students in my 6th period Adobe Illustrator class. Although she was absent a lot, when she was in class she worked hard and completed to perfection all her projects. Nearly always in a good mood, she was unusually pleasant and polite. Her extremely attractive face more than compensated for her short stature. She wore very tight clothes that accented her impossible to ignore body that just happened to be shaped like a Kalamazoo electric guitar. She was a real looker and got a lot of attention from the boys.

As I had already done in all my other classes today, I announced to my students the formation of the Alma Vargas Memorial Club and told them to come to this room after school tomorrow if they were interested in participating. Several asked questions about it and only a few seemed disinterested. Most of the questions had to do with what would take place during club time. I told them that Ricardo would tell them all about that at an informational meeting tomorrow. Michelle asked if it was just for Hispanic students and I said absolutely not.

"I liked Alma. She was cool. She had this place figured out!" she commented. A few other students expressed interest and then they went back to work on their assignments.

The rest of the day went by quickly. At 3:30, I walked over to the library, signed-in, and picked up an agenda. The meeting's topic was on how to use data from standardized testing to better serve our students. There were several handouts showing sample student scores sorted in a lot of different ways like ethnicity, grade, and subject area. I found out that they called this disaggregating the data. Among other things, the data showed that our Southeast Asian students were performing better on these tests than the African American and Hispanic students. The Star test as they call it in California classifies a student as advanced, proficient, basic, below, basic, and far below basic in math, language arts, and social studies. Almost all LBJ students minus a few exceptions were classified as far below basic or below basic in all subjects.

Standing in front of an LCD projector with a Diet Pepsi in his hand, stood the highly-paid consultant Martin Burke. The

98

opening slide to a PowerPoint presentation was projected on a large white screen that Mr. Chirac had set up. It read "Backwards Planning" with the subtitle "teaching from the standards". More teachers began to stroll languidly in. Some rolled their eyes and complained that they wished they could use this staff development time for departmental meetings. "Be nice if they spent this consultant money on teacher salaries for a change," added Mr. Martelaro in earshot of Mr. Burke.

The consultant appeared nonplussed as he took a sip of Diet Pepsi. I imagined he was used to resistant teachers forced by administrators to attend his workshops when they were most tired. He probably had developed a layer of thick skin to deal with it and the fact that his workshops netted him more than 300 grand a year must have helped. I sat down at a table with Jerry Cheasty and Judy Rosales. At 3:30, Principal Ramos came and looked around as if to see if anyone was missing. I looked around too. Several teachers must have had other things to do as the turnout was low. As usual, Mr. Duckworth was nowhere to be found.

Mr. Burke began his presentation on backwards planning but after the first few minutes that defense mechanism that had protected me from boredom since childhood kicked in. My mind began to wander. I was thinking of how Alma had appeared in my dream and how it seemed real. Even though it couldn't be, I felt like I had met her. I wondered if Rosanna had climaxed last night. I thought about the idea of her joining Tantei Man. I looked at Mr. Cheasty and Ms. Rosales and they appeared to be completely tuned in to the lecture. Not me though. I found myself sitting on the beach in Brazil with a group of friends admiring the scenery. I then started thinking about Alma's diary and the journey she took to get here. I went from one thought to the next and the thoughts weren't always connected. One thing was absolutely clear. I had my ADD back. My mind was drifting like it always had.

Suddenly Mr. Burke stopped lecturing and conversations began to take place at the tables scattered around the library. It appeared we were supposed to be discussing something in groups but I had no idea what it was. Based on what Jerry and Judy were discussing, I figured out that we were supposed to come up with a concrete example of backwards planning in our subject matter. Typical, I thought. This guys making big bucks as a consultant so what does he do? He lets his audience come up with ideas for him.

Pretty sweet gig if you ask me. After a little thought, I came up with an idea for my class and waited until he called on our table. By the time everyone was finished it was time to end the workshop. That was an easy $1,500 Mr. Burke must have been thinking to himself. After he left, I chatted a while with Mr. Cheasty. I mentioned the Alma Vargas memorial club plan but he didn't think it was such a great idea.

"You know, these kids have to deal with obstacles that we can't even begin to imagine. I know you mean well by sponsoring this club but I'm afraid it might increase the cynicism of our students," he paternally advised.

"What do you mean? From what I understand, Alma was a positive force on the campus. I'm not doing this to be morbid. I see it as a celebration of her life, not her death."

"Just be careful. Alma was a controversial figure here and you may be unknowingly opening up a problematic can of worms."

"I guess we're willing to take that chance for the betterment of the school." I took the high moral ground.

"All I'm saying Harley, is that when wounds are in the process of healing, don't go picking at them."

I was starting to get annoyed so I changed the angle of the conversation.

"Did you ever have Alma as a student?" I asked as if I didn't know.

"She was in my geometry class last year and in my calculus class this year. I had to find alternative curriculum for her because she wasn't challenged by what most students consider difficult. She's the kind of student that keeps a teacher on his toes." With that he smiled, picked up his backpack and headed out the door.

I walked back to my room to get ready for the next day and to meet Ricardo. During period 7, he asked me if I wanted to go to Portumex for a meal. I didn't have any plans so I said yes. Portumex is a restaurant on 23rd St. near Burbeck Ave. run by a Portuguese guy married to a Mexican. In spite of the part Lusitanic name, the food is strictly Mexican. It was only a few blocks away from LBJ High so we decided to walk. On the way there, I couldn't help thinking that this was the same route that Alma took to go home. It was a little after five when we arrived. Like in many Mexican restaurants, you order at the counter and then take a seat. I was surprised to see that one of my students was at the cashier and another was in the kitchen cooking. No wonder they never did their homework, I thought. Juanita looked at me and said, "Mr. Butler, what are you doing down this way?"

"Just visiting my old stomping grounds," I joked. Actually, I did spend a lot of time in the area as a child. My grandmother had lived right around the corner and my father had sold Christmas trees on a vacant lot a few blocks down the street. It had never been a rich area but back in the 60s and 70s, it was more populated by European immigrants. Now, the Mexicans were clearly in charge of 23rd St. I ordered a three taco combo, a Corona and Ricardo ordered a burrito and a Pepsi. I pulled out a 20 dollar bill to pay for both of us but Juanita insisted that the meal be on the house. Can't beat the price, I thought.

After a few minutes, my other student Felix delivered the meal to our table with a smile. I asked him what time he got to bed. He said about 1:30 usually. During the meal, Ricardo and I talked about how to go about the first meeting of the memorial club. A couple of times his eyes filled with tears but he was able to express his plans clearly. He was determined to make the club a vehicle for positive change at the school. After the meal, we walked back down 23rd St. At Barrett Ave., he went left towards his family's pizzeria and I went right back towards LBJ High and my lonely Corvette, the only car left in the teachers' parking lot.

I decided to take a drive down 23rd St. to retrace the way Alma would had normally walked home. I was kind of superstitious that way. Perhaps seeing what she saw on a daily basis would somehow make me more in tune to her thought processes. It was about 7 o'clock and already dark. The street looked like it could have been in any town in Mexico. Taquerias were everywhere. The auto body shops all had Spanish names. Old large American-made sedans from the 70s and early 80s were headed up and down the street. As I was getting close to Lincoln Ave., I looked across to see where my dad's old Christmas tree lot used to be near the old Scalice Music store. There were now other shops in its place.

Near the corner of McBryde Ave., I noticed three girls standing on the sidewalk wearing extremely short mini skirts and tight tank-tops. I instantly recognized that one of them was my 6th period student Michelle Saechao. As I pulled over to say hello, she quickly walked over to my passenger window and bent over in such

101

a way that her breasts became clearly visible. She looked at me with detached, glazed eyes.

"You want a date?" she asked.

"Michelle, it's me."

She gave me a second look over and her eyes widened. "Mr. Butler, what are you doing down here?" She covered her mouth as she laughed.

"Just going for a drive."

"Oh, sure you are," she laughed again. "Tell you what, how about I give you the teacher discount? You look like you could use a blow job." She opened the door and sat down next to me. Then she put her hand on my leg a little too close to my privates for comfort. The animal part of my brain was getting excited. After all, she was beautiful with curves that wouldn't quit. I took a deep breath.

"Listen Michelle, I'm not down here looking for sex. I'm really just taking a drive. How about I give you 100 bucks and take you home?"

"300 bucks and it's a deal," she countered.

I opened my wallet and started counting the 20s. I had about 115 dollars in cash. I handed it to her. " How about I give you this? You go home and we'll talk about career options tomorrow. Trust me on this one. There is easy money to be made in this world but don't sell your soul in the process. The price is too high." She slouched down in my seat and stuck her high-heeled shoes on my dash.

"Drive!" she commanded. I drove off and started heading down side streets. I was thinking about the consequences if I got pulled over. I could already read the headlines. - Teacher Pays Student for Sex –

"Thanks for caring Mr. Butler but really what are you doing down here?"

"Just like I told you. Taking a drive. I had dinner at Portumex with Ricardo and thought I'd drive down 23rd to see how it had changed. Then I see you. Simple as that."

"This is a nice car. You mind if I take a little snooze?" She put her head on my lap and lightly rubbed my legs with her hands. I could feel her face and warm breath on my penis. I couldn't do much to stop her as I was driving. She then began to massage my erect penis. When she unzipped my pants, I hit the brakes.

102

"That's enough. I can not. I will not. This is not right," I stuttered.

"Your mind says no but your dick says yes," she smiled and continued rubbing. With that, I grabbed her hand.

"Enough! I'm taking you home. I'm a teacher and my position is sacred! I'm here to help you find your future, not contribute to your delinquency!" She yawned and began shaking her head.

"You know my mother works in a massage parlor. I do this. It's a family tradition," she smiled faintly.

"Look Michelle, I know how the world works. I know you need money to survive and you'll make a lot more doing this than say working at McDonald's. But you're young, smart and beautiful. You could have so much if you just put your mind to it. Sometimes, when you make a wrong turn in life, it's hard to get back on the high road but you still have time to change before something really bad happens." I was preaching. She took a deep breath, held it in, and then released it all at once.

"I'm confused. Please take me home. Here's your money back." She tossed it on my lap. I picked it up and tossed it back.

"No, you keep it. Think of it as a gift to get you started on a new life journey. Tomorrow at the club meeting we can talk about setting goals and then how to take steps to reach those goals. Don't worry, I won't let anyone at school know I saw you doing this."

"Don't worry. Everyone knows I'm a slut," she said while laughing cynically.

She showed me the way to the apartment complex where she lived on Carlson Blvd. As she got out of the car, she thanked me and placed a kiss on my forehead. I felt awkward. She was my student after all. "I look forward to seeing you tomorrow Mr. Butler. Goodnight." I watched as she wiggled quickly up the stairs to the third floor.

I drove back down 23rd St. to finish retracing Alma's route home. The two girls that I had seen with Michelle were no longer there. At Alfreda Blvd., I turned left and drove the block and a half to where Alma's home stood on the left side of the street. I parked across the street and just looked at her house for a few minutes. It was an old house, built more than 80 years ago I imagined. Her parents could afford it because they were sharing the rent with relatives. I couldn't begin to comprehend the pain they must be

103

going through. They came to America hoping for a better life for their kids and their beloved daughter ends up getting murdered so brutally.

I decided to head back to McDonald Ave. to visit the site where Alma's body was found in Nicholl Park. It was dark and probably not the safest thing to do so I took my pistol along just in case. I knew the exact area because I had seen all the photos and coordinates. Her body was found on the grass not too far from where the old bird exhibit used to stand. I sat down on the sacred spot and said a prayer. I closed my eyes and tried to visualize the moment. As I did, those same intense, golden rays of light I had seen the night before at Rosanna's house began flickering behind my eyelids. The light was penetrating Alma's chest. I could hear her repeating several times in Spanish "a person of trust". I opened my eyes and the images and sounds were gone. I walked back to my car thinking what a strange thing the mind was.

Back at home the first thing I did was check my messages. The first one was from my Doctor. "Harley, I got your message about wanting to stop Concerta. Never make decisions like that on your own. You need to set up an appointment so we can discuss your regimen and how to adjust it."

If you only knew doc, if you only knew, I thought to myself. I called Rosanna back and we chatted for about an hour. She seemed like she was getting serious about the private detective profession. I took a shower and went to bed. As I lay there, my mind traveled to and fro like it always had. The old Harley was coming back. I wondered if I would dream.

CHAPTER 7

I awoke an hour and a half before my alarm went off after a night of intense vivid dreams. I felt restless and energetic. I got the coffee brewing and jumped into the shower. Feeling refreshed, I poured a cup and boiled an egg. I dug out Alma's diary and sat down on the lazy-boy.

February 10, 2007

Today I had one of those strange life coincidences. I am the leader of the new student orientation committee. It was my idea to begin with. When new students enroll at LBJ High, they are simply given a class schedule loosely put together based on their transcripts. They are not interviewed about their future goals. They are not given a tour of the facilities. They are thrown into the ocean and expected to swim. I decided to organize a group of students into a committee to help these students when they arrive. When a new student arrives, we meet with them and do our best to make them feel at home. We talk with them, eat lunch with them, introduce them to people, and check to make sure they are taking the classes they really need. What was the coincidence, you ask? Well, today during 1st period one of the counselors, Ms. Sakae called me in to meet a new student. The committee had arranged with the counselors to have one of our members present when a new student was given their class schedule on their first day of school. When I walked into Ms. Sakae's office my eyes nearly popped out of their sockets. Sitting on a chair looking completely lost was Ruth, the girl
I met in Juarez. I often had thought of her and the terrible thing that happened that night with the coyote. She had made it to America! There were so many things I wanted to ask her but couldn't in front of Ms. Sakae. When she first saw me, she gave a double look as if to say - is that really you? I couldn't get over her Mona Lisa smile. Ms. Sakae introduced her (as if that was necessary), gave me a copy of her schedule, and off we went. I gave her the grand VIP tour of LBJ High. She looked like a lost puppy. I asked her how she got to America and she said that this time they took a plane. Her grandmother had died and their family had received a small inheritance. With the money, they bought round trip tickets to LA

105

with the intention of never using the return part. Now, that's a lot easier than the way she did it the first time. Her schedule included an ELD (English as second language) class and her other classes were all SDAIE (Specially-Designed Academic Instruction in English). The idea behind SDAIE is to make regular classes more understandable for those who don't speak English well. They put me in SDAIE when I first got here but I quickly transferred out. Anyway, after the tour, I dropped Ruth off at her 1st period class. At lunch, I introduced her to a few classmates. She seemed shy at first but after a while started opening up. I couldn't stop thinking about how strange it was that our lives had crossed paths again. In the end, I think she'll be okay here. I didn't mention that night in Juarez at all. Some things are better left unsaid.

February 15, 2007

I took 1st place at the debate competition today! Not bad, given that it was my first competition ever. The topic was "should public school students have to wear school uniforms". We had to take a stand either for or against. Although I am personally against uniforms in schools, Mr. Duckworth made me take a stand for. According to him, taking a position that I didn't believe in would help me understand the power of rhetoric. If you can persuade someone about something that you didn't believe in, imagine what you could do if you did, he says. Anyway, knowing all sides of an argument helps you understand the issue better and that can't hurt. The debate took place in the auditorium at Piedmont High. I couldn't believe the neighborhood. It was full of million dollar houses with well-manicured lawns. I bet the only Mexicans living in Piedmont are the maids and gardeners. After the debate, I talked to my opponent for a while. He couldn't believe that I'd been in the country for less than a year. You could tell by the way he talked that he came from a rich family. In spite of this, he was a nice guy and a good loser. (laughing) When I got home, Papa put the trophy on the mantel in the front room. He was beaming with pride. Today was a good day.

February 16, 2007

Guess what? I got my picture in the paper. There was an article about the debate competition on page three of the Times. Most of it was about Mr. Duckworth and how he has worked wonders with us poor ghetto kids. My name was mentioned as the first LBJ High student to take 1st place in 23 years. That feels good. The picture showed a close-up of my face speaking into the microphone. I showed Papa and Mama when I got home and they asked me to translate. Papa reminded me that we were still illegal and that although he was proud of me, he recommended taking a lower profile. I wish the world didn't have borders.

Feb 23, 2007

Just got back from a snow trip to Lake Tahoe. What a beautiful place! Ricardo and I rented a sled at a place called Boreal. It was a blast. I highly recommend it. The only downside was having to sleep in his truck. I would have been miserable if I didn't love him. As you can imagine, I didn't get much sleep. I'm exhausted!

March 3, 2007

Today, when Mr. Duckworth introduced the new topic for the May debate competition, I almost fell out of my chair – Should illegal aliens be allowed to stay or be deported? I hope he lets me choose the side I want this time.

March 18, 2007

Today I got called into Mr. Ramos's office and he was not happy with me at all. I'll make a long story short. I took the list that we brainstormed in the debate club about problems at LBJ High and discussed them with Mr. Franco at Destinos Latinos. He in turn has been hounding Mr. Ramos and district officials to fix these problems. Mr. Ramos explained to me that there is only so much money available for services and maintenance in the district. He said we are doing the best we could with what we have and complained that I was giving the school a bad reputation by

107

advertising its dirty laundry to outsiders. He forgot to mention that he had been approached by our club about these problems long before we turned to Destinos Latinos. If the problems had been addressed, there would have been no need to turn to outsiders as he calls them. He finished by telling me he was disappointed in my judgment. To hell with him.

April 1, 2007

I have spent almost all of spring break practicing for the upcoming debate. Mr. Duckworth has been showing up everyday of his vacation to help out the few dedicated students who want to improve. Today, when he arrived he told us to be quiet as he had a special announcement. He said he had heard from district officials that they would spend 5 million dollars to fix some of the problems on the list that we submitted to the Assistant Superintendent. We applauded until he told us to be quiet again. He yelled out "April Fools!" April Fools is what the Americans call the Day of the Innocents. I'm not sure I liked his cynical joke. Tonight Ricardo and I will go to the cinema. We haven't decided what to see yet but I've heard the Kung Fu Hustle was funny. It's now 1 in the morning. The movie was hilarious. I mean I still crack up when I think about some of the scenes. After the movie, I went to Ricardo's house. His family was out so we had the house to ourselves. That's all you need to know.

April 5, 2007

I got called into the Principal's office again today. He is beginning to treat me like I'm some sort of discipline problem. He keeps telling me; go to him first before going to outside agencies. I told him we already had. He tells me fixing these problems take time. I asked him what steps had he already taken. He says he had personally checked to make sure there was toilet paper in the bathrooms and there was. I say that's great but what are you doing to increase course offerings. He says there are only so many slots available to each school in the district. I asked him, if that's so why do public schools in Lafayette and Piedmont have so many more offerings than we do. He says the answer to that is complicated. I said it shouldn't be. He went on and on about how I was stirring up *trouble and hurting the school's image. Imagine that, after all the positive publicity I have brought to the school by winning the debate. A principal should work to support student involvement, not suppress it. Mr. Ramos even called my home and talked to Mama. Mama said he mentioned something about a local immigration sting and to be careful. What a leader! He is trying to scare my family to get to me. I now know something with 100% certainty. We can not count on our Principal to support us. We'll need to count on ourselves and a few good teachers.*

April 20, 2007

I've started thinking about university. Sure, I have one more year of high school but now is the time to really get serious. I took something called the SAT test last month that Mr. Franco had arranged. I scored an 800 on the Reasoning Test and above 770 in all other areas. Your SAT score is one of the things universities look at when considering your application. Mr. Franco said that my scores were excellent and that when combined with my grades should help a lot in getting me into a good university. He said that one of the disadvantages I have is that the Advance Placement offerings at LBJ High are very limited and that kids at the richer schools will have more variety of coursework on their transcripts. The other disadvantage is being illegal of course and that's a big one. I'm not sure how I should apply. Papa says that since I don't have a social security number, I can't attend university. He's been worried about us getting deported ever since Mr. Ramos scared Mama the other day. Papa thinks I should just get married and be a wife but I have dreams and will not give up. Mr. Franco told me there are ways to attend university for undocumented people like me due to some law called AB540. I'm not sure how that works but I will try to find out more. I also have no idea how I will pay for tuition or qualify for financial aid. There are road-blocks ahead but I will crash through them.

In spite of having gotten up early, I arrived at LBJ High with just 10 minutes to spare before the period 1 bell. Ricardo had posted flyers advertising the club meeting yesterday but for some reason they were all torn down. There was a note in my box advising me to see Mr. Ramos as soon as possible. I stuck my head in his office and told him I could drop by during my prep period. The first half of the day went well. The students worked hard and seemed more motivated than usual. After lunch, I knocked on Mr. Ramos's door. He was eating a sandwich and talking on the phone at the same time. Mr. Ramos was tall and slender with a thick black goatee and mustache. He looked like a young Vincent Price who was going for that distinguished look but somehow it just didn't work.

"Mr. Butler, come on in." He was smiling. "How are your classes going?" he asked.

"I think I've gotten most of the students on task except for a few holdouts."

"I've been hearing good things about you," he complimented.

I had the feeling that wasn't the reason he called me in so I got right to the point. "You said you wanted to see me?"

"There's a couple of things I need to talk to you about. Yesterday, I noticed flyers around campus advertising your club meeting. It's a district regulation that any flyer that is posted on school property needs to be approved first by the administration."

"Fair enough," I responded. "I had seen so many other flyers around campus that I just took the liberty given the fact that it was for a student club."

"That gets me to my next point. Any club activity also needs to be approved by the administration." He handed me a club application form that looked quite simple. It had a spot for club objectives and club activities.

"I could fill this out and get it back to you in just a few minutes," I offered.

"I'm afraid it is not that simple. This club idea of yours has been getting a lot of people talking. You know, these young people witness a lot more violence in a year than most of us do in an entire lifetime. Ms. Vargas's death, as tragic as it was, was not the first student we have lost to violence and regrettably won't be the last."

I wasn't sure where he was going with this so I didn't interject. "Frankly, I think you should reconsider this memorial club idea. You teach computers, right? How about a computer club?"

I was at a lost for words. I remembered from Alma's diary that Mr. Ramos was not always a happy camper when it came to student activism. This club idea was probably bringing back sore memories for him. I thought carefully. "I can promise that all activities conducted by this club will always be constructive and with the school's best interest in mind."

"I've said what I had to say," he said impatiently. "I hope you take it into consideration." The phone rang. When he picked it up, it was my cue to leave. When I opened the door, Mr. Cheasty was standing right there in front of it. I wondered if he had been eavesdropping. He gave me a nod and then I headed back to my classroom. Just yesterday, he had given me the same advice as Mr. Ramos.

I had a decision to make. Should I call in Ricardo and discuss canceling the Alma Vargas Memorial Club idea or ignore Mr. Ramos's advice altogether? What if I were fired? Would I lose the bonus the Richmond Police Department had promised me? Would the case go unsolved? I could call Randy and ask for his opinion.

"Fuck it," I thought. I would go through with the meeting today. I would tell the students who showed up that the administration didn't think the club was a good idea and get their input. After all, it seemed like a reasonable risk to take. The possible rewards outweighed the downside. I'd never heard of a teacher getting fired for sponsoring a club before but that didn't mean that it hadn't happened.

The afternoon classes went well. The students were a little more rambunctious in the afternoon but not terribly so. Michelle Saechao worked quietly on her projects. Neither of us mentioned anything about the night before. Several students confirmed that they would be showing up at the club meeting after school. I kept thinking about the potential hot water I was about to get myself into. At 3:15, the final bell rang and I waited.

Ricardo was the first to arrive. He had prepared an agenda for the meeting and I quickly reviewed it. By 3:30, 13 students had arrived and it was time to begin. My function as a sponsor left me on the sidelines but I would butt in when I found it necessary. Ricardo pulled out his notes and looked around nervously.

"Welcome to the Alma Vargas Memorial Club. As most of you probably know, my name is Ricardo Oliveira and it was my idea to start this club. Alma was very special to me but that's not the reason I'm here. At least, it's not the complete reason. Alma touched us all because she wasn't afraid to speak the truth. She saw

111

things that weren't right and tried to get them fixed. I see the true purpose of this club as to keep Alma's good work alive. Sure she pissed some people off, mainly the administration but in the end she succeeded in getting a spotlight shone on LBJ High and what that light revealed was not always pretty. Still, she didn't do these things just to complain or because she wanted attention. She wanted a better life and opportunity for all of us. In my opinion, we have a duty to pick up where she left off. I can't think of a better way to honor her memory than to start this club. Before we get to work there is one more thing I'd like to say. Those responsible for her death have not been caught yet and that bothers me deeply. I have no idea who could have done such an evil act but maybe if we work together we can somehow help out in the investigation. It won't bring Alma back but she does deserve justice."

This was exactly what I wanted. Now, I'd have 13 assistants unknowingly helping me out. I didn't expect Ricardo to use the club as a way to help solve her murder but I wasn't surprised. After all, it's human nature to want justice. Some say it's human nature to want revenge but revenge always brings civilization down a notch. At least that's what Gandhi preached.

After Ricardo's introduction, the students gathered into two rows and got into social mode. I walked over and told them what Mr. Ramos had told me. They looked irritated and asked me what I was going to do. I turned the question back on them and asked them what they thought I should do.

"It's your call Mr. Butler," Caleb Jones commented. Caleb was about 6'6" and built like a linebacker. "You can be a kiss-ass if you want. It's up to you," he continued.

As I scanned their faces, I came to a realization. Just the fact that these students showed up today, demonstrated that they cared about more than just their hard day to day lives. They wanted to be part of something positive and were crying out for direction. Where could they go for this direction? A lucky few find it in sports. Others find it in a favorite teacher. There were a lot of outside organizations like Making Headways or Destinos Latinos that appeared to want to help but as far as I could see, this help was fragmented. These students came to the Alma Vargas Memorial Club meeting of their own free will because Alma represented hope. I felt selfish for even having considered for a minute not sponsoring them to save my financial package. A couple of other students made remarks expressing their disappointment in Mr. Ramos. Rather than waste more meeting time, I interjected.

"I know the school administration for whatever twisted reason thinks this club is a bad idea. I sure don't. I know that you don't. Yes, I have been advised not to sponsor the club but that doesn't mean it won't go on. I have an idea. Let's create an alias. How about calling ourselves the Networking Club? Sure, we'll still be the Alma Vargas Memorial Club but on paper we'll be the NC."

There was a few seconds of silence and then Ricardo spoke.

"Does it a matter what name you give the administration? All they're interested in really is preserving the status quo. Ramos's first priority has always been himself with the local press running a close second. Students have always been on the bottom of the totem pole around here. What do we have to lose? All those in favor of giving a bullshit name to Mr. Ramos, raise your hand."

With that, all 13 students raised their hands high. The show would go on come what may. The students present at the meeting represented the diversity of LBJ High. There were six Latinos, four African Americans, two Southeast Asians, an Indian, and one white kid. Ricardo proceeded to take control again.

"Before we get into planning club activities, let's all introduce ourselves and explain why we're here. I know we already know each other but let's get to know each other better, if you know what I mean."

Ricardo appeared to be a natural leader. I could see that he wasn't going to let this group become just another trivial social club. The students clearly looked up to him. You could tell by the way they looked at him when he spoke. He continued.

"I come from a city called Goiania in Brazil. A little after I was born, my father took a vacation to California and never came back. We were not reunited again until last year when my mom, sister, and I came to California where my father worked at a pizzeria. At first, I was homesick for Brazil but after a year I began to make friends and now this is my home. I met Alma in the summer of 2006 in an English class. We hit it off immediately. She was the love of my life and always will be. I'm convinced she's sitting in this room with us right now and her spirit will guide us." He wiped a tear from his eye.

113

"Hey, I'm Caleb Jones." He did something funny with his hands the way rap singers do. "Last year, I was about to get in a fight with this big Mexican gang-banger dude. Anyway, we had already gone to blows when Alma gets in the middle of us. She really caught us off guard. I mean I had never seen a student try to stop a fight before. Most of the time, when there's a fight, people come running thirsty to see blood but she jumped right in the middle of us with both hands in the air yelling something about conflict resolution. By the time we figured out what she was talking about, our tempers had cooled down. I'm not sure if it was what she said, the way she said it, or the compassion in her eyes that calmed us down but whatever it was, it worked. He left with his homies and I left with mine. The next day I get called out of class and they take me to a small room in the back of the library. Sitting at the end of the table was Alma with a notebook in her hand. On one side of the table was the Mexican dude I wanted to kill the day before. I sat right across from him. She set the rules for the meeting. Only one person could talk at a time. We couldn't ask questions to each other. Things like that. Anyway, to make a long story short, by the time we left the room, we both realized that a fight was in neither of our best interests, and that we had a lot more in common with each other than we thought. After that day, I talked to Alma any chance I could. She was different and I mean that in a very good way."

A tall student with intense dark eyes who I knew from my graphic design class stood up. "Greetings comrades. My name is Pedro Montano and I'm the Mexican gang-banger dude that Caleb just told you about." A few students laughed loudly.

"After I met Alma that day in conflict mediation, I began to think seriously about my life. She kept an eye out for me and made sure I stayed out of trouble. You know, she may have been the only person out there at the time who gave a shit about me except my mom. She made sure I came to school and tried to get me to study but what I remember most was the question she kept asking me. *How do you see yourself Pedro?* At first, I found it annoying but she kept persisting with the question. It's not easy to think about who you really are but everyone should do it because we only got one life. Anyway, when I finally blurted out a bunch of crap about who I thought I was she just sat there real calm like and said, *Perceptions are not set in stone. You are not who you think you are. You only need to change the way you see yourself.* Over time, she helped me change how I thought about myself and for that I will be forever grateful." Pedro's eyes were watering.

Hello friends. "I'm Josh Anderson and I knew Alma from the debate club. All I can say is that she was a great friend and the best debater who ever set foot on this campus. I'd be happy, if I were half as good as she was. What I miss most about her is the way she questioned everything. If you weren't making sense, she'd let you know it. When she saw that something was wrong, she just didn't complain, she did something about it." Josh was the only Caucasian present.

"Hi everybody. It's me, Diane Phan." The students said "Hi Diane" in unison. "I had heard about Alma and saw her around but the first time I got to know her was in Mr. Bergman's American Government class. We were assigned as partners and had to do a biography about each other's life using PowerPoint. Man, she took it seriously. I mean I was the kind of student that did just enough to get the grade but Alma wasn't that way. She took it to the next level. She visited my house, interviewed all my relatives, and took a ton of pictures. She even called the Vietnamese embassy to ask questions. When she was done, I think she knew more about my family than my family did. My project did not even come close to hers but she inspired me to do better next time." There was some laughter and she continued. "She helped me in some other private ways that I can't talk about. All I know is that I miss her and I want to be a part of this club."

Pedro gave a nudge to a cute, quiet Hispanic girl to stand up. She hesitated but finally called up the courage. "Hi. My name is Ruth Orozco." She stopped, blushed and looked around. "I met Alma in Juarez and again here at school. She help me a lot." She sat back down. This had to be the Ruth from Alma's diary. She didn't say much, probably due to her limited English ability. I couldn't help thinking of the horrible rape she had experienced in Juarez. I remembered that Alma in her diary had described Ruth as having a Mona Lisa smile. She hit that one right on the nail.

The rest of the students present introduced themselves. There was Armando Jaime who said Alma was helping him prepare for college. There was Miriam Lopez, one of my graphic design students, who said she used to walk home with Alma and took driver's education classes with her. The extremely thin Mariana Suchil talked about how Alma visited her at Juvenile Hall and

115

inspired her into not dropping out of high school when she was released. Byrisha Washington explained how Alma had showed up on her doorstep at 7:30 a.m. and asked her why she hadn't been attending school. Byrisha said she was so shocked that a student would care enough about her to visit her apartment that it inspired her to get her act together. Carnell Smith, a lanky African American student with dreadlocks, told a story about how Alma talked the district out of expelling him for fighting. Michelle Saechao ended by talking about how Alma simply made LBJ High a warmer place to be.

Ricardo took the floor again. "As you can see from all your stories, Alma has impacted all of our lives in more ways than one. We have got to pick up where she left off. Yes, we are sad about her death but we don't want this emotion to rule our spirit. Let's remember how she lived and keep up her positive work. This club will help us do that. In our next meeting, we'll get into the details on how we are going to do that. I suggest we meet every Tuesday after school. All those in agreement say Aye." There were no dissenters.

The meeting ended. Some students left and others hung around the lab for a while. At around 5, I told them they had to go home so I could lock up. I thought the first meeting had been interesting and it was great that these students had a club they could call their own. It was moving and inspiring to see how a young girl could have such a powerful impact on so many people's lives. I was still worried though about the flack this was going to cause with the administration. One thing was certain; the next few weeks would be interesting.

It was already getting dark when I arrived in the teacher's parking lot. I decided to head to Albany to visit my office to check up on things. Besides a little dust, the room was the same as I left it. As usual, the answering machine was full of messages from people inquiring about my services. I hoped this sabbatical wouldn't have a negative effect on my business but it was too late now to stress about it. Perhaps I could get Rosanna to help man the phone and return some of these calls. I sat down on my comfortable, leather chair, closed my eyes and began taking yoga like deep breaths.

"Om ah hum benza guru padma sidi hum," I repeated in my mind over and over. A Tibetan friend had taught me that chant years ago and it stuck in my memory like a foreign language dialogue memorized from middle school. I forgot what the words meant or even why one was supposed to repeat them but for some reason they just popped in my mind at this quiet moment in my office. Slowly, the weight of my body began to disappear and for a brief moment my spirit was free. At least, I had the illusion it was free. Is this what becomes of us after death? I guess I'd have to wait to find out. If this was it, death wouldn't be so bad after all, I predicted.

I'm not sure how long I stayed in this meditative state but I was brought back to reality by the sound of someone moaning in the room next door. It was the kind of moan that could have been from either pleasure or pain and from its mid-tone range; it was difficult to distinguish the sex of the person. This was the first time I had ever heard any noise coming from the office next door and was hoping this wouldn't become a regular occurrence. Was some kind of therapy taking place? I still didn't know what somato-emotional release meant. Anyway, either the pain or the pleasure of the person was increasing as the moans became louder and longer. Finally, a spasmodic scream could be heard that vibrated the walls. It lasted about 10 seconds but then gradually decreased in volume until there was complete silence. I could hear muffled conversation coming through the walls but couldn't make out what was being said. I turned on the computer and quickly googled somato-emotional release therapy. Turns out this therapy is based on the concept that our tissues and muscles actually hold memories of past experiences including traumatic experiences like car accidents or assaults. Apparently, through a combination of physical and mental therapy these tissue memory issues could be addressed. Was this some sort of California pop culture, new age nonsense or a legitimate therapy? I wasn't sure. Whatever was happening behind those walls was intense though. Maybe Ms. Weinstein was simply having sex with a partner. The truth was, it was none of my business.

I did a little dusting and then headed out the door. Ms. Weinstein's door opened at the exact moment I passed it startling me. A tall, scruffy-looking teenager with long hair and torn jeans walked out the door carrying a skateboard. "See ya Ms. Weinstein," he said not looking back as he exited the main door. He looked to be about 16 years old. As soon as he reached the sidewalk, he set his skateboard on the ground and took off noisily down Solano Ave.

117

There were a few awkward moments of silence as Ms. Weinstein and I looked at each other trying to figure out if we should exchange pleasantries.

"How's the detective business these days?" she asked to break the ice.

"Keeps me busy. How are things with you?" I wondered if she was trying to determine if I had heard the sounds coming from her office.

"Sorry if we disturbed you in any way. This kind of therapy has its intense moments," she confessed. Ms. Weinstein looked to be in her mid 30s but her face was wrinkle-free. She had light brown hair, a tall and slender body and wore a long, conservative, navy-blue skirt that was slightly disheveled. I thought she looked more dressed for Manhattan than a town in the Berkeley area but she did appear professional. That thought led me to a question.

"How long have you been operating out of this office?"

"Oh, not long. I moved here from New York a few months ago and just recently set up my practice." My Manhattan impression was dead on target.

"Did you have a practice back in New York?"

"Oh, I had a practice alright and I really miss my patients. There are a lot of established therapists in the Big Apple but I was able to find a niche. I had some family difficulties that were starting to get in the way of things so I moved out here for a fresh start."

"I think we have quite a few therapists out here as well. After all, this is the West Coast."

"That's true but I think it's easier for someone to get started here than back east. In New York, you need to worry about the petty jealousies of your competition. Out here, I get the feeling that people will just let you be if you offer a useful service."

I had no idea what she meant and still couldn't get those moaning sounds out of mind. "Do you do traditional therapy? I inquired.

"It depends on what you mean by traditional. My specialty was Cranio-Sacral therapy with an emphasis on Somato-Emotional release. I was trained to treat the victims of physical trauma but discovered over time that the methods I used could be used to help people realize their full potential. That's why I went beyond my training and developed a unique practice."

She had my interest. "You mean that sign on your door is not correct?"

"Well, yes and no. It's part of what I do but it's not the full picture. I see it as my job to help folks find their core, their soul if you will, and become attuned with their animal essence. At the same time, I help them get in touch with the implicit and unspoken ideas behind their physical actions."

I suddenly had a feeling of déjà vu. Where did I hear that before - implicit and unspoken ideas? My curiosity deepened. "So the Somato-Emotional Release therapist sign is basically a cover for something much more grand?"

"I mean if my plaque read Soul Healer or True Identity Finder I'd be written off as just another New Age Mumbo-Jumbo practitioner. You're right. It is a cover. But in the end, aren't we all more than our professional titles suggest? I bet you do more than just investigate."

She was right about that but I still couldn't stop thinking about the moaning I heard and the teenage boy that I saw. What was going on in there? Due to patient confidentiality, there was no point in asking and I'd probably never find out. We engaged in small talk for a while. She seemed pleasant and non-assuming and asked some general questions about my practice. We ended up exiting the main door and walked a few blocks together. She told me she lived in a studio in the Rockridge area of Oakland and had few friends in the Bay Area. When we bid farewell on the corner of Tulare St., she mentioned getting together for lunch someday.

Back at home, I cooked dinner and had a meal while watching TV. Rosanna and Joãozinho dropped by unexpectedly. She was excited about starting a career as a detective and would start out under my direction at Tantei Man. I could get her working on some of the cases that were coming in and communicate with her by cell from LBJ High. She could earn the hours she needed for a license quickly that way. With her natural inquisitive nature, I had a feeling she'd make a good detective. Was I ready for a partner? I wasn't sure but it looked like I was going to find out

119

CHAPTER 8

The next few weeks were uneventful at LBJ High. The Networking Club met only once more before the two week winter break. I did not hear any more comments from the administration on our rogue club so I assumed that everything was okay. There was a teachers' meeting and a couple of what they call staff development meetings that I attended in December but I drifted off at these so I couldn't tell you what they were about. Mr. Duckworth visited my room the day of the club meeting and mentioned that he had some video of Alma from one of the debate competitions. He promised to make a copy for our club.

After school, I usually met Rosanna at Tantei Man to go over some of the light cases I had recently felt comfortable taking on. She was a fast learner and had enrolled in the courses she'd need for her license. I kept a record of the time she spent working for me which averaged about ten hours a day. At this pace, it wouldn't take long for her to accumulate the 6,000 hours needed for licensing. Needless to say, my life was getting busy.

The holidays came and went and it was time to get back to work at LBJ High. The Networking Club would have its first meeting of the new year on the 16th.

As promised, Mr. Duckworth dropped a video tape in my box to share with the club. The title on the case read, May 2007 Debate Competition Acalanes High School – Illegal Immigration. I decided to take it home and review it before letting the club see it.

It started out with some shaky video of the location, a gymnasium. On one side, I could see that the bleachers had been pulled out and were filled to capacity. The voice narrating the tape was that of Mr. Duckworth. He panned across the floor. On one side of the gym, three tables placed side by side had teachers who were designated as judges sitting behind them. On the other side, facing the judges were two podiums placed about 20 feet apart. There was nobody standing at them. He did a few more scans of the facility. Alma and Ricardo appeared briefly and then there were random images of the floor. Mr. Duckworth had apparently forgotten to turn off the camera. I fast-forwarded to the next scene. A couple of students from other schools were debating the illegal immigration question. This was cut off after about a minute and the next image showed Alma standing behind the left podium. A quick pan revealed a male student dressed in a blue suit standing behind the one on the right. He was giving his opening statement. Alma was dressed in a light grey skirt that went to just above her knees. If a young Sonia Braga and a young Bridgitte Bardot were mixed in a blender and then put back together again to yield the best result, you still wouldn't have someone approaching Alma's beauty. She was truly captivating but the conservative suit she was wearing contrasted oddly with her natural beauty.

An MC who was standing next to the judges' table spoke into a microphone. He introduced the debaters and restated the topic. Should illegal aliens be deported? He went over the rules and then asked the young man, a senior from Acalanes High, to begin his opening statement. The camera panned back to the student.

"Good Morning. My name is Joe Rabin and I am senior at Acalanes. Thank you for allowing me the opportunity to express my views on the topic of illegal immigration. Three months ago, a car on Highway 4 in Hercules crossed over the double-line and hit another car head-on, killing a family of five. Last month, the owner of a hamburger stand on San Pablo Avenue in El Cerrito was shot to death as he was leaving work and robbed of 55 dollars. Two weeks ago, an elderly man in Berkeley was beaten brutally and robbed of his wallet. He is still in a coma. What do these horrible crimes have in common, you ask? Well, I'll tell you. They were all committed by illegal immigrants. These incidents, as despicable as they are, represent a mere drop in the bucket of the cost of illegal immigration to the average American citizen. Local city officials all over the Bay Area are reporting a garbage dumping problem. People pick up illegal aliens every day in front of places like the Home Depot, pay them to dump their garbage and give them the money to take it to city recycling centers. (The camera panned to Alma. She was taking notes.) Nine out of ten times this money is pocketed by the illegal alien and the garbage dumped in places like school parking lots and scenic country roads. Who pays for the clean-up? We do. Who pays when thousands of illegal aliens each week arrive in hospital emergency rooms all over the state? We do. Who pays for the education of illegal immigrants? We do. Who suffers from the thousands of crimes committed by illegal aliens? We do. (A section of the mostly white audience yelled out "we do" in unison.) You may be asking yourself, aren't we a nation built on immigrants? The answer is yes of course. The problem is that there

121

is a big difference with the immigrants of the past and those of the present. (applause could be heard) The soul of the United States was built on the backs of our hardworking Anglo-Protestant ancestors. (Another pan to Alma who was covering her mouth as if to hide a laugh) The Christian values of these early immigrants included respect for the law, individualism, and the pursuit of happiness. Contrast that with the current immigrants from south of the border who apparently have no respect for our laws and reject the goals and dreams of the individual to join the conformity of the street gang. There is no pursuit of happiness here. There is only destruction of happiness. Uncontrolled immigration from south of our borders is now in the process of ruining the very quality of life that has made America a beacon of hope for the world. Our only hope in preserving this great country is to begin the politically incorrect process of deporting those that are here illegally."

The audience in one of the bleachers erupted into a standing ovation applause. The pan to Alma showed a composed girl with a relaxed smile on her face. The MC asked Ms. Vargas for her opening statement. Alma took a deep breath, slowly scanned the audience and began her introduction. The expression on her face reminded me of the way she had turned and looked at me in my dream.

"Buenos Días. Mi nombre es Alma Vargas y yo voy a la secundaria LBJ High y estoy en el tercer año. (Nervous laughter could be heard) Don't worry. I can speak English. (She smiled and glanced down at her notes) Good Morning and thanks for taking the time to attend. I'm Alma Vargas. (She smiled widely) I'm a junior and proud to be representing LBJ High at this debate competition. In 1844, James Polk, ran for the office of president on a platform of expansionism and won. At the time, all or most of the states of Arizona, California, Colorado, New Mexico, Nevada, Texas and Utah were part of greater Mexico. About this time, the term "Manifest Destiny" came into fashion among Americans. The term refers to what Americans thought of at the time as their God-given right to expand and take territory. To make a long story short, the Mexican war ended with the U.S. and Mexico signing the Treaty of Guadalupe-Hidalgo. For a mere 15 million dollars, the United States acquired an unbelievable amount of land including Alta-California. Does anybody here know where that is? (She paused, smiled and looked around) Beep! Time's up. (She jumped) That's

122

where we are right now. My point is that there is something very cynical about wanting to deport people from a land that in a way was once theirs. Illegal Mexican workers have played a key role in developing the California economy by doing the work Americans won't do. Describing these hardworking people as criminals as my opponent has is criminal in my opinion. (Subdued laughter could be heard) There is no doubt that immigration should be controlled and that immigrants involved in illegal activity should be deported. The reality though, is that most immigrants are hardworking people like my father who does back-breaking work everyday to support his family. My opponent has given a few examples of recent crimes committed by immigrants to instill fear in you. This technique of exaggerating the negative qualities of an ethnic group to create an atmosphere of xenophobia has been used throughout time. Hitler did it with the Jews. (She held up a newspaper and pointed to the front page) Look at this headline. "Irish Catholic Priest arrested for rape." Do I hear an outcry to deport Irish immigrants? (She put her hand around her ear as if straining to hear. A couple of laughs could be heard) You could make a negative case out of any ethnic group, by arbitrarily showing only the negative aspects. Latinos are easy targets because they are poor and often dark-skinned. Should we rewrite the tablet on the Statue of Liberty to read, Give me your tired your poor, Your huddled masses yearning to breathe free but don't forget to deport the hard-working Mexicans. (Laughter could be heard as she pounded on the podium to emphasize) The beauty of the USA and especially California is in its diversity. This is what makes it a beacon of hope. Let's keep it a beacon of hope by allowing those who obey its laws to legally reside and eventually become citizens."

There was polite applause that paled in comparison to the ovation her opponent received in spite of the fact that her opening statement seemed better prepared and much more animated than his. He had the home field advantage for crowd support. That was for sure. Besides Ricardo, I saw no other evidence on the video of other LBJ students in attendance. Knowing what I knew of Alma's past, I found it astonishing how polished her English was. Her vocabulary was that of a graduate student and her slight accent simply added charm to the equation.

The two exchanged points and counter-points over the next 15 minutes of tape. Alma was clearly getting the best of him. He mentioned the fact that illegal aliens were a financial drag on health care. Alma countered that a recent Urban Institute report had concluded that immigrants actually contributed more in taxes than cost of services received. He mentioned that aliens took jobs away from American citizens. Alma countered that the A.C.L.U. had reported several studies that showed immigrants actually created jobs. She had obviously done her homework and was ready for anything that was thrown at her. I was certain she would win the debate. At the end of the closing remarks, the MC took the microphone.

"We will now take a five minute break to give our judges time to score."

In the next scene, Ricardo had his arm around Alma. He was pointing his finger at the side of her head saying she kicked butt. You could hear Mr. Duckworth behind the camera saying she did, she did, she did.

The next scene was a pan of the judges' tables and the two podiums with Alma and her opponent standing behind them. He focused the camera on the MC who was now standing between the podiums.

"Ladies and gentleman, we have reached the end of this part of our competition. We will now ask the judges for their results. Mr. Cohen, please rise?"

"I have Mr. Rabin 10 Ms. Vargas 9."

An electronic scoreboard immediately displayed the totals.

"Mr. Levy?"

"Rabin 9 Vargas 8."

"Mr. Katz?"

"Rabin 9 Vargas 7."

The scoreboard read 28 to 24. Alma had lost but for the life of me, I couldn't see why. Was there something they saw differently than what I saw on the video? I felt like a parent at a little league baseball game frustrated by an unfair call by the umpire. The game was clearly rigged. Alma walked gracefully towards the podium of her opponent. Smiling, she shook hands with him. You could make out that she said "congratulations" even though she wasn't holding a microphone. She turned around, smiled again and waved to the crowd. I could see that she was not only a great public speaker, she knew how to lose with grace.

In the last scene, Alma and Ricardo could be seen goofing around in the parking lot. They seemed to be having a good time and she appeared to be completely unaffected by the loss. I ejected the video and put it back in its case. The club would enjoy this, I thought. It was strange how Alma's voice on the tape appeared to be the same voice I had heard in my dream. At least, I thought it was but how could that be? It was probably just my mind playing tricks on me.

At the club meeting, all members showed up and watched the debate video. Several made the comment that Alma should have won. A few of the girls began sobbing including Ruth. A little while later, Ricardo presented an action plan for school reform and had all members sign it. What a guy! While they were talking about what to do about all that was wrong with the school, I couldn't help thinking about how Principle Ramos had been so quiet over the past couple of weeks. I had passed him in the hallway several times but he didn't even acknowledge my existence. I tried to make eye contact but he would have none of it. Was he just preoccupied with running the business of the school or was I getting the proverbial cold shoulder for going against his wishes?

Around 5, Ricardo walked me to my car. I quickly jumped into the driver's seat but as soon as I got in he began rapping on the window. I stepped out and he pointed to the two tires on the passenger side of my Vette. Both had been slashed and were as flat as could be. Was this one of the benefits of being a public school teacher that I had heard so much about? Report cards wouldn't come out for a couple of weeks so it couldn't have been in retaliation for a bad grade. I hadn't given anyone a referral for discipline since I'd been there. I thought the students liked me. Maybe someone was just jealous of my old Corvette, I theorized. That's when I noticed a small piece of dirty folded paper tucked behind my windshield wiper. I unfolded the paper carefully. It turned out to be some wrapper from Jack in the Box. On the inside, there was a message written in Spanish in sloppy cursive. It took awhile to make out the letters but I finally figured out what the message said. La ave que deja el nido muy pronto va a alcanzar la muerte. The fledging that leaves the nest too soon will fall to its death. What the? I felt my blood began to boil with anger. Someone was playing games with me. I showed the message to Ricardo and he just shook his head.

125

"I don't think a student wrote that," he offered. "The student body at LBJ High is just not that into proverbs."

Ricardo tried to grab the note to look at it but I pulled it away from him. There could be useful forensic evidence on it, I told him. He advised me that slashed tires in Richmond were not serious enough to get the cops off their butts. Of course, I wasn't thinking just slashed tires. I called up my State Farm agent and they arranged a tow truck that would be there in the hour. Looked like they'd pay for the towing but since I had a $500 deductible policy, the tire cost would be my expense. Shit!

We walked back to my classroom through the empty hallways. I peaked in the Teachers' Room and noticed that a few teachers including Mr. Cheasty and Ms. Rosales were taking a Spanish lesson. I waved and then headed to room 207. I logged on to my computer and Ricardo logged on to his. He decided to keep me company during this hour of killing time. I checked my e-mail and a few news sites when it occurred to me that I should probably step outside and give Randy a call to tell him what happened. He arranged to pick up the mysterious note at my office later on and take it to forensics. I felt better when he told me that the department would probably cover the tire expenses.

Back in room 207, I noticed that Ricardo was on a web site that was full of pictures of Alma. "What are you looking at?" I asked.

"It's the Alma Vargas Memorial Site that I set up on Myspace."

"What's the URL?" He scribbled it on a piece of notebook paper and handed it to me. I typed it in the address field but a St. Bernard software message came up instead. *Your organization has chosen to limit viewing of this site due to the rating of its content (adult).*

"Looks like the district filter software blocks Myspace but if I can't get on with administrative privileges, how the heck did you get on as a student?"

"Now, Mr. Butler. You're asking me to give up useful intelligence that our troops have gathered over time." He laughed. "I'll tell you what, if you promise not to reveal it to your superiors, I'll let you in on it."

"In the name of discovery, I promise."

"We use what are called anonymizers. Basically, it's web site on a server that allows you to type in a web address and then surf from this proxy site just as you would regularly. The only difference is you type the URL in a special field, not the browser's address field. Here, I'll show you." He typed in the address of the anonymizer and a simple web site popped up. There was a field where he typed in the URL for Myspace and up popped the site.

"That's nice to know," I said. "Why doesn't the filter block the anonymizer site too?"

"Oh, it will. We have to keep finding new anonymizers all the time. This one is working right now but there is no guarantee it will tomorrow. It's a real cat and mouse game, you know. There are some things that I agree shouldn't be available at school like pornography but blocking off social networking sites like Myspace or Facebook? That's kind of like saying, you can't hang out at school with your friends. We'll always find a way."

He was right about that. I kind of thought of filters as a necessary evil. Some kids will head down the path of least resistance and go off task if given the opportunity on the computer. A filter has the potential to keep students from going astray but if they knew how to get around them, what was the point of using them? Anyway, I was about to use an anonymizer to bypass our district's filter and visit Alma's memorial site. The main page had a nice black and white photo of Alma's face where she appeared almost heroic. This was not your usual Myspace cheap snapshot that most people post. The gradation of tone and enigma of her expression reminded of an Imogen Cunningham portrait.

"Who took this photograph?" I asked.

"I did."

"Have you studied photography?"

"Not officially. Mr. Martelaro occasionally talks about different photographers' work in art class and I do a lot of study on my own. I forget who it was but he gave us a presentation on a photographer who talked about the difference between taking and making photographs. I liked that idea and took it to heart."

"I'm not sure I know what you mean by that – take vs. make?"

"Take implies that you are stealing something. A lot of photographs are just that, stolen pieces of reality. I will not pull that trigger unless I have clear connection with my subject."

127

I was impressed by the insight considering his age. "You obviously had a connection here." I praised.

"Thanks, but the truth is no photograph could do Alma justice."

I nodded and began clicking the links. There were hundreds of messages posted and according to the meter; the site already had more than seven thousand hits. I read a few of the messages and looked at the pictures. There was a picture of Alma dressed warmly next to a snowman. I remembered the diary entry of the Lake Tahoe trip. Suddenly, my cell phone rang. It was the tow-truck driver waiting for me in the parking lot. We went out and watched as he jacked up and hoisted my Vette onto the flatbed. My insurance agent had arranged to send it to a Big O Tires in Berkeley to get the tires replaced. They were not reparable. I rode along in the cab and then just hung around the reception area at Big O until my tires had been replaced and aligned.

I drove back to Albany and got a bite to eat at Barney's, a hamburger joint across the street from my office. Back at the office, I found a note from Rosanna explaining who had called and what she had been doing. In the quiet of the room, I began thinking about the tire and note experience. Would this little inconvenience turn out to be a blessing? I hoped it wouldn't become a daily occurrence. That could get costly.

Suddenly, I heard it again. It was the sound of moaning and just as before I couldn't tell if it was from pleasure or pain. This time the voice seemed slightly lower than before but just as before, the moans increased in intensity. It couldn't be the same kid, I thought. Unfortunately, it looked like I was going to have to get used to this sound invasion.

The thought entered my mind that the same person who slashed my tires could have keyed my car as well. I was getting annoyed by the noise so I decided to take a walk outside to check it. I looked it over closely on all sides and didn't see anything more than a few supermarket dings.

When I returned to the office, the main door swung open suddenly right when I was about to turn the knob. Out walked this well-built and tall African-American teenager smiling from ear to ear. As soon as I recognized that it was Caleb Jones, I tried to pretend I didn't see him and started walking up Solano Avenue.

"Mr. Butler, Mr. Butler. It's me Caleb."

128

"Hi Caleb. Whatcha up to?"

"Just taking care of some business. Shouldn't the question be, what are you up to?"

"Just taking a walk," I said nervously. I was thinking my cover could have been blown.

"It's alright Mr. Butler. We all have our needs. I gotta get back home and do some work now. See you tomorrow." With that, he walked off whistling a tune. He had an air about him that said he had just made love with the most beautiful girl in the world and was walking on clouds. Or maybe it was just Ms. Weinstein's excellent therapy working its magic? Something didn't feel right about the picture though. My biggest concern was with Caleb finding out that I was a detective. Since the sign outside read Tantei Man, he had no way of connecting me to the detective business unless he saw me enter my office which he didn't. At least, I think he didn't. There was also the possibility that he had been there before and seen me but I doubted that. Anyway, there was no point in getting paranoid.

I decided to do some grocery shopping at the Safeway down the street. By the time I finished, Caleb should be long gone. I bought some canned goods and a 12 oz. bag of Peets coffee beans and got into the longest line to kill time. When I got back to my office, it was completely quiet. I reviewed Rosanna's note again. Just when I was about to call her to clarify something there was a knock on the door. It was Randy, dressed casually and sporting his usual Oakland A's cap.

"What a day, old buddy," I exclaimed. "First, I get my car vandalized and then I see one of our students leaving my office building."

"Has your cover been compromised?" He looked worried.

"I don't think so. I bumped into him right as I was about to open the door. It looks like he had business with the lady in the office next door."

"She's a therapist, isn't she?"

"I think so," I replied.

"You mean you have your doubts?" He laughed.

"She calls herself a somato-emotional release therapist." He looked puzzled. "I know. I had to look it up to find out what it meant. You know, I've spoken to her and she looks and talks like a professional. The only thing that seems out of the ordinary is the sounds."

129

"What sounds? Does she play loud music?"

"No. The last couple of times I've been here, I heard the sound of guys moaning. The moans increase in intensity and then taper of. Sounds like sex to me man."

He chuckled. "You said she looks and talks like a professional. Maybe that therapist thing is a cover for prostitution."

"I meant she dresses and talks like a well-educated person. There's nothing about her presence that would suggest she was a whore."

"Except the moaning?"

"Yeah. That's a mystery alright. Strange thing is the clients that I have seen have all been young. One was a lanky white teenager on a skateboard and then today it was one of my students, Caleb. I'm going to have to get some sound proofing if this keeps up. It affects my concentration."

He laughed again. "I'll have one of our newbies on the force run a check on her. It could just be some intense therapy going on but it concerns me that one of your students was here. Usually families from the hood can't afford private therapy."

"I'd appreciate that." I pointed out the love letter I received on my windshield earlier.

He put on some rubber gloves and picked it up carefully by the edges the way one would hold an old vinyl record. "We'll have it checked for prints and DNA evidence ASAP. Anyone else touch it besides you?"

"Don't think so."

"Good. This may or may not be a break. It could just be a malicious student. Teachers get their cars vandalized all the time but usually vandals don't leave behind a proverb."

We reverted to small talk. I mentioned to him about Rosanna wanting to become a detective and he told me he was still seeing Kátia. He talked about some of the recent cases he had been working on and I explained to him a little about the day to day life at LBJ High. When he left, I started thinking about Caleb Jones and Ms. Weinstein. That was weird. I had not seen a single LBJ High student in Albany since I started working at LBJ High and now I see one leaving my office building on the same day that my tires get slashed.

130

CHAPTER 9

From where I parked my Corvette near the base of the Statue of Liberty, I could see LBJ walking his dog. The beagle appeared excited, sniffing all around the pedestal. Suddenly, it hiked its left leg and peed.

"That's no way to treat Lady Liberty old boy," said LBJ loudly. "She's telling the world to send their wretched refuse." He let out a cackling laugh and got down on his knees. He held his dog by the skin of its neck with one hand and looked him straight in the eyes. "That's all we need is more garbage. You know what happens when you pile garbage on garbage, old boy?" He paused a few seconds as if waiting for the dog to respond. "Well, I'll tell you little buddy. You get a very big garbage dump." His voice had a paternal sound to it as if he was passing on the wisdom of the ages.

I tried to open the door to get out and talk to him but it was jammed. The window would only open a quarter of the way down. I began knocking and screaming. "Hey LBJ, give me a hand over here. It's not a dump." He turned his head as if he had heard, looked over in my direction and then spoke with that same paternal voice. "Listen closely Harley. The Great Society is in your hands now. You know it's only as great as you make it. Remember, that was just a speech. That's what us politicians do to get folks on our side. Some people took that one way too seriously though. You just do what you can with what you got Harley. That poor girl is counting on you."

He laughed out loud and disappeared on the other side of the pedestal. The dog began to bark the way dogs do when they sense an intruder. Suddenly, it stopped and from the same side of the pedestal that LBJ had disappeared behind, stepped out Caleb Jones sporting that unforgettable smile. He cupped his hands together, made the shape of a megaphone, and yelled out in a deep powerful voice – I can help! I can help!

The digital clock on the nightstand read 3:37. I got up to pee and contemplated taking notes on my dream while it was fresh in my memory. Otherwise, I'd forget it or it would simply become convoluted with memories of other dreams. Since stopping Concerta, they had sure come back with a vengeance. In my experience, dreams could either be good, bad, or neutral. I wasn't sure what this one was. That laughing LBJ was a bit disturbing. If I took notes, maybe it'd be useful someday in therapy. I reminded myself that I didn't think much of therapy and went back to sleep.

When I arrived in room 207, the first thing I did was turn on my computer as was my usual routine. By habit, I reached for the mouse but to my surprise it wasn't there. I looked around my desk to see if it had fallen off but it hadn't. I checked the mini din connector on the back of the computer and discovered that the mouse had been removed. At 6:00 p.m. yesterday I was sitting right here using this computer. Whoever removed it did it sometime between then and now. No big deal, I thought. Mr. Chirac could get me a replacement. That's when I looked around the classroom. Shockingly, every single mouse had been stolen.

I walked into Mr. Chirac's room to see if he was making some kind of change like upgrading to optical mice but he wasn't. He appeared to be just as surprised as I was. The mice in his room hadn't been touched. He said he had a few extras he could give me but not enough for the whole class. I'd have to talk to Mr. Ramos about ordering some more. I walked down to his office but as usual he was not in. I left a note explaining what had happened. I told Ms. Perkins about the theft and she said I'd probably have to file an incident report. With the five mice that Mr. Chirac had given me, I decided to just use one for my computer. I didn't want students fighting over the work-stations that had mice. Today's lesson would have to be about how to navigate your computer using the tab key.

The incident report had to be a brief summary of what happened. Since it'd be another 30 minutes until period 1 started, I decided to get it done.

Incident Report

Wednesday, January 18, 2008

Harley Butler – LBJ High School

This morning, upon arriving in my classroom, I discovered that every single mouse had been stolen. I was in the room until 6:00 p.m. the night before and everything was okay. I discovered the theft this morning at 7:30. The theft took place sometime in that 13 and half hour period. I was at the school so late because two of the tires on my car had been slashed and I was waiting for a tow truck.

I printed it out and took it over to Ms. Perkins. She scanned it hurriedly. "You've been having a run of bad luck, haven't you?"

"Comes with the territory I guess. What happens next?"

"Your incident report will be looked at and signed by Mr. Ramos, then filed away. This isn't serious enough to file a police report."

I nodded and got back to class a few minutes before the bell rang. The rest of the day was a struggle. Students complained and had trouble getting things done using the tab key. One even asked me why I was the only one who had a mouse. I couldn't offer a good explanation. During lunch, I discovered a note in my mailbox that read "See Mr. Ramos immediately after school."

At 3:30, I knocked on Mr. Ramos's door but he was not in. I asked Ms. Perkins if she knew where he was. She said he'd be back shortly. I sat down on one of the folding chairs, waited, and thought about what Mr. Ramos was going to throw at me. Teachers passed and smiled. Students looked at me with curiosity. A Mexican man sat down next to me after asking a question in broken English to Ms. Perkins. Mr. Bergman and Mr. Cheasty strolled through smiling enigmatically as if they had just heard an inappropriate joke. 25 minutes passed. Just when I was about to give up and leave, Mr. Ramos arrived. The Mexican man obviously wanted to meet with him but was told by Mr. Ramos in Spanish to wait for a few minutes.

I entered his office and sat down in the seat opposite him. We both took deep breaths. His eyes glanced around the room nervously but he didn't look at me. Even though I was 39 years old, sitting in this office brought back painful childhood memories of being sent to the Principal on discipline. He fiddled with some papers on his desk and then made eye contact with me for the first time. His eyes darted once more around the room before he spoke.

"Part of being a good teacher is classroom management. As I'm sure you are aware, we have limited funds for technology and we need someone who can keep the kids from destroying what equipment we do have. So far, you haven't been able to do that."

It took a few seconds to digest what he had just told me. "If you are talking about the missing mice; that was totally beyond

133

my control. They were stolen between 6:00 p.m. and 7:30 a.m. when there were no students on campus."

"So, you say but the fact is they were stolen. Maybe you didn't lock the door when you left. Maybe you left it slightly ajar by accident. Maybe, Maybe, Maybe. The bottom-line is that there are 26 mice missing and now our students are suffering. Classroom management involves taking care of the equipment as well as controlling the students."

In spite of my natural instinct to fight for fairness, there was no point in challenging his reasoning. After all, I was at LBJ High to solve a case, not as a career move. I knew this little meeting had everything to do with the Alma Vargas Memorial Club and nothing to do with the stolen mice but I had to play the game.

"In the future, I will triple check the door to make sure it's locked," I said apologetically.

"It's not just mice that I'm worried about. I'll be straight with you Mr. Butler. There are procedures in place here at LBJ High. If I let every staff member just do whatever they wanted we'll have chaos. Just like you expect your students to obey your classroom rules, I expect my staff to adhere to professional standards. I need to run a tight ship here for the good of the students. That's all I wanted to say." He stood up quickly and opened the door, an obvious cue for me to leave.

I went back to my class to straighten up. Chuckling, I triple checked my classroom door to make sure it was locked. Those mice weren't stolen because I left the door ajar. Somebody with key access to these rooms took them. Could one of the maintenance men have done it? Don't think so. Why would anyone want so many mice? I doubted a hot mouse would get more than 50 cents on the street. Slashed tires and stolen mice? It was clear I was being harassed but by whom? Obviously someone who had access to my room and who felt threatened by my presence at LBJ High.

As I was walking towards the teachers' parking lot, I ran into the lead janitor Julius Wilson. Julius was an African-American man who had been a maintenance man in the district since his mid-20s and was now approaching 60. Whenever I met him, he would always mention something about his impending retirement.

"When I retire, there ain't no looking back for me," he would say. "Kids just ain't the same as they used to be. They throw trash on the ground even if there is a garbage can three feet away. I won't miss this shit. Believe me."

His beer belly and weathered face made him look closer to 70 than 60 but his over-sized shoulders projected strength. He was genuinely a warm person, did his job well, and was liked by the staff. I enjoyed chatting with him. I told him about the mice incident and he just shook his head.

"Ain't that a bitch. Tell ya one thing Mr. Butler. I was here Tuesday night until around 7:00. There wasn't no kids around far as I could see. I don't think students would have stold your mice Mr. Butler."

"You got any idea who might have done it?" I asked.

"Not for me to say. Don't think no maintenance folk would have done it."

"I wasn't implying that one of your staff may have -."

"Don't bother me none. I've had bad apples working under me before. Right now I got a pretty good staff though, everyone on the up and up around here. Anyway, wonder why someone would want to steal so many mice. Don't make no sense to this old man." He wished me good luck with a smile and then went about his business.

I drove straight to my office. Rosanna was just about ready to leave when I got there. She was dressed in tight blue jeans and a red and yellow t-shirt. There was French writing on the front of it but I had no idea what it meant. All I knew was that she looked magical. Just like that night in her bedroom, the light had a way of finding her. There wasn't much light that came through that old skylight but what little did managed to illuminate Rosanna's face. I told her about the noises I'd been hearing from the office next door and she just laughed.

"Finally, someone getting their money's worth with a therapist," she commented.

"It's been kind of getting on my nerves to tell you the truth. I mean if this continues, it could be a problem. Clients may feel uncomfortable and take their business elsewhere."

"I've got an idea," she said. "Let's give her a taste of her own medicine." She moved towards me and gave me a nice, warm kiss.

135

"This could spiral out of," she slipped her tongue in my mouth before I could finish my sentence. "I think we need to think of this office as a place for work, not -" She inserted her wet tongue again before I could finish. I did not want to make love in my office. It just seemed unprofessional to me. I would have no moral high ground to stand on if I confronted Ms. Weinstein about the noise. That said, Rosanna had a way of leading me down the path of least resistance. I tried again to gain control of the situation.

"Listen, my love. Just this time I will do anything you want. The office is the office and the home is the home if you know what I mean."

"I don't really but I guess I'll have to accept these limitations you've imposed," she responded with a laugh. Maybe it wouldn't hurt just this one time to bend the Harley Butler work ethic, I thought. I decided to let her have all the pleasure since she'd done so much for me in the past. Her blues jeans came off easily considering how tight they were. I had her sit on an empty area of my desk. She leaned her head back and I proceeded to do things to make her happy. While I was in the act, I couldn't help thinking that her moans were increasing in intensity similar to the way Ms. Weinstein's clients were. Could those moans coming from her office have been anything else other than an expression of sexual pleasure? Since I wasn't an expert in the world of psycho-therapy, I had no idea of the powers and secrets of the trade. Rosanna had a nice tension release and then began laughing. We slow danced around the office to the ambient sounds of the world for a while and then took care of a few business details. A second after she left, the phone rang.

"Tantei Man, at your service," I answered.

"Hey Buddy, this is Randy. Just wanted to let you know that we're still waiting on the lab results for the proverb note. I'll let you know if it leads anywhere but that's not why I called. It's about your therapist neighbor."

"I'm all ears."

"Well, I checked the California Board of Behavioral Sciences to see if her license was listed. I found quite a few Weinsteins but no Helen. All the other Weinsteins were registered in different cities so it couldn't have been just a name variation. At that point, I knew at least she was practicing without a valid California license. Since, you told me she used to practice in New

136

York I took the liberty to check the Office of the Professions there. Again, I found quite a few Weinsteins but no Helen.

"Looks like the lady next door is a fraud," I said the obvious.

"Let me finish. It gets even more interesting. Just to be diligent, I also took the liberty to phone a couple of the Weinsteins practicing in Manhattan. Guess what? I found her older sister actually is a well-respected, psycho-therapist and has a popular practice in downtown Manhattan. I was able to get in direct touch with her. I called on the pretext that I was an old friend looking for Helen. She had no idea where her little sister was and was worried sick about her. She told me that Helen had a way of getting herself into trouble due to what she called her unusual perspective on things. When I asked her what she meant by that, she didn't elaborate."

"Well, thanks Randy. Not sure what to do with that information but it's good to know."

"We could have her arrested. That would definitely solve your noise problem," he suggested.

"No, don't do that. Not yet anyway. I'd be grateful if you could keep what you found out confidential. In the grand scheme of things, I don't think she is doing any serious harm and anyway I'd like to talk to her about it myself."

"You've got a big heart Harley. I'll wait to hear back from you. Let me know if you need anything."

We discussed the Vargas case and the recent events at LBJ High until I was interrupted by a knock on the door. I hung up so I could answer it. A heavyset middle-aged lady greeted me with a smile and handed me a brochure that read School Care – Support Albany schools. Before I could say I wasn't interested she began her well-rehearsed speech.

"Hi, I'm Teresa Glass and I'd be grateful if you could give me just a few minutes of your time. I've been visiting local businesses in Albany to remind them how good schools benefit the community. As everyone knows, our schools are under funded. If we didn't have an organization like School Care, our kids would be denied music classes, counselors, speech therapists and many extra-curricular activities that our organization supports. Good local schools create desirability for housing and that improves the market

137

value of homes. Good local schools have a direct correlation with low crime."

She went on and on espousing the benefits of good schools but the whole time she was talking, my ADD mind kept thinking about what Mr. Duckworth had told me. The more affluent areas keep the poor areas down because organizations like School Care only support the local schools. Since they can adequately subsidize their children's education, they feel no urgency to fight for state-wide or national education funding reform leaving the poor schools perennially under-funded. When Ms. Glass got to the part where she was going to show me how I could make a contribution I interrupted.

"I'm sorry but I've already dedicated my school donation budget to another school district." She gave me a "how could you" look and marched out of my office.

To tell the truth, I wasn't sure Mr. Duckworth's views were on target even though they did make a lot of sense. Perhaps it was just his persuasive rhetoric. He had a way of presenting his ideas in such a clear and forceful way, that one would leave the room converted to his way of thinking. Were the haves really keeping the have-nots down indirectly as Mr. Duckworth espoused or were there other more significant factors at play? I wasn't sure. Whatever the reasons for the economic disparity, it was clear from my short time at LBJ High that more funding was needed. But if you were to ask me what I thought would make the biggest difference in these kid's lives right now, I'd say a loving family with expectations. Since you can't buy love, you can buy the next best thing – youth programs with strong adult mentors. Anyway, if I were to make a donation to schools it would be to support the disadvantaged, not the advantaged youth.

A few days later I ran into Ms. Weinstein in the hallway. I asked her if she had a moment to spare.

"My office or yours?" she replied gingerly. I agreed to her office as I was curious to see the inside. The first thing I noticed upon entering was the large comfy-looking leather chair in the middle of the floor. It resembled something between a lazy-boy and a reclining dentist chair. It had an earthy-brown color and just looking at it, made you want to try it out. There were a few other comfortable looking chairs around and she asked me to take my pick. Although the chair I chose was comfortable I felt anything but. I was nervous because I had no idea how she was going to react to what I was about to tell her. She took a seat in a nearby chair. There were a few awkward moments of silence before I spoke. "I'm really sorry for what I'm about to tell you." I hesitated and looked at her face for reaction. She looked completely at ease. "As you know, I am a detective and I."

"For god sake stop beating around the bush Harley," she interrupted. "So you had me investigated and you found out I wasn't licensed. You even talked to my arrogant sister about me. Hooray! Hooray! So what do you want me to do? Get out of town by sunrise?" Her face remained serene but my jaw dropped. Her directness caught me completely off-guard. I took a deep breath.

"Look. As I was saying, I'm a detective and the sounds coming from your office made me think that more than therapy was going on in there. I had my partner do a routine check. That's all."

"And what exactly did your partner find out may I ask?"

"It looks like you already know. Is there anything more you want to tell me?"

"I have no problem telling you but I'm not sure you'll understand. What I really want to know is why people can't just let me be and do my good work. I've never had an unsatisfied client."

"Look Helen. I'm not here to judge you. I'm just trying to keep you out of trouble here if I can." I tried to regain her trust. "Tell me about your older sister," I prodded gently.

"So you know about Samantha?"

"Not really. All I know is that you have an older sister practicing psycho-therapy in Manhattan who seems to be doing well for herself."

"Seems to be doing well you say? She stood up and paced back and forth across the room before she sat down again. It was the first time I'd seen her lose her poise.

"I guess that depends on how you define doing well. She makes a lot of money. That's for sure. A lot of lost souls come to her for help. Most leave more messed up then when they arrived but I don't think she really cares about that as long as she gets paid. She knows the major trick of the trade. String your client along and always schedule that next appointment before they leave the office. Samantha's really no different than the rest of them. Ninety-nine percent of all therapists are a farce. That's a simple fact of life. They get into psychology initially because they're confused,

139

depressed, or unhappy and think it will help them figure themselves out. I know that was the case with Samantha. The problem is they end up projecting their unresolved issues on their clients. That of course does the patient more harm than good. These same therapists see somebody like me who actually helps people as a threat to their livelihood."

I just sat there quietly listening. She was obviously no dummy and was operating from a core that at least she thought was on higher ground. I finally decided to challenge her.

"Don't you think we need guidelines to prevent just anybody from practicing therapy? I mean think about it. Teachers need to be certified. Lawyers need to pass the bar. Doctors need to get through medical school and pass exams. If as a society, we let anybody do anything, wouldn't that just lower the bar across the board?"

"I don't argue with that. Sure we need guidelines but we need to be tolerant to those exceptions out there that can excel in these professions in spite of not being licensed. Why should we let these people practice? Because they do good and really help people. Trust me on this one. In any given profession, only 10% do it for love. The rest just play the game and collect their paychecks. Think of teachers for example. We all know there are people out there that can relate to and teach kids and are willing to expend a ton of energy in doing so. Would a parent rather have a certified teacher who just hands out assignments and sits on her ass or an uncertified person who really loves and cares about her kid and is also competent in the subject matter? It's a no brainer, don't you think?"

"Yeah, sounds great but how do we practically allow these good exceptions into the system without allowing the bad, predators in schools for example?" I asked.

"Simple really. Each profession should have an Unusual Talent Clause that allows people with talents in the profession to practice. The biggest criteria should be the satisfied client and content knowledge. Of course, the person would need to demonstrate knowledge in the subject matter of the profession."

"Do you think you meet these criteria?"

"I'm positive I do. The problem now is, because of that arrogant sister of mine, I have a criminal record."

"I'm sorry. I didn't know that. Do you want to share that with me?"

140

"No big deal. I was operating a successful practice out of a small office in Greenwich Village. Basically, I started with nothing just like I'm doing here but within a few years I had more clients than I could handle. Big sister practicing in uptown Manhattan could no longer handle the fact that little sis was doing so well and eventually had me arrested for practicing without a license."

"How'd you know it was she who turned you in?"

"She confessed it to me when she bailed me out. She said she wanted to nip the problem in the bud before it got out of control. In reality, she was just jealous. A couple of her regular clients switched over to me and I think that's when she decided to make that fateful call."

"Sounds like a classic sibling rivalry gone amuck," I said.

"It's hard for me to forgive her for what she did. She not only hurt me, she hurt all the clients who were benefiting from my work."

"And that's why you moved to California?"

"How'd you guess? But now you're going to get me in trouble here. Man, this world is upside-down."

"The world's a lot of things, even upside-down sometimes," I agreed. " Listen Helen, I like you. After hearing your side out of the story, I really don't think you're harming anybody but I am curious, how did you get started in this therapy business in the first place?"

"It all started when I was in high school. Samantha was a graduate student at the time majoring in Psychology at Cornell. I was bored to death with high school and all the bullshit that goes along with it. I mean really bored! I didn't fit into any of the cliques of the day and only had one good friend. I cut class half the time and got poor grades. I would spend the weekends at Helen's apartment. While she was out with friends, I would nose through her notebooks and read her textbooks. When she got home, I would discuss what I read with her. While a lot of the material had to do with theory, I was intrigued with the possible practical application of what I was reading. I think Samantha thought of herself as superior and was jealous and annoyed that her little under-achieving sister grasped the material she was studying at a prestigious university as well as or better than she did. I began cutting school more often but not to hang out with boys like a lot of girls my age. No, I snuck into Cornell's library and would spend the entire day

141

reading books and abstracts about psychology and psycho-therapy. I was especially interested in hypnotism. One day, I was relaxing in the student union when I noticed a flyer posted on the wall. The Department of Psychology was looking for student volunteers to participate in a study that had something to do with hypnotism and thus began my life of crime." She let out a controlled laugh.

"Let me guess. You used a false identity to enroll?" I speculated.

"You're a good detective Harley. I won't go into the details but I ended up being chosen for the study. I was told that it was possible that we would feel some discomfort and could experience some significant pain. The point of the study was to demonstrate if subjects could be made not to experience pain under duress during hypnosis. The result was it worked with about 90% of the participants. It is a fact that some people just can not be hypnotized."

"Did it work with you?" I asked.

"Oh yeah. I found out later that while under hypnosis I had been pinched with a pair of pliers and shocked with progressively increased voltage. Apparently, I kept a smile on my face the whole time. The interesting part for me was the fact that not only did I not feel pain, the marks left behind by the physical intrusions were minimal when compared to a control group that was not under hypnosis. That was a real epiphany for me. The mind could actually control the body. I got to thinking about the healing potential of hypnosis and psycho-therapy."

"Did you ever consider pursuing a traditional degree? I mean it seems that would have been a piece of cake for you."

"In a perfect world that's the way I would have gone. Remember, I had poor grades in high school and I almost didn't graduate. My parents had all but disowned me as a result. Where was the money for college going to come from? Grants and loans wouldn't pay for everything and I had to survive in the real world out there. My first year out of high school I shared a small studio with my best friend Ana and took odd jobs to make ends meet. It was after waiting tables for 6 months at TGI Fridays that I got to thinking that there had to be a more rewarding way to survive. I had taken some workshops in hypnotherapy and decided to try my luck at it. I posted a few fliers around town and put an ad in the Village Voice. It took a while but after a few months I could afford to quit my waitressing job. Within a year, you could say I was doing well. Word of mouth spreads quickly."

"So your clients were happy with your work? Did they ever inquire about your background?"

"A few asked where I went to school and other questions about my background but I had anticipated this and was prepared. A few licensed therapists answered my ad and faked that they were interested to see if I was legit but I had prepared responses for them too. Life was good and getting better. Almost all of my clients claimed that I had helped them in whatever their particular problem was and word got around about my practice. I initially did consultations in the homes of my clients but after a year and a half, I was able to afford the rent for my own office in Greenwich Village."

"So what went wrong? Why'd you move West?"

"Let me finish my story. You see, I had a successful practice going for 15 years at my little office in the Village. I had no complaints from clients. In fact, I had to turn people down as my schedule was always too full. Then came that fateful day. I got a call from the Office of the Professions asking me about my background. I pretended to be busy and told them I'd call them back. I knew something was up but was hoping for the best. About a month later, my office was raided by the NYPD and I was arrested for practicing psychology without a license. At my trial, several of my clients showed up testifying on how I had immensely improved the quality of their lives but it was to no avail. The law is the law. Luckily, a good lawyer got me out of having to serve time but I did have to pay a hefty fine and was warned sternly never to do it gain. The saddest part for me from the whole experience was learning that it was my sister who had tipped off the Office of the Professions."

"Do you have any idea why she did it?"

"I know exactly why! Simple primal jealousy! Over the years, she had learned to accept the fact that I had found a niche that made me useful to society. Sure she had always bugged me about getting a college degree but that was the extent of her intrusion into my personal space. Somehow she found out that a few of her unsatisfied clients were jumping ship over to my office in the Village and that's the straw that broke the camel's back as they say.

143

I can forgive her but I can not forget. I hope your cop friend didn't tell her where I was."

"I don't think he did. He called her on the pretext that he was looking for you."

"That's good to know. Can you be straight with me, Harley? Am I going to have to leave the Bay Area?

"I don't think so Helen. Although I find what you do quite unorthodox, I don't think you are doing any real harm to anyone. Perhaps you are even helping people. I don't know that for sure but I will give you the benefit of the doubt. The fact that you are breaking the law leaves you at risk though."

"I know that all too well. Recently, I've been thinking of pursuing a degree through distance learning just for the peace of mind."

"That sounds like a good idea. There's still something that's bothering me though."

"Spit it out. I have nothing to hide."

"You know, I don't really understand this therapy thing but based on the sounds I've been hearing coming through the walls, there must be a sexual aspect to it," I speculated.

She smiled from ear to ear. "Now, I get it. You think I'm a call girl and that's why you had me checked out."

"I have to be honest and say I did have my suspicions."

She remained poised and drew in a deep breath. "A lot of the angst going on in people's lives has a sexual element to it whether they are aware of it or not. When I have a person under hypnosis, I bridge the gap between what the person perceives as their problem and the sexual nature of it."

"It sounds like you are really good at doing that." I tried to be funny.

Her face remained unchanged by my comment. "Sorry if the noise disturbed you but the landlord told me that the walls were thick enough to block out sound. Obviously, they weren't. I'd be glad to add some sound-proofing if it's unbearable for you."

"I'm sure we can work something out but I'm curious. Are your clients under hypnosis when they go into moaning mode?"

She smiled again. "Yes. It takes a while to get them there but once they submit, there's no turning back. Under hypnosis, I can help bridge the gap between who they think they are and who they really are. Sometimes the experience is painful, other times there is immense pleasure. Regardless, I want them to feel lighter when they leave my office."

I remembered that kid on the skateboard and Caleb's face as they were leaving her office. They had an enchanted expression like they had just experienced the Magic Kingdom for the first time. In reality, I had never been a big fan of the field of psychology or psychotherapy. I had always thought of therapy as a luxury excess of the bourgeois class. Get a pedicure and then go talk to your shrink about your misbehaving husband who doesn't understand you. Something in my core told me that Helen was different. Maybe she really did have something to offer. I didn't understand it but I trusted her. That hypnotism she did sure had me intrigued. Maybe that could be useful in my detective work some day. I was still bothered by the fact that Caleb had visited her office but wasn't sure how to confront her about it.

"Do you ever see people who can't afford to pay you?" I asked.

"I have a friend who works for the V Team. The V team is an NGO that sends college-age psychology majors into public schools to help out with counseling for kids with issues. She has referred a few kids to me and I worked with them for free. I think I'm making some real progress with a couple of them. I'd like to do more of this work but I have to survive in the real world now, don't I?"

"I understand. Listen, I'm going to call Randy and have him bury anything he found out about your past. You're safe for now but I would pursue that degree you were talking about. Why spend your life looking over your shoulder?"

"Good advice and thank you from the bottom of my heart. Sorry for the noise. I'll get to work on getting my room sound-proofed."

I spent a few minutes talking with her about the potential for hypnotism in detective work. She offered to help in any way she could. I had a feeling she was going to be a good office neighbor from now on.

CHAPTER 10

Although I was still my usual distracted self, by mid-February I was thinking of calling it quits at LBJ High. I was reminded by Randy that the Richmond PD had invested quite a bit of their budget into the investigation. When I told him that I felt more like a teacher than a dick, he just laughed and asked what difference is there. Jokes aside, we discussed potential suspects and motives. I mentioned that Principal Ramos seemed like an agitated fellow and that Alma had been a pain in the ass to him. Randy thought he had too much to lose given his rags to riches background. Ramos had come to California at age 10 with just the shirt on his back. He credited a few great teachers in inspiring him to go to a university. His first goal was to become a lawyer but he switched majors in mid-stream to education. He worked hard to get where he was and wouldn't do something stupid to blow it all, said Randy. I told him that this too much to lose theory could work the other way as well. I worked my ass off to get where I am today and am not going to let a loud–mouthed teenage girl take it all away from me. We both agreed that the mice theft and my car being vandalized could turn out to be a blessing but weren't sure how yet. There was no DNA evidence found on the proverb note left on my car. All we had to go on was the handwriting sample.

On Monday, the 11th of February, there was a note in my pigeon hole requesting my attendance at an IEP. It was going to take place during 5th period, my prep time, so I really didn't have an excuse for not attending. IEP stands for individualized education program and is part of Special Education. The student being reviewed was no other than Pedro Montano, one of the Alma Vargas Memorial Club members. Special education students are evaluated at least once a year to make sure goals are being met and to set new goals if necessary. I found out that Pedro had been diagnosed as ADHD in middle school and had been receiving special education services since the 7th grade. I agreed to attend.

We met in a small isolated room right near the library entrance. Seated at one side of the table were June McCracken and Betsy Brey, two of the Special Education teachers. On the other side sat Pedro and his mother. I pulled out a chair next to his mother and introduced myself. I had only seen these two teachers at faculty meetings and had no previous contact with them. Pedro gave me a nod like one friend to another and I reciprocated. Both McCracken's and Brey's eyes appeared glazed as they fumbled through paperwork. It looked as if they were both medicated on a strong antihistamine. McCracken fumbled through some more papers, found the one she was looking for and spoke.

"We've been getting some reports back from teachers that Pedro has been off task quite a bit in class."

She had sad, bulgy bloodshot eyes and spoke like she was reading a script on autopilot. "I've gotten reports back from Ms. Rosales and Mr. Bergman. Both state that Pedro is in danger of failing and that he often disrupts class," she continued. Pedro's mom sat quietly. Her face showed no reaction. I wondered if she understood what McCracken had just said.

"I've been noticing a change in Pedro's behavior too. He seems to be having trouble focusing and staying on task," said Ms. Brey. "Pedro told me the other day that he decided to stop taking his medication. Ever since, I've noticed some negative behavioral changes." Ms. Brey was a heavy-set woman with a large Mediterranean head. She was in her early 20s but her tired expression made her appear older. Pedro's face suddenly turned serious. He looked towards me as if searching for support and then towards Ms. Brey angrily.

"I'm just tired of being controlled. I know I have a lot of energy but that should be a good thing. Schools should learn how to use that energy in good ways. I don't care what the doctor says. I don't care what a few teachers say. I'm not going to take that Ritalin shit anymore. Keep the wild Mexican boy under control. That's all they are trying to do." There were a few awkward moments of silence and then his mother spoke.

"Excuse my poor English. I want you to understand something. Pedro is a good boy. He no want to hurt no one. I don't want to give him that medicina any more. He no need that medicina. I love him the way he is." She smiled and sat calmly with her palms held together on her lap.

"The problem Ms. Montano is that Pedro is not the only student in his classes. A teacher's responsibility is to the class as a whole. We can't have one student disrupting the education of the many," preached McCracken.   Even though her words were passionate, her tone of voice was anything but. It was like she had

147

been through this routine many times before and knew exactly what to say.

"That's bullshit," blurted out Pedro. "That's just your opinion and you know it. Ask the students if they think I'm disrupting them. Just ask them. This is all about control and you know it. Nothing more. Nothing less." Looking annoyed, McCracken glanced up at the clock and then looked at me.

"Do you have anything you want to add Mr. Butler?"

"Well, I've had contact with Pedro in my Graphic Design class and in the club I sponsor. He has always participated positively and I've enjoyed having him. I think he is a great kid with tremendous potential. It's my opinion that he could get by just fine without the Ritalan given proper support." Both Pedro and his mother smiled. Ms. Brey rolled her eyes and began shaking her over-sized head.

"I didn't know we had a doctor on our staff. Thanks for your professional opinion," she said sarcastically. I thought about my experience with Concerta and how it made me focus on trivial details and kept my mind from wandering. Unlike Pedro, I made the decision to take the medicine and then stop it of my own free will. Pedro was trying to free himself of the medication but was up against people in positions of authority discouraging him from doing so. He clearly needed support here.

"Pedro is 16 years old now. He obviously feels strongly about stopping Ritalin and I think we should respect both his and his mother's wishes."

"Mr. Butler, you need to know that a lot of times these medications are given in the context of civil responsibility," offered McCracken. "They're a small price to pay for the benefit of the whole." Pedro shook his head and his eyes glared with anger again.

"I've been paying that price ever since middle school and I'm not going to pay it anymore." Pedro picked up his back pack and stomped out of the room. His mother's face showed the first sign of nervousness since she'd arrived.

"I'm sorry," she said. "Pedro really no want that medicina."

"Let me clarify my position on this," I said. "I'm not an expert on when to use or not use Ritalin. All I know is that we over-medicate in this country and the only real beneficiaries of this are the pharmaceutical companies. I'm not saying that drugs like

Ritalin don't have therapeutic value. I'm sure they do in some cases. The problem lies in the magic pill mentality that permeates our culture. I read recently that 10% of American school-age children are taking psycho-tropic drugs. That's a crime in my opinion. Take Pedro, for instance. The fact that he has been performing well in my class in spite of not taking his Ritalin should be evidence that he can do well without it. Sometimes we need to look at the context in which the student is performing poorly and not just target the student with an easy pharmaceutical fix. The real scary thing is that we really don't know the long term affect of using all these magic drugs, do we?" Both McCracken and Brey glanced at each other with an expression that asked - what are we going to do with this guy? I was expecting some sort of rebuttal but all I got was glazed stares as they stuffed paper-work back into manila folders. Finally, they stood up, shook hands with Pedro's mom and left the room. Mrs. Montano gave me a sweet smile and a hug. I reassured her that Pedro was a great kid and went on my way. As I headed back to my classroom, I wondered if I'd ever get invited back to an IEP meeting.

I saw Pedro again after school as we had a Networking Club meeting scheduled. He thanked me for taking his side and said he owed me one. The club didn't know it yet but I was looking at this meeting as a golden opportunity to take the investigation to the next level. I knew I had to start taking more risk and what better way than utilizing these ready foot-soldiers. By 3:35, we had 100% attendance. Ricardo gave a brief summary of the club's school reform efforts and Carnell asked about progress on getting more Advanced Placement classes. Miriam Lopez asked Ricardo if he had heard updates on Alma's murder investigation and he said he hadn't. This was the signal for me to get started.

"Excuse me for taking the floor but I have a few things I want to talk to you guys about. Although I didn't know Alma like you guys did, I feel that I have come to know her through you." They looked up at me with interest. "I am sickened that this crime has gone unsolved and will not sleep well until her killer is behind bars. The trouble is the Richmond Police have limited resources. I know they are trying but this case looks like it's a difficult one to solve."

"How do you know they are trying?" interrupted Carnell Smith. The golden grill he was wearing on his front teeth glittered as he spoke. "She was Mexican. The cops just don't care that much about Mexicans and blacks."

Carnell would have been surprised to find out just how much of the department's resources were being spent on this case but of course I couldn't tell him. There was definitely some truth to his statement though. If a blonde teenaged girl from Piedmont had been found dead in Nicholl Park, the response would be different than if it were a nameless gang-banger. I decided to agree with him although I knew there were cops like Randy who cared deeply about the community.

"I think you are on to something Carnell," I said. That's why we need to start doing some investigating ourselves. Now, I've heard that Alma was drugged before she was killed." Ricardo raised his eyebrows. "We know that Alma shook up the boat here at LBJ High. Although she was loved by many, she angered some who felt threatened by her. I was able to find out through a connection that her body had traces of the drug Restoril when she was found."

"That's why I'm 100% certain she wasn't killed during a robbery," said Ricardo. "The cops asked me a ton of questions about drug use. It really annoyed me because I knew Alma did not take drugs. Believe me, if she was taking aspirin she would have told me about it." He thought for a moment. "Come to think of it, they did ask me something about Restoril. I wasn't sure why. I wasn't thinking clearly at the time as you could imagine. Anyway Mr. Butler, what do you mean start doing some investigating ourselves?"

"I have list of all the staff here at LBJ High. I want to be able to eliminate them all as suspects. Let's start by taking an inventory of what they keep in their desks. I'm especially interested in pill bottles. Write down the prescription name if there is one. I know this is a strange thing to tell students to do but we have to take extraordinary efforts for Alma's sake."

"How are we going to get a chance to look in a teacher's desk?" asked Michelle Saechao.

"Hey, come on. You guys are students at LBJ High. There are lots of ways. Create a diversion. Ask to use the room to work on your assignments during lunch. Be creative guys. You can do it."

"This is the first time I've heard a teacher ask students to do something that could get them in trouble," said Josh Anderson

150

the white kid. "You know you could get fired if the administration found out Mr. Butler."

"I'm willing to take that chance and the blame if any of you get caught but don't get caught," I said chuckling. "Be quick and efficient and put things back in their place. Don't forget to take a notebook and note down anything of interest that you see, got it?" I continued.

"Why are we doing this?" asked Caleb.

"In the rare chance that the killer is one of our own," I answered. "Think of it as a science experiment. One of the first steps is gathering data. Remember, I've got your back. Let's meet back here this Friday after school and go over your findings.

For the rest of today's meeting, I want you to take this list of the LBJ High staff and decide on the who, what, and when. Make sure everyone gets covered." For the rest of the meeting, they made plans on how they would gain access to the desks and storage cabinets of the teachers and staff. They all agreed that the administrators would be the most difficult but even they would not be impossible. At around 5, the meeting was adjourned.

"That's the coolest homework assignment I've ever gotten," said Mariana Suchil as she walked out the door. "I'll do my best Mr. Butler." Even the quiet Ruth Orozco was smiling and gave me a puzzled look before saying I'll try.

Once all of the students had gone, I began to have doubts about the craziness of what I'd just asked them to do. In the silence of my room, I wondered if I had just crossed an ethical line that I would come to regret. I had always lived my life on the up and up, I thought. I had a strong sense of right and wrong due to my strict Irish and Portuguese upbringing. But what had I done here? I had just encouraged some impressionable youth to sneak through property that wasn't theirs. I closed my eyes and meditated on the essence of Alma. She was like a prophet to these kids at LBJ High. Finding her killer was a higher good and some lines could be crossed to get there. I made a note to myself to discuss these delicate boundaries with the members at the next club meeting.

Friday came quickly. The students were more energetic than usual because this was the last day of school before Presiden t's week. Mr. Prince more than matched their enthusiasm. He patrolled the hallways like an Abrams Tank, sweeping up any student that was still there after the second bell. The punishment was the

151

dreaded Saturday school. He would yell as loud as he could - this is a lockout over and over again. When he said this, students would start running to class to avoid getting caught in the sweep. During a lockout, teachers are told to lock their doors after the second bell rings. Students who missed by seconds would sometimes pound on a door hoping to be saved by a sympathetic teacher. Although, Mr. Prince's methods were effective in clearing out the halls, his militaristic presence made it feel more like a jail than a school. A lot of the Hispanic students thought they were unfairly targeted by him but others felt he was needed to keep order in a school that could easily go out of control. I was curious what Alma thought about Mr. Prince.

Would any of the club members even show up today given that the coming week was off? When the final bell rang at 3:15, I waited and one by one every single member of the Alma Vargas Memorial Club aka the Networking Club arrived. What dedication! Each was holding a blue folder that contained the raw data that they had gathered. I gave a brief pep talk about how what they were doing was usually wrong and was only acceptable now because of the higher good involved. They nodded as if they understood and then Ricardo took the floor.

"I am pleased to report that our operation was successful. We suffered no casualties and only a couple of our soldiers reported close calls. Bottom-line is we own this place." There was a loud round of applause before he continued. "For the rest of this meeting we will take turns reporting the details of our individual findings. Ms. Lopez, could you take the minutes for us?"

"Yes, Captain," replied Miriam. She opened up a notebook and pulled out a pen from her backpack.

"Who wants to go first?" asked Ricardo. All except the shy Ruth raised their hand.

"It looks like I will have to call on you," he said chuckling. "Let's start with Ms. Chanthanasak. Diane, could you give us a summary of your findings?"

"Sure. Michelle and I were in charge of the science department." She glanced down at her notebook. "We checked the desks of Mr. Proszenko, Ms. O'Conner, Mr. Bayod, and Ms. Goodman. In Mr. Proszenko's desk, we found a prescription for Lexapro and Vicodin. I could not find anything in Mr. Bayod's desk or jacket pocket.

I knew that Vicodin was a potent pain killer like Oxycontin but wasn't sure about Lexapro although the name sounded familiar. I had probably heard it on one of the many drug commercials on TV that were so common nowadays. I told Ricardo to log-on to one of the computers so we could google the drugs that we didn't know.

Michelle Saechao raised her hand. "Ms. O'Conner had a bottle of Claritin. I know what that is. It's for allergies. Ms. Goodman had a prescription for Levoxyl and Cytomel whatever those are."

"I got it. Lexapro is an antidepressant," interrupted Ricardo. He paused and clicked away at the keyboard. "Levoxyl is taken for hypothyroidism and so is Cytomel. Hypothyroidism ring a bell Mr. Butler?"

"I believe that means you have an under-active thyroid gland. That's a pretty common illness from what I understand," I answered. Suddenly, the absurdity of what we were doing made me stop and think. "Before we go on, as club sponsor, I want to make something perfectly clear. We really do need to respect the privacy of the staff. Let's not ever forget why we are doing this. We are looking for the drug that was in Alma's system when she died." The members nodded their heads in agreement.

"Good job soldiers. Pedro and Mariana - are you ready to report your findings from the Math department?" asked Ricardo.

Pedro stood up and spoke for his team. "We covered the rooms and desks of Mr. Cheasty, Ms. Maldonado, Mr. Souza, and Mr. Larkin. In Mr. Larkin's desk we found a bottle of Adderall. Don't look it up. I already know what it is. It's for ADD."

"I didn't know teachers took ADD medicine," commented Miriam.

"Since most of them push it, they might as well take it too," laughed Pedro. He continued. "In Mr. Souza's desk we found a bottle of Frovatriptan. That's for migraine headaches. In Ms. Maldonado's closet, we found a tube of Preparation H and a bottle of Daflon. Both of these are for the treatment of hemorrhoids." Miriam covered her mouth with her hand to hide a smile.

"What are hemorrhoids?" asked Ruth.

"It's something you get from sitting on your ass too long," answered Ricardo smiling. That got a laugh from the group.

"Finally we did a thorough check of Mr. Cheasty's room," continued Pedro. "We discovered quite a bit in there. We found a bottle of Cialis, Celexa, Norvasc, and Yohimbine."

"Never heard of any of those except Cialis. Somehow that one sounds familiar," said Ricardo while tapping away at his keyboard. "Okay, got the first one. Cialis is for erectile dysfunction. Anybody experiencing an erection lasting longer than four hours should seek immediate medical attention," joked Ricardo mocking the Cialis TV commercial. The group laughed again. "Celexa is an antidepressant. Those seem to be popular among staff. Norvasc is for the treatment of high blood pressure and let me see what I can find about Yohimbine. According to drugs.com, it increases the amount of blood that is allowed to flow into the penis. Ol' Mr. Cheasty is working on his mojo."

"Come on guys. Remember what I said about respecting privacy. Let's keep it clean and stay focused."

"How about Mercedes and Byrisha? What'd you find out about our fantastic P.E. teachers?" asked Ricardo. Byrisha stood up and read from her notebook.

"In Mr. Seitenbacher's office, we found human growth hormone tablets, Viagra, and a bottle of Trimox. Don't bother checking Ricardo. We already have. Trimox is a kind of Penicillin. In Mr. Zimmerman's desk, we found a spray called Clobetasol. That's used to treat psoriasis. In Ms. Alvarez's coat pocket, we found a bottle of Oxycontin, a painkiller. We couldn't find anything in Mr. Walker's office."

"Good job girls. Caleb and Josh. You're up."

"We were in charge of Art and Music," said Caleb. "We couldn't find any drugs in Mr. Martelaro's room but did find a jar full of strange looking mushrooms. In the music room, we found a bottle of Prozac in Mr. White's saxophone case. That's all we have to report."

"Great Caleb! Armando and I were in charge of the English, ELD, and the Special Ed. Department," said Ricardo. "Armando tell them what we found."

"I'll start with the English teachers. Ms. Rosales was clean. Couldn't find a thing of interest in her desk except lesson plans and books. Ms. Sandal, on the other hand, had a lot of meds. In her desk, we found Adderall, an ADD med and in her jacket pockets we found a bottle of Zoloft, an antidepressant and a bottle of Vicodin, a

154

painkiller. In Mr. Bateman's jacket pocket we found a bottle of Paliperidone. That's an atypical antipsychotic whatever that means. In the English as a Second Language department we found Vicodin in Ms. Wexler's desk and Cymbalta, an antidepressant. We also found a bottle of Adderall in Ms. Chatman's desk. What's up with all these teachers with ADD and depression," asked Armando.

"That's an interesting question and we'll talk about it later," I said. "Let's get through with everybody first. What about the Special Education teachers?"

"We found Celexa in both Ms. McCracken's and Ms. Brey's drawers. That's an antidepressant by the way."

"Carnell, the lone soldier, are you ready to report your findings on the foreign language department?" asked Ricardo.

"You got it! Mr. Gonzalez has migraines. I found a bottle of Topamax in his jacket pocket and in Ms. Legard's closet I found a bottle of you guessed it, Adderall. That's it for me."

"Okay, we are making progress here," said Ricardo "Almost finished guys. That leaves just Ruth and our note-taker Miriam."

"Me and Ruth investigated the history department," said Miriam smiling.

Miriam was a very attractive and articulate student. She had cat-like green eyes and a soft-agreeable personality. One of the few students that I considered well above-average; she was definitely on track for the UC system..

"We split responsibilities," she continued. "I covered Mr. Bergman and Mr. Wong, and Ruth covered Mr. Duckworth. I am pleased to announce that both Mr. Bergman and Mr. Wong were drug-free, although I did find some funny smelling tea in Mr. Wong's closet. Now, I'll give the floor to my good friend Ruth." Ruth looked down at the floor with that enigmatic smile of hers and then at her peers nervously. Her English although improving was still very limited.

"I check Mr. Duckworth's desk. I find some medicina," said Ruth.

"Did you write down what kind of medicine it was?" asked Ricardo. She smiled and unzipped her backpack. She pulled out two pill bottles. Everybody's eyes enlarged.

"Ruth, you weren't supposed to take the pills. You were just supposed to take notes," said Byrisha. Miriam translated that into Spanish and Ruth's eyes began glaring at the ground.

"I'm sorry. I didn't understand," she said softly.

"It's okay. We'll try to find a way to get them back to him. I'll take the responsibility for these from here," I said. "No te preocupas Ruth. It's just a small misunderstanding," I added. I could see that she was feeling remorse and embarrassment for her mistake. She handed me the bottles and I smiled to give her reassurance.

"If you guys don't mind, I'd like to talk to you about something," I said glumly. "Under most all other circumstances, I would classify what we did here as wrong. People, and yes teachers are people, have a right to privacy and we invaded that privacy. I don't want us to laugh or gossip about any teacher or administrator based on what meds we found in their possession. I don't want us to forget why we did this."

"You got to have faith in us Mr. B.," said Miriam. "We're doing this for Alma and that's all. We don't really care what meds our teachers are taking". The others nodded in agreement. There was no need for me to continue with my Ward Cleaver type lecture. These kids got the message and understood it. At least, they seemed to.

"You said you were going to talk to us about teachers taking medicine for ADD and depression. I think we can talk about that without talking about specific teachers, can't we," asked Pedro articulately.

"Here's my take on this whole teachers and meds thing," I said. "I don't really think teachers are taking any more meds than the rest of American society. I bet if we were to check the desks of workers down at City Hall, police officers, lawyers, whoever, the results would be similar. A few of the meds you found were for physical conditions but most were for perceived conditions like ADD and depression. Why are so many people taking these drugs? Just turn on a TV any time of any day. What do you see? Commercials advertising every kind of drug under the sun. Want a better sex life? We got just the pill for you. Not as focused as you could be? We have just the right thing for your ADD. Feeling blue? How about this great new antidepressant? Intelligent people think they are immune to this commercial bombardment but they

156

aren't. Advertising works. In the end, it's all about a competitive pharmaceutical industry keeping the stock prices rising."

"That makes me even madder," said Pedro. "Someone planted a seed in my head in the seventh grade that I needed Ritalin to function. Take this and your life will be better, they said. If I knew then what I know now," he lamented. "Never again will I be fooled."

There were a few moments of silence and then Ricardo stood up suddenly from behind his monitor. "I think our efforts have been in vain, Mr. Butler."

Why would you say that?" I asked.

"Restoril is a drug to treat insomnia. This is not the kind of drug that you would take to work. It would be taken right before bedtime."

"You got a point there Ricardo but I was thinking that a predator would not be using the drug the way it was intended. Anyway, we had to do this as a first step. Let's talk about what we need to do next. We still haven't checked the administrators."

"Actually, I did," said Ricardo. "They are completely clean. At least at school. Mr. Ramos asked me to come to his house this weekend and set up his internet. I can snoop around in his medicine cabinets when I get there."

"Good thinking," I said. "Is that MySpace page you set up for Alma still getting a lot of hits?"

"Over 10,000 now. Why do you ask?"

"I just thought there might be a possibility that the killer would be tempted to drop by if they knew it existed." I said.

"Okay. But even if the killer visited the web site, how would we ever know it?"

"You wouldn't right off the bat," I explained. "It could help us narrow down the number of potential suspects though. Let's say those 10,000 hits represent 1,000 people. You know a lot of the same people will go to the site over and over again. We could then break down those 1,000 people into categories like frequent vs. infrequent visitors – message posters vs. non-message posters. You get my drift?"

"How about regular message posters vs. psycho-message posters?"

"Sure, why not but why would you say that?"

"There's somebody who keeps posting negative shit on the message section."

"What kind of negative shit? Can you show me?" By this time, the club members had spread out all over the lab and the group meeting was over as far I could tell. I pulled up a seat up next to Ricardo as he navigated to the Alma memorial site that he had sat up on MySpace using an anonymizer.

"I created a group called the Alma Vargas Memorial Site on MySpace. To post comments, you have to join. There is no administrating of the group so anyone can join. The comments are listed here over on the right." He clicked the "view all" hot link. "Look, there are hundreds of messages," he said pointing.

I read through a few of them. We love you Alma, We miss you Alma, Thanks for being a friend, Viva Alma Vargas, You will be in my heart forever. They went on and on. Some were long and drawn out. Others were short but there were sure a lot of them. The pictures of the posters appeared under the messages and I recognized quite a few of them. Even with our super fast T1 line connection the page took a long time to open completely. "Show me what you meant by psycho-message poster," I requested.

He scrolled up and down through the messages. "Here's one of them." *Well what did you expect? You came here for a free ride and you got one.* The poster's name read Bobby Bernard and instead of a picture of a person, there was a picture of the American flag blowing in the wind.

"That's sick," I said.

He kept scrolling until he found another post. *If you didn't like the way things were here, you could have crossed the border back into Mexico. You got what you deserved.*

"That's enough," I said. "The problem with these online forums is that anyone and their sister can post. Anonymity empowers the weakest and sickest among us. Don't let this idiot get you down."

"I won't. How do you know it's a him though?"

"I don't. It must be some kind of gender bias thing I got going. I just can't imagine a her being that malicious. You are right though, we need to think objectively and not assume anything."

"Is there anything we can do to find out who the poster is? It may lead to something, right?"

"Well, technologically speaking it would be very easy to find out where the person is posting from. It's really quite simple to trace an I.P. address nowadays. The problem is I doubt if MySpace would give it up. They would most likely quote privacy concerns. I imagine the only way they'd give in is with police pressure and to get that we'll probably need more evidence. Remember, this is probably just some asshole with a complex so let's not obsess with this guy."

At around 5, all the students had left and it was time for me to wrap it up and go home. I stopped back at my office and talked about my day with Rosanna. I showed her the Alma Vargas memorial site on MySpace and some of the comments including those by the poster Bobby Bernard. We did a Zabasearch for Bobby and Robert Bernard and found more than a thousand people with that name. The truth is most posters online don't use their real name when posting but it was worth a try. Rosanna was getting her feet wet with a few cases I had taken on so after a quick dinner at Barney's, I decided to head home and give her some space to work.

I was almost asleep in my lazy-boy chair when the phone rang. I decided to let the answering machine take it. I could hear Rosanna's voice coming from the speaker but couldn't make out what she was saying. The only thing I thought I recognized was the name Bobby Bernard. After a quick shower, I played back her message. *Harley, call me back as soon you can. I found something in the files about Bobby Bernard.* What could she possibly be talking about? I didn't remember ever working a case involving a Bobby Bernard. Thinking she could still be at the office, I called but just got the answering machine. I called her house but got an answering machine there too. I'd have to wait until tomorrow to find out what she had discovered.

In the morning, when getting dressed I noticed the two bottles of pills in my jacket pocket that Ruth had taken from Mr. Duckworth. I had completely forgotten about them. The labels read Paxil and Blocodine. I knew Paxil was an antidepressant but wasn't sure what Blocodine was. Mr. Duckworth didn't strike me as the kind of man that would take an antidepressant but who was I to judge. Anyway, I needed to find a way to get these back to him before he discovered them missing if he hadn't already.

When I got to LBJ High, the first thing I did was to trace down Ricardo. I thought it would be easier for him to access Mr.

159

Duckworth's desk so I gave him the task. He said he'd do his best but couldn't guarantee anything. I tried to reach Rosanna a few times during the day but she didn't pick up. That caused me to spend the whole day thinking about this Bobby Bernard and what could possibly be in my files about him. During period 7, Ricardo told me that the opportunity didn't present itself to replace Duckworth's meds but he'd try again after school. He did note that he seemed unusually agitated and that he wasn't his usual self. When the final bell rang, I only stuck around a few minutes and then headed straight for my office.

Seconds after I entered the door, Rosanna came through huffing and puffing. "Sorry I didn't get back to you but I had an emergency. Joãozinho fell off the washing machine and cut his chin open. The poor thing needed seven stitches. We spent 6 hours at Kaiser Richmond waiting to see a doctor. Do you believe that? I was in such a rush when I left my house that I forgot my cell phone."

"Don't worry about it? Is he alright?"

"He's taking a nap right now. I think he'll be fine. Kátia is watching him at my house."

"What was he doing on the washing machine?"

"Just being a boy testing his limits."

"I'm glad he's alright. By the way, I got your message about Bobby Bernard but for the life of me I can't remember working a case involving anyone with that name."

She stood up and walked over to the old file cabinets that were up against the wall, the ones I had inherited from Roger and Bill. She opened the B cabinet, shuffled through some folders, picked one out and tossed it on the desk in front of me.

"How about if I go up to Peet's and get us some coffee while you review it," offered Rosanna.

"I'd appreciate that. Thanks."

There were just a few sheets in the folder. The usual client information page listed the client as East Bay Construction. Next to reason for services was the following in Roger's cursive: Owners have been harassed and threatened by unknown individual or individuals. Employees have been threatened with deportation. Construction sites and equipment including a tractor have been vandalized at significant cost to company. I jumped ahead to the resolution page: Perpetrator determined to be lone individual Bobby

Bernard, a minor 17 years of age. According to Mr. Bernard's aunt with whom he lives, Bobby suffers from MPD. Client has decided not to pursue charges. There were a few pages of notes from stake-outs and a couple of faded, grainy photos. From what I could tell, Mr. Bernard was tall and athletic. He had long straight hair and was wearing a t-shirt and blue jeans. Other than that, you couldn't tell much from the photos. The date stamped on the document read June 17, 1991. Heck, this happened more than 15 years ago. A few minutes later, the door swung open and in stepped Rosanna carrying a tray with a couple of coffees.

"Were the files of any help to you?" she asked as she twisted the cups of coffee out of the tray.

"Too soon to say. Do you have any idea what MPD is?"

"I saw that too. I'm sure it's some kind of dysfunction or disorder. You Americans have a million of them. Let's google it and find out."

We switched seats and Rosanna opened the Safari browser and navigated to the Google search engine. "Hold on a minute," she said. "There's something called a Myeloproliferative disorder." She clicked a link and began reading silently. "Appears to be some kind of blood cancer. The prognosis doesn't look that good for this disease so I doubt that someone that had it in 1991 would still be a alive today."

"Maybe this is just a coincidence. This is the wrong Bobby Bernard," I said.

"Hold on. Patience Harley. Let's see." She navigated back to google. "Music Player Daemon, Metropolitan Police Department, Minneapolis Police Department, The MPD Programming Language, Memory Protection Devices, Multiple Personality Disorder, MPD Racing – I can go on and on if you like."

"Hold on a second. The only one so far that sounds like an illness is the first one you mentioned and maybe Multiple Personality Disorder. I guess the only way to find out for sure would be to call Roger and Bill in Mexico. Could you open Skype for me?" I had an account with Skype that allowed me to make international calls directly to people's phones abroad for a few pennies per minute. We switched seats. I put on the headphones and clicked Roger Smith's number from my contacts list.

"Bueno," a male voice on the other end said. I guess that's how Mexicans answer the phone but the strong American accent told me that this wasn't a Mexican speaking.

"May I speak to Roger?"

"What do you need Harley?" he said laughing. It was Roger. He still recognized my voice after all this time.

"How's the easy life going?"

"I'm not complaining but sometimes I miss the old detective life. You know what they say, once a dick-"

"Always a dick." I finished his predictable joke. "You know Roger - I found something in your files that may be related to a case I'm working." Rosanna pinched me and whispered *you found something.*

"You know Harley, my old memory is not as keen as it once was but I'll give it a shot. What do you need?"

"Does the name Bobby Bernard ring a bell?"

There were several moments of silence. I could hear him repeating the name to himself as if to ignite a memory.

"Oh yeah, Bobby Bernard. Bobby fucking Bernard. How could I forget? That had to be one of the strangest cases in my 50 years of detective work."

"Really?"

"Strange and sad. He was just a teenager but what a mental case. He had that same mental disease that Sybil had."

"Who is Sybil?"

"Maybe that was a little before your time. There was a book and movie made about her in the 70s. She was some chick that was abused as a child and that apparently led to her having multiple personalities. It was like there was a whole bunch of different people living in her body. Different stimuli would trigger these different people to come out. They all had their own names and identities. It's freaky as hell man."

"You wrote on the resolution page that the subject suffered from MPD. That must mean Multiple Personality Disorder. Right?"

"You got it. At least that's what his aunt told me. It's all starting to come back now. I remember his aunt was the nicest lady. She was a Principal at some low-income elementary school in Oakland, a real warm person. Apparently, the kid was abused as a child by his father, a right-wing ex-Marine, who had this crazy, irrational, hatred for immigrants, especially Hispanics. She told me

162

the guy was a real nut case and would beat his son just for being friendly with Mexican kids his own age at school. It was hard to obey his dad because 80% of the kids at his school were Mexican. The abuse was severe and persistent. It went on for years until the father was arrested for murder and sent to the Big House. I believe he killed a Hispanic man in a bar fight in San Leandro."

"Where was the mother during all this?"

"Oh yeah, I remember asking the same question. The aunt he went to live with after his father's arrest was his mother's sister. She said her sister died of a heart attack when Bobby was three. She thought it was strange because there was no history of heart disease in her family but life went on. He was 14 I believe when his father was arrested for murder. The aunt said she didn't have much of a relationship with Bobby before because she and his father didn't get along. Visits were few and far between."

"Why did he move in with his aunt then?"

"From what I understood, she was the only person in the world who gave a shit about him."

"Seems like it would be a major life changing event, adopting a teenager with a severe mental illness," I said.

"I don't think his MPD had presented itself at that point. I remember the aunt saying that he was a nice kid, a little nervous but good natured. She enrolled him at one of the better high schools in Oakland. He was a star athlete on the football and baseball team and was a very popular student. The girls loved him. She said it wasn't until his junior year that the persona Bobby Bernard was born."

"What do you mean? His real name wasn't Bobby Bernard?"

"No. I mean we filed the case under the name Bobby Bernard because that was the personality causing all the havoc for East Bay Construction. His aunt said that she came home one day and he was sitting on the couch ranting and raving about how Mexicans were ruining California."

"Sounds like Lou Dobbs," I said jokingly.

"Sounded more like the kid's father, she thought. She said it was totally out of character for him. She asked him if something had happened to him at school that caused him to change and that just made him more aggressive. When she called him by his regular name he said something like - Don't call me that. That's not my name. My name's Bobby! That's when she realized that something was seriously wrong. When he reverted back to the person she knew, she immediately sought professional help for him and from what she said, he was very cooperative and welcomed the help."

"What was his real name?"

"You know, I really don't remember. That was 17 years ago. I'll ask Bill tomorrow and see if he recalls. I think the aunt's name was Ms. Richardson or Robertson but I'm not sure about that. I'm sorry I couldn't be of more help Harley. What's this all about anyway?"

"Just working a lead on a case. It may not be important but I've got to follow through. You know how it is."

" I hear you Harley. I'll give you a ring if Bill can add anything."

"Well, what finally happened with the case?" I asked.

"It was a simple case to solve really. After a few days of surveillance, we caught him in the act of vandalizing a construction site. We were never sure why he chose that particular construction company to target. As you know, tons of construction companies use Hispanic labor but understanding this MPD thing was not really our business. The folks at East Bay Construction didn't even bother pressing charges after talking to his aunt. I remember the owner saying he felt sorry for the kid. I think the aunt may have forked over some cash to pay for their damages. That was the end of the story as far as we and they were concerned. It was a minor case really. I probably would have forgotten all about it if wasn't for the multiple-personality element."

"Keep on living the good life Roger. I owe you guys big time for all the guidance you gave in my early days."

"You were a natural Harley. That's why we took you on."

After hanging up, I thought about this Bobby Bernard character who had been posting on Alma's MySpace Page. It had to be the same guy but what did it mean? Due to the efforts of Destinos Latinos, Alma's case had been in the papers more often in the past few months. If the guy or should I say part of the guy who hated immigrants still lived in the area, he could have easily become aware of the Alma Vargas story and then targeted the web site. That didn't mean he was the killer though. This could turn out to be just an annoying distraction. I hoped Bill could shed some light on the matter. Anyway, we needed to find out as soon as possible who the mother-ship was that this Bobby Bernard character was occupying.

CHAPTER 11

On Friday, Ricardo dropped by after school and told me that he was able to get Mr. Duckworth's meds back in his desk in such a way that he might think they had been simply misplaced. That made me feel better especially given the fact that Friday was the last day of school before what is known as President's week. I'd have a week off from LBJ High to unwind and gather my thoughts. I was just about ready to pack it up for the day when Duckworth coincidentally dropped by my classroom with a little cassette in his hand.

"Thought you might like to see this."

"What is it?" I asked.

"It's a video that Mr. Chirac took of a workshop last year. The theme was something like how to make school more relevant for Hispanic youth. It was meant for teachers but a few students including Alma attended and helped host the event."

"Well, thank you. Do you mind if I take it home and bring it back after the break?"

"Not at all. Take your time."

We talked about how we would spend the time off. He mentioned something about getting some surfing in and I told him I'd be getting things done around the house. He left as quickly as he came in. His short visit reminded me that we still hadn't checked one of the drugs that were found in his desk.

I pulled out my notebook that contained the pharmaceutical notes and found the ones relating to Duckworth. What the heck is Blocodine, I thought to myself as I googled it. The screen read, Did you mean: Bloodline? I checked my spelling and tried again but the same message popped up. Most of the drugs that we googled earlier came up quickly with several links. It was easy to find out what the indications were. Not a thing came up for Blocodine though. Nada. Maybe I'd call my doctor early next week to see if he knew anything about it. I could check the library but if nothing came up on google, I doubt I'd be able to find anything there. As unlikely as Jake Duckworth was a viable suspect, I couldn't leave any stone unturned.

I put the video in my backpack and headed out the door for a nine day vacation. On Monday morning, I had an e-mail in my inbox from Ricardo. He had been to Mr. Ramos's house over the weekend to help set up a new internet connection.

Mr. Butler, I was able to check the medicine cabinets at Mr. Ramos's house. I found a bottle of Xanax. That's the same class of drug as Restoril. The bastard did it. I know it. Could you call my cell phone? Ricardo

I took a deep breath. I had learned from experience that jumping to conclusions could cloud the mind and lead one astray. I got on the computer. Yes, Ricardo was right. They were both benzodiazepines and are usually prescribed to treat anxiety and insomnia. I called Ricardo immediately.

"What's up?" he answered.

"This is Harley Butler. I got your message about what you found in Ramos's medicine cabinet. I want you to stay calm on this. You hear me? We can't jump to conclusions or we could blow the whole case."

"What do you mean? We got the evidence now."

"That was good work Ricardo but we need more evidence. Both Xanax and Restoril are commonly prescribed drugs. Remember how many teachers had the ADD drug Adderall in their possession? Just the fact that he had a drug similar to Restoril would not even be enough to get a search warrant. That's what they call weak circumstantial evidence in the criminal justice world."

"So we need more?"

"You betcha! A lot more. I know you want justice for Alma but we've got to do it right."

"Shouldn't we tell the police?"

"Let's hold off on that until we get some more on him. Calling the police could do more harm than good. If he feels like he is becoming a target, he could go on the defensive and we could lose some golden opportunities to gather more evidence."

"Do you think he did it?"

"I really don't know Ricardo. Let's keep trying to find out."

After we disconnected, I thought about the things that had happened to me – the slashed tires, the obscure message in Spanish, the stolen mice. Mr. Ramos would have had access to my room. He could have slashed my tires or had someone do it. Still, he was a principal and I had a hard time reconciling in my mind that someone in charge of the education and well-being of so many students could commit such a dark crime. I had heard of principals and teachers being convicted of murdering a spouse or another adult but never a student.

On Tuesday, I went to the doctor for a routine check-up. I explained to him about the side effects I experienced on Concerta. His response was simply that the drug is not for everybody. I asked him if he knew what Blocodine was prescribed for. He said he had never heard of it but if he had time he'd look into it and get back to me.

That evening I decided to watch the video that Mr. Duckworth had dropped off. I inserted the cassette into my digital camera and plugged it into the USB port on the front side of the computer. The first scene was a pan of the LBJ High cafeteria. Teachers were seated all around at circular tables. I recognized Alma among a group of students seated at a table on the far left. The camera panned to the guest speaker who was standing in front of a screen. A PowerPoint slide read, Lowering the Hispanic Filter. The Assistant Principle, Mr. Calloway took the stage and reminded the staff why they were lucky to attend this workshop put on by Jaime Rodriguez, author of the book Strategies for Teaching Hispanic Students. He started out his presentation by talking about how the Hispanic student-age population was growing in California and how important and imperative it was to address educational issues facing this population. He went on and on about how teachers need to examine their own cultural biases so they can better understand and help their Hispanic students. There were comments and questions from teachers but no argument or challenge to the ideas presented by the speaker. Mr. Rodriguez was preaching to the choir. My ADD kicked in. I was getting bored by the predictability and was wondering why Mr. Duckworth had loaned me the video in the first place. So far, Alma had only appeared in a brief pan of the camera. I clicked the fast forward button to 15 times normal speed. A few seconds later, I noticed a pan to Alma's table. I pressed the stop button and then rewind for a fraction of a second. Mr. Rodriguez was wrapping up, summarizing the main points of his presentation. He ended by saying something like teachers should strive to learn as much as possible about the culture and language of the students they teach. Doing so would lower the Hispanic filter and turn more kids on to school. The teachers gave him a loud round of applause. That's when the

167

camera panned to Alma who was standing with her hand raised high. There was a placard on her table that read Leadership. When the applause died down the camera panned to Mr. Calloway who was also standing.

"Before we leave, one of our student representatives has a question." All eyes looked in her direction.

"I have a few comments about today's workshop," she said calmly.

"I hope you found it rewarding," said Mr. Rodriguez grinning, "By the way, where are you from?"

"I'm from the state of Chihuahua," she said, appearing slightly irritated with the question. "And yes, I did find the workshop rewarding but probably not for the reasons you think." The room got quieter. She looked around at everyone as if gathering her thoughts and testing the waters. "I'm sorry but I can't help thinking that all this talk about catering to the Hispanic student will ultimately hurt Hispanics."

"I'm not sure what you mean by that," said Mr. Rodriguez.

"Take me for example. If you feel a need to classify me, I am a Hispanic student with all the cultural and language characteristics that you have been talking about for the past hour. I don't expect nor do I think it is important that my teachers understand my background. If they do, that's fine. If they don't, that's also fine. We don't need our education spoon-fed to us. We should be challenged to do our best by teachers knowledgeable in the subjects they teach. Busy teachers should be going to workshops to improve their skills and knowledge in their subject matter, especially with the limited resources facing school districts today. Einstein said there was so much to do in so little time. We shouldn't take precious time away from our busy teachers especially to try to get them to perceive Hispanic students as somehow different. We are all different. Just check our fingerprints!"

The teachers who just a minute earlier were applauding Mr. Rodriguez were now applauding Alma but much louder. A pan to his face revealed that it was turning a dark red. I wondered if he was contemplating if the consulting fee he had negotiated for the gig was worth it.

"I think after you spend some time studying how students learn you may appreciate a workshop like this," said Mr. Rodriguez into the microphone.

"I hope not," said Alma who could be heard clearly. "Once you start to compromise and patronize, you lower the bar for others and yourself. I pray that never happens to me."

Mr. Calloway took the microphone and reminded everyone that the workshop was over. The videotape ended with a shot of Mr. Rodriguez looking very perturbed.

Brilliant, I thought to myself. A student who questioned with passion everything that was thrown at her. I wished I could have met her. What a jewel!

I called Mr. Duckworth to ask him about this Rodriguez character. Jake said that the guy is on the payroll of several school districts with similar demographics. It's sickening how many of these numbskulls who don't teach kids get paid so much money to show those who do the job on a daily basis how to do it, he said. He asked me if I wanted to play some shuffleboard at the Hotsy Totsy Club this Saturday to unwind. The Hotsy Totsy Club is a fun dive on San Pablo Avenue in Albany that I had been to once or twice. They offer cheap drinks and a non-pretentious atmosphere. I agreed to the plan.

The next few days were spent in the office. Rosanna was working a few cases, clocking up the hours and I would offer guidance when needed. We went out once with Kátia and Randy to Picantes in Berkeley for Mexican food. I hinted to Randy that I had some leads but didn't go into the details. Sometimes I just don't like mixing work with leisure. For the amount of time it took to finish a pitcher of margaritas, we unwound and left the work world behind us.

On Thursday, I ran into Helen Weinstein in the hallway. I hadn't heard much noise coming from her office recently and wondered what she had been up to. She thanked me again for not reporting her. During our conversation, I brought up the subject of Blocodine. She closed her eyes as if trying to retrieve something hidden deep in the files of her mind.

"Blocodine, Blocodine, where have I heard that before," she whispered.

"Ring a bell?" I asked.

"Where have I heard that before?" she ignored me and repeated the question as if asking again would refresh her memory.

169

"I did a google search on it and didn't find a thing," I said. "Usually if anything at all has been published about a drug, you can find at least something about it online."

"No, I've heard that before. Where have I?" she stopped this time in the middle of the question and her eyes opened wide.

"Yes, I remember now. I read an abstract several months ago in the UC Berkeley library. I mean I just briefly looked at it. I do that every now and then you know. Go to the university libraries and read dissertations, master theses, preliminary research abstracts. I know. Get a life. But sometimes you find a jewel amongst all the intellectual drool. That's why I do it."

"What do you remember about the blocodine abstract? Was it a jewel?"

"I remember it described a small controlled study with just three subjects. It caught my interest because the new compound was designed to treat Multiple Personality Disorder. Although I've never treated anyone with this disorder, it has always fascinated me. Anyway, the more I learn about how the mind functions the better. I'm the consummate non-licensed professional."

My jaw dropped. Case solved, I thought to myself. I couldn't believe what I was hearing. Jake Duckworth and Bobby Bernard were the same person. It just didn't fit. Mr. Duckworth seemed like the least likely person in the world to be afflicted by something like this.

"Are you alright? You seem to be lost in thought," she said.

"Yeah, I'm fine. You can not imagine the value of what you've just told me. You just helped me solve a very important case. At least, I think you did."

"Always glad to be of service to my friendly neighborhood gumshoe. I'm curious though. How could an abstract about a drug to treat MPD help solve a case? I'm dying to find out if it's not confidential."

I didn't respond. My mind was drifting to tomorrow's plan to have drinks with Jake at the Hotsy Totsy Club.

"Tell me more about the study. Did you read anything about the subjects involved?"

"All I remember is that the subjects were chosen because they were not in denial of their illness and wanted treatment. I also think I read something about them being well-educated. I guess in a

170

small study you want to make sure you have people responsible enough not to miss a dose. Otherwise, there goes your small study."

"Makes sense. Did the abstract explain how Blocodine worked?

"I don't remember much about it except that it had something to do with smart cells targeting specific areas of the brain, stimulating some areas while sedating other parts. Very fascinating."

"Did they reach any conclusions?"

"Yes. They highly recommended further studies and were excited about the preliminary results. All three subjects responded well with a minimum of side effects."

"Do you think it would be possible that after the study was complete, they would allow the subjects to continue to use the drug?"

"It's unlikely because the researchers would have been worried about liability. What if one of the subjects died from the drug? On the other hand, since the drug was so effective one of them could have felt it was their ethical responsibility to allow a suffering patient to continue its use. It's hard to say."

"The reason I ask is because I think I know who one of the subjects is and I happen to know that he is still taking Blocodine."

"You're putting me on, aren't you?"

"Absolutely not. Believe it or not, he may be the killer in a case I'm working on."

Her eyes opened wide with curiosity. I decided to open up to her because I thought there was a possibility she could help me out.

"I have a question about hypnosis," I said gauging her eyes as I spoke. "Would it be possible to get someone with MPD to change from one personality to another under hypnosis?"

"Yes, in theory and as long as the person wants to be hypnotized."

"Would the fact that the person is on the drug Blocodine affect the experience?" I asked.

"You want me to hypnotize a murderer, don't you? What kind of girl do you think I am?" she asked jokingly. "Anyway, I have no idea what affect if any Blocodine would have."

For the next 30 minutes, I went on to give her a summary of the case, my suspicions that Jake Duckworth and Bobby Bernard

171

were the same person, and that I suspected he was the killer. As a person who dedicated her life to trying to help people, she said she felt awkward and uncomfortable using her skills to help get someone arrested. When I told her the story of the very special Alma Vargas, she agreed to give it a shot.

"I'll have Randy and his gang set up hidden cameras and microphones. Don't worry. Just be yourself. I'm not even sure I'll be able to get him to show up or under what pretense but I'll figure something out before tomorrow. I'll call you tonight with all the details."

She loaned me a key to her office so I could let Randy's team in to do their job in the morning. I walked down to The Pub, a beer and cigar bar two blocks from my office to have a beer and think. I ordered a Bass, sat down in a nice soft chair next to the fireplace, closed my eyes and tried to visualize how tomorrow would play out. How could I get Mr. Duckworth to agree to visit her office? What would I say to him? A guy in a fleece jacket sitting next to me was talking on his cell phone to someone about how stressful his day had been and how he was unwinding at The Pub. That's when an idea popped into my ADD infected mind. Teachers have a high-stress job. There's no doubt about that. What if I told Duckworth that I knew a hypno-therapist that could relive his stress and do it for free? I wondered if he would go for that. I played out the scenario in my mind. I'd tell him I knew someone that was running a therapy practice, was developing some new therapy techniques, and was willing to try them out free of charge with people she knew. I could say that she had hypnotized me an hour earlier and I came out feeling refreshed as a newborn baby. It may not work but I'd give it a try. How else could I get him to recline on Ms. Weinstein's lazy-boy?

I called Helen and immediately told her about my idea. She hesitated but then reluctantly agreed to go along with my story remembering that she owed me a favor. Deceiving someone in my practice goes against my very nature, she said, but I guess solving the murder of that young girl should take priority.

I had one more Bass to help calm my nerves. Knowing that Duckworth was the probable killer of Alma Vargas made me uncomfortable inside. The beer helped me relax and think. It just seemed so unlike him, I thought. How could such an articulate, socially-conscious person like Jake have this Bobby Bernard devil in their brain? This MPD syndrome was just hard for me to fully comprehend. All I could do now was to put on my best acting face for tomorrow night and prepare the best I could. Perhaps assuming that he was innocent would help me stay calm but that would be difficult. After the beer, I drove home and went to bed early. I wanted to be rested for the next day's events.

I was awakened by a strange dream in the middle of the night. I dreamed I caught up with Alma outside the white church where I saw her exit in a previous dream. She was hovering about ten feet in the air. A bright halo-like, circular light was shining behind her head that made it hard to see her face but her eyes were clearly visible. The scene reminded me of one of those paintings depicting the apparition of the Virgin Mary but this person was clearly Alma and I was the person close to Earth in awe. She had her arms spread out like the Christ the Redeemer statue in Rio and her eyes gazed off into the distance with a peaceful, compassionate expression. Little by little, her honey-brown eyes moved until finally she was looking directly at me. She smiled a smile that could only be described as perfect.

"The essence of man lies hidden in the spaces between his thoughts and actions. Until you can truly appreciate the shadow cast by a distant unseen flower, you will not be complete. Do your job but don't be too quick to judge," she spoke the last sentence slowly and deliberately as if she wanted to make sure I understood.

That's when I woke up. The last time I saw her in a dream she told me a person of trust had betrayed her. Now, she was speaking in proverbs. What did she mean by that? Was I crazy for even taking these dreams seriously? Anyway, I didn't have time to contemplate. There was a lot of work to do.

I met Randy's crew in the morning at Helen's office. They put a few hidden cameras and microphones in strategic locations and set it up so we would be able to monitor what went on both visually and audibly from my office next door. I did a few checks of the system after they left to make sure it was working. After that, I went to the Albany YMCA to workout. I figured the more physically exhausted I was, the more relaxed I'd be when I met Duckworth.

Finally, the moment of truth had arrived. I was chilling in my lazy-boy at home when the phone rang.

"Hey Harley, this is Jake. Ready for a five star experience tonight at the Hotsy Totsy Club?"

"I'm all in. What'cha been doing all day?"

"The usual – grading essays, preparing lessons, walking the dog. Got a little blue thinking about our winter break nearing its end."

"I hear you man. You won't believe what I did today. I just got hypnotized."

"What the hell are you talking about Harley?"

"I know it sounds weird but this friend of mine just started this practice in Albany. She does something called hypnotherapy to relieve stress."

"To each his own," he said as if uninterested.

"Well, she hypnotized me for free and I came out of it feeling like a new born baby. Every muscle in my body feels relaxed and loose. I highly recommend you try it."

"Who knows? Maybe some day I will."

"Here's the deal Jake. This is expensive therapy. Really expensive. Normally, it would cost several hundred dollars just for one session. Not something within a teacher's budget really. This friend of mine told me she wanted to refine her technique before marketing her business and asked me if I had any friends she could practice on. Basically, you could have this luxury service performed tonight for free."

There were several moments of silence before he spoke.

"Sounds interesting Harley but my idea of therapy is a cold draft beer at the Hotsy Totsy Club."

"I hear you man but it would take just a few minutes and just imagine how good that beer is going to taste when you're completely stress-free."

"You make a strong sale. What's in it for you?" he asked with a laugh.

"I look at it as doing a favor for two friends. How about I meet you at Starbucks on Solano at 6:30 and then we can walk down to her office? She's a wonderful, smart lady named Helen."

"You're not trying to set me up with her, are you?"

"No, I'm not but she is good-looking. I think you'll like her."

"I'm not sure what you're getting me into Harley but I'll give it a shot. I'll probably get there around 6:45."

174

"See you in a bit."

I hung up the phone, congratulated myself for pulling it off and then called Helen to tell her we were on. We discussed the kind of information I wanted to get out of him and how crucial it was for her to bring out the Bobby Bernard sub-personality in the session. She said she couldn't promise anything but would do her best.

I arrived at Starbucks at 6:30. Given the fact that I was already nervous, it probably wasn't a good idea to put any caffeine in my system but I ordered a cappuccino anyway. Come to think of it, my coffee habit and my so-called ADD were probably connected. I learned early on that coffee helped me focus and am now a complete addict. At least, it doesn't take complete control of my system like that crazy medication did. Even though caffeine is a stimulant, maybe it has the paradoxal ability to calm me down. That's what my doctor said that ADD drugs did. Anyway, I knew I had to be on top of my game tonight and didn't think a little caffeine would hurt. I sat down in one of the soft seats in the center with my back to the door. I didn't read or look around. I just sat there thinking about how the night would play out.

"Harley!" someone said in a loud voice.

I turned around. Looking right at me was a tall Caucasian skinhead smiling at me like I was his best-friend. I felt uneasy until I realized that the skinhead was Duckworth.

"What the hell did you do? Join the Marines?" I asked.

"Nope. Just a local monastery. I'm officially a monk now."

"So no Hotsy Totsy Club tonight?"

"Are you kidding? I belong to the Pale Ale Order. Drinking beer is fine."

"You're messing with me Jake."

"No shit Harley! Now let's go see that therapist you're trying to set me up with."

"That's not quite what I had in mind."

"I'm just messing with you Harley. Relax."

We exited Starbucks, crossed Solano Avenue and walked the few blocks towards Helen's office. Duckworth seemed to be in a jovial mood but I couldn't get over his new appearance. With his wavy hair, he looked like a typical fun-loving California golden boy surfer. As a skinhead, he looked menacing and unapproachable.

At the door, he read the signs out loud. Since I did not include my personal name anywhere on the building's façade there

175

was no way he'd know that this was my office too. That didn't stop me from being nervous that someone who knew me would spontaneously show up and blow my cover. I quickly opened the main door and went inside. Jake followed.

"Helen Weinstein. I've heard that name before. This is that therapist that Caleb Jones was seeing. I thought you said she was trying to get established."

"I meant in the field of hypnotherapy."

"I see. Caleb told me about her. He said getting therapy with her was one of the best things that ever happened to him."

"Well there you go my friend. Now she has two recommendations."

"How long will this take?" he asked.

"Probably about a half an hour to an hour but it should feel like just a few minutes. You won't remember anything when you come out. It'll be like taking a short nap."

"Alright, let's get it done with."

I knocked on Helen's door. Helen was dressed in the same navy-blue skirt that I'd seen her in before. She looked more like a professional salesperson than a therapist but by any measure was very attractive. She led us both into her office and directed Jake and I to sit in a couple of upright chairs that were up against the wall. After we went through formal introductions, she spoke.

"I guess Harley explained to you what this is all about Jake. I'm developing some new techniques in hypnotherapy and wanted to refine them a bit before trying them out on clients. I appreciate the fact that you volunteered your time and want you know the process is totally harmless. There is one catch though. To be hypnotized, you need to want to be hypnotized. If you resist, it won't work."

"I think I want to," he said laughing. His eyes darted from Helen to me as if looking for approval.

"Well I'll let you guys get down to business. I'm going up to get my car and head back home for a few minutes. Give me a call on my cell when you're finished."

I waved to both of them and closed the door behind me. As I went out the front door, I made a point to make as much noise as possible. I walked about a half a block down the street, stood there for about a minute and then went back. I opened the outside door as quietly as I could, walked softly past Helen's door and opened mine. Randy was already sitting there looking at some monitors with headphones on. He nodded to me but did not say anything. The device he was sitting in front of consisted of four small screens and a larger one imbedded in the middle. Each small screen showed a different angle of the room and by pushing a button below any of the small screens, that image would be transferred to the larger screen. The entire device was set up awkwardly on my desk and left little room for anything else, not even the cup of coffee that Randy was drinking.

He handed me a set of headphones as I pulled up a seat. Jake was still sitting in the same chair he was when I left and Helen was still explaining the process to him. Suddenly, Jake stood up, stretched a little, and walked over to the reclining lazy-boy chair. The camera angle changed and Randy pressed the button to make the new angle appear on the large screen. I adjusted the volume so I could hear better. Here is a transcript of the session:

H: You are walking uphill on a narrow cobblestone road. It is a pleasant perfect day with a turquoise blue sky. You are completely relaxed. There is no hurry. You have all the time in the world. You take slow deliberate steps taking in everything around you. You notice that your vision and hearing has improved and everything you see and hear relaxes and comforts you. You make it to the end of the road where there is a small white cottage. You open the door and go inside. There is nothing in this cottage that can harm you. You are welcome and belong here. You sit down and lean back in a very comfortable chair. In front of you is a white movie screen and in the middle of the screen is a golden circle. The golden circle relaxes you even more and wants to draw you in. Now is the time for complete and total relaxation. Stare at the golden circle. Let it draw you in. You are getting more and more relaxed. More and more relaxed. Relaxed. (Helen's voice fades)(8 minutes and 33 seconds of silence pass.) Before we go further, you need to release more tension. The golden circle is now transforming into the person you desire. (Jake's face contorts and then relaxes.) You are now making love with this person with all the passion you have at your disposal. (Jake begins to moan and wiggle in his chair)

Your bodies are hot and sweating. Your penis slides deeper and deeper into the hot, wet universe. The pleasure is unbearable. (The moans increase in intensity. Jake begins to hump up and down rapidly) (Randy covers his mouth with his hand to avoid letting out

177

a burst of laughter.) (Finally, he seems to come to a climax. His entire body shakes. For a few seconds, all that can be heard is heavy breathing that gets increasingly slower.) (1 minute and 55 seconds of silence pass.) You are now ready to explore the various channels of your mind. If something is uncomfortable for you, remember it is just a movie and can not harm you. There is no reason to be afraid of anything you see, hear or encounter. (Jake nods slightly and grunts something incomprehensible.) You are now in a complete state of relaxation. Let's get back to that golden circle you saw earlier. Do you still see it?

J: Yes, I see it.

H: Good. The golden circle is the doorway into your unconscious mind. It has a screen that can open and close. The screen is now opening and the movie is about to begin.

J: Okay.

H: Your student Alma Vargas is standing there in front of you.

J: Yes, I see her. (His body contorts slightly)

H: Do you have anything to say to her? (He shakes his head back and forth nervously.)

J: I'm sorry I couldn't protect you Alma. I just couldn't - (He doesn't finish the sentence.)

H: Who do you want to protect Alma from Jake?

J: Oh no no no no. I can't go there. (His voice becomes strained like he is in pain. He moans.)

H: Remember Jake, there is nobody here that can hurt you. It is just a movie. Now, relax and tell me who you need to protect Alma from. (He shakes his head violently.)

J: It's Bobby. Bobby shouldn't be allowed to come out but sometimes I can't stop him. I tried very hard to stop him. (He covers his face with his palms.)

H: Don't worry Jake. It's just a movie remember. (She pauses a few seconds) By the way what's Bobby's last name?

J: It's Bernard. I can't let him out of the house. He'll do bad things. (He shook his head again.)

H: Does Bobby live with you Jake?

J: I thought I'd gotten rid of him for good but he came back uninvited.

H: So he still lives with you?

J: I'm not sure.

H: Is there anyway I can talk to Bobby?

J: That wouldn't be wise. He's dangerous.

H: Why do you think he is dangerous Jake?

J: Bobby is full of hate. He does things to hurt people.

H: Do you think Bobby could change if he got help?

J: I don't think so. Bobby needs to just disappear.

H: Okay Jake, but since Bobby keeps coming back maybe it would be better if we could try to change him. That way he might be easier to get along with and not cause so much trouble.

J: I don't know if that is a good idea.

H: It doesn't hurt to try Jake. Remember, everything beyond the golden circle is just a movie. (30 seconds of silence pass)

H: You still see the golden circle. Keep concentrating on the golden light. It keeps drawing you in deeper and deeper. There is now a remote control in your hand. Click it once to change the channel. (Jake makes a movement with his thumb as if clicking a remote.) We're on Bobby's channel now and we're going to try to help him. (Jake's heavy breathing can be heard clearly.) Bobby is now in control of your body and mind. I'm going to talk to Bobby now. Can you hear me Bobby? (Jake makes no response and just lies there as if he's in a trance.) (1 minute and 14 seconds pass.) Bobby, I know you are there and I want to talk to you. If you can hear me say yes.

(From this point on Helen has been successful in accessing the Bobby Bernard persona. However, we still use J for Jake)

J: Yes. (Voice has deeper intonation. Doesn't sound like Jake.)

H: Now Bobby, you can see the golden circle, can't you?

J: Yes, I can. (Spoken matter-of-factly.)

H: Good Bobby. Beyond the golden circle is a film screen that will present movies to you at my suggestion. Remember nothing can harm you. It is just a movie that has a beginning and an end. (37 seconds of silence pass.) The first movie is going to star Alma Vargas. Can you see her now? (18 seconds of silence)

J: Yes, I can.

H: Where is she?

J: She's at Nicholl Park lying on the grass?

H: What's she doing at Nicholl Park?

J: That's where I took her.

H: Do you know what time it is?

J: Not exactly sure. I know it is around dawn.

H: Is Alma having a good time?

179

J: Hell no! I drugged her up pretty good.

H: Why did you drug her up Bobby?

J: So she wouldn't scream and try to escape.

H: Why would she want to escape?

J: Because I'm not Jake. I'm doing a real service for California.

H: How do you help California, Bobby?

J: It's all about scaring the Mexicans. Make them know California is not safe for them. That's how I help.

H: How did you kill Alma Bobby?

J: With a baseball bat. I whacked her pretty good several times. Got her in the head the last time. (Helen's face becomes visibly disturbed. She paces back and forth a few times) (43 seconds pass.)

H: Okay Bobby. The movie is going to go back in time to when you first saw Alma. Do you remember where she was?

J: All I know is that I found myself sitting in the McDonalds on 23rd St. and she was sitting across from me with an American Government book open. The dumb-ass thought I was her teacher. (He laughs.)

H: So what did you do? Did you tell her that you weren't her teacher?

J: Hell no! Why would I do that?

H: I don't know Bobby. Do you remember what time it was?

J: It was around dinner time, maybe around 6:00 p.m. I was eating a Big Mac and fries and she was eating some chicken nuggets.

H: So you don't remember arriving, you just suddenly found yourself at McDonalds?

J: Yep, that happens to me sometimes.

H: So what did you do after you ate at McDonalds?

J: Well, she wanted help with a school project so I invited her back to my place. It was easy. I told her I'd get her home by 8:00. She jumped right in my car.

H: When she jumped in your car, did she still think you were her teacher?

J: Hell yeah! (He laughs loudly) She was not suicidal.

H: You mean she had no suspicions at all that you may not be her teacher?

J: Not exactly. She just kept asking –is something wrong Mr. Duckworth - and I kept answering - I'm just fine and dandy. She thought I was him.

H: So where did you take her?

J: Back to my house of course.

H: Where is your house Bobby?

J: On Marin Avenue in Albany.

H: Okay, so you both walk into your house. What do you do once you get inside?

J: Well, she sits down on the couch and starts talking about Habeas Corpus or something. I had no idea what she was talking about so I had to change the rules of the game.

H: How did you change the rules Bobby?

J: I took her in the bedroom and tied her up. That's how I changed the rules. (He speaks casually as if it was the most normal thing in the world to do.)

H: What did Alma think about you changing the rules?

J: She didn't like it at all. She was shocked. She kept saying – Why are you doing this Mr. Duckworth? I told her I ain't fucking Mr. Duckworth. Finally, she shut up and started crying. She kept begging me to stop. That's when I duct-taped her mouth shut.

H: Once you had her tied up, what did you do?

J: She kept wiggling and fighting so I made her drink about 10 shots of tequila.

H: How could she drink tequila with duct-tape on her mouth?

J: Oh, that was easy. (He laughed) I used one big piece for her mouth. It was thick enough to cover her little mouth easily. I just pulled if off, poured the tequila down her throat, and put it back on again. That way I made sure she swallowed it all.

H: Did you give her any drugs to go with it?

J: Yeah, I did. I grabbed some stuff from the medicine cabinet. I think I made her swallow three or four pills. Anyway, she spit them out the first time but I don't give up that easily. I just got faster with the duct-tape.

H: Do you remember what kind of drug it was?

J: Umm, I know it was still in the box because I remember reading some of the information pack that came with it. It was some kind of insomnia drug. There was a warning about drinking alcohol with it. (He let out a chilling laugh.)

H: So it was a drug for insomnia but you're not sure of the name of the drug?

J: I think it was Restorafed. Something that started with R.

H: Do you mean Restoril? That's a drug used for insomnia.

J: Yeah, that's right.

181

H: Okay, let's get back to the movie. Alma is tied up and you're getting her drunk. How did she end up in Nicholl Park?

J: I took her there. Why would I leave her in the house? If I kill her in the park, the police won't know who did it. They'll think she was just another victim of gang violence, another dead Mexican in Richmond. Time for a donut break. (He laughs.)

H: Why did you wait until the dawn to take Alma to the park?

J: So no one would see me finish her off of course.

H: So how did you spend the rest of the night with Alma.

J: I did some things with her. That's all you need to know.
I scrubbed off the duct tape real good right before I took her to the park.

H: Why did you need to kill Alma Bobby?

J: I was just doing California a favor. I thought I already told you that. (He appears agitated with the questioning.)

H: I see. After you killed her in the park, where did you go?

J: I just started driving away up McDonald Avenue. That's all I remember. (Helen looks stressed out. She puts her face in front of one of the cameras and mouths, 5 more minutes making a hand signal.)

H: Did you keep anything of Alma's as a souvenir?

J: I trashed her backpack but I kept that notebook she had out.

H: Where is it now?

J: It's in the secret hiding place.

H: Could you tell me where the secret hiding place is?

J: Of course not.

H Okay Bobby, the movie is almost over. There are a few more things we need to look at though. Where do you stay when Mr. Duckworth goes to work?

J: I'm one stealth dude. I'm always in the background even though Mr. Duckworth may not think so. Dad always liked me better and he hates me for that.

H: Did you ever go to work with Mr. Duckworth?

J: Like I said, I try to show up at work but he tries really hard to keep me boxed in. Sometimes the line between him and me gets blurred. I can see things happening at work that he's oblivious to.

H: What is he oblivious to Bobby?

J: Well, I know there are people at his job who are out to get me but he has no idea about it.

H: Who is out to get you Bobby?

J: Well, that new computer teacher they call Mr. Butler. That guys a phony! He ain't a teacher, I can tell you that. He's at the school for one reason only - to catch me. I'm trying to scare his ass away anyway I can.

H: What have you done to scare him away?

J: Just basic harassment stuff to make his stay as unpleasant as possible. I stole the mice from his computer lab. (He laughs loudly and pauses to think.) Oh yeah, I slashed his tires too and left him a message in Spanish.

H: Do you speak Spanish Bobby?

J: I can get by with it. Dad always said know thy enemy. I just wanted to get that nosey bastard nervous.

H: Okay Bobby, keep watching the golden circle. It's time to say goodbye. You are getting very sleepy. There's a remote in your hand. You are going to change the channel. Jake Duckworth is slowly going to come back. Jake can you hear me? (There is no response.) Jake, you are still in that comfortable cottage. Can you hear me?

J: Yes, I can. (The tonality of his voice reverts back. He shakes his head as if waking up from a nap.)

H: Okay, Jake. Keep watching the screen. I am going to count backwards from 10. When I reach 0, you are going to be back in my office relaxing comfortably. You will not remember a thing from the session and will feel completely refreshed, as if waking from a satisfying nap. (15 seconds of silence.) Okay, lets, begin. With each number you are going to be a step closer to awakening. Ready. Ten, nine, eight, seven, six, five, four three, two, one, (She pauses briefly.) zero. (His eyes open wider.) We're finished Jake.

J: What do you mean?

H: I mean the session is over. You were a great subject. Thanks for your time.

J: Wow! How long was I here?

H: About 40 minutes.

J: I am feeling great. Thanks for whatever you did. I guess I'll call Harley so I can get out of your hair.

H: Oh that's alright, let me get you a cup of tea while you're waiting.

That was my signal to leave the building. I said goodbye to Randy, walked down the street to Safeway and waited for the vibration to go off in my pocket. It didn't take long.

183

"Hey Harley, this is Jake. The session is over and I'm feeling great. Thanks for setting that up."

"Alright, I'll be right there. Sit tight."

I walked slowly up Solano Avenue digesting what I'd just seen on camera and the prospect of Duckworth's impending arrest. A search warrant would be issued soon. Evidence would need to be gathered and plans would need to be made on when and where to arrest him. In the past, when I solved a case that resulted in an arrest I felt a sense of satisfaction in that some sort of justice would eventually be served. This case was different. Duckworth was basically a good man with one horrific flaw. That flaw made him a clear and present danger to society. I wished there was a way I could use a pocketknife to cut out the Bobby Bernard part of his brain, put it in a jar, and take it down to police headquarters. We've got your man, I'd say as I handed over the jar. That way Duckworth could continue to inspire students at LBJ High while the evil slice of Bobby Bernard's brain matter could be preserved in perpetuity in formaldehyde. Perhaps it could even be studied by scientists to better understand MPD. The truth was Duckworth would be locked up for a very long time and the students would never see him again. Maybe the insanity defense could get him committed to a mental institution but anyway you shuffled the cards, he'd be looking at decades if not life behind either walls or bars. I was sad for Alma and I was sad for Mr. Duckworth.

Suddenly, I remembered what Rosanna had said about that book she was reading, The Gift of Death. She said it had something to do with understanding the implicit and unspoken ideas behind one's actions. Duckworth was taking a medication to try to block some of those ideas from coming to the surface but maybe that was futile. Was Bobby Bernard a complete separate personality or just a sub-folder in the complex file system of Duckworth's brain? I couldn't say. Maybe the only difference between him and any so-called normal person was the degree of disconnection between the outward self and those implicit and unspoken ideas. It just happened that in Duckworth's case, those unspoken ideas were extremely disturbing.

I made a quick call to Randy and told him I'd brief him on our night out at the Hotsy Totsy Club. He seemed worried about me knowing what the guy was capable of. He wondered if the hypnosis session may have somehow loosened up the Bobby Bernard persona, a persona capable of murder. I assured him that I would carry my pistol just in case.

I entered the main door and walked the short distance down the hall to Ms. Weinstein's office and knocked on the door. Sitting in a chair with a cup of tea in his hand was Duckworth smiling as if nothing had happened.

"Thanks for turning me on to this lady," he said gleefully. "I'm feeling totally relaxed and refreshed."

"He was a great subject. Not everyone is that easy to hypnotize," said Helen.

"Well, I'm glad it worked out for everybody," I said. "Maybe we'll all get together someday for drinks," I lied.

After a few minutes of small talk, we bid Helen farewell, walked back to our separate cars and headed down to the Hotsy Totsy Club on San Pablo Avenue. I ordered a draft beer and sat down at the first of four rectangular tables. This was a bar that smelled of wear and tear. The leather wrap around the bar counter and the bar stools was well-worn and faded. There were people scattered all around the main bar. A lonely barfly sat on the corner stool nursing a beer like it was his mother's breast milk. A Mae West poster on the wall behind him read Every day's a Holiday. Three guys on the stools near my table were having a loud debate on which was better, satellite or cable TV. The walls were covered with kitsch like mirrors advertising everything from the Oakland Raiders to Budweiser, the King of Beers. Right below me against the wall was a shuffleboard that no one was playing. There was a flat panel TV screen on the back wall that was broadcasting a Golden State Warrior's game. The room behind the main bar sported an old pool table and a cabinet full of ancient sport trophies. It was a dive alright but a comfortable and non-threatening one.

When Jake walked in, all heads turned in his direction. His shaved head made him look like a cross between a white supremacist and an anemic Buddhist body-builder. The patrons seemed to be watching him from the corners of their eyes as if the night wouldn't go back to normal until they were absolutely sure that this guy wasn't going to go on a rampage. When he sat down and spoke to me I could see the relief in their eyes. I walked up to the bar and ordered a draft beer for him.

"First one's on me," I said.

185

"Thanks man. Here's to hypnotherapy and winter break," he said while raising his glass in the air.

"I hear you. A couple of more days and back to the old grindstone. Let's enjoy what we have left."

We both took a healthy swig of cold beer. I couldn't help thinking to myself that my life at LBJ High was coming to an end and secretly made a toast to that with another healthy swig. I don't think I had ever finished a beer that quickly before and was ready for my second. I ordered another one for both of us even though he still had half of his first left. Maybe it was because of what I had just seen in Helen's office but I was at a loss for conversation.

I kept my eyes focused on the Warrior's game. I remembered the part in the therapy session when he said that he knew that I was at the school to spy on him. I wasn't sure how the Bobby Bernard persona could be aware of that and not Jake but it made me nervous. Maybe he was just playing me and was waiting for the right moment to put the whack on. The thought made me nervous enough to go to the bathroom and take my gun off safety.

"How about a game of shuffleboard?" I asked when I got back to our table. "I haven't played this game in years." I thought keeping busy would calm my nerves.

"I'm pretty good, you know. I hope I don't embarrass you," he bragged.

"It won't be the first time, I've lost face," I said faking a laugh.

I picked up a disk and slid it gently. It landed right in a scoring zone.

"Not bad, Harley. Haven't played in years, huh?

"Beginners luck, I guess."

He slid a disk gently across the board knocking me out of the scoring zone and into the gutter.

"Sorry about that but I play to win," he said smiling.

My second disk almost went into the gutter but hung about half way over the edge.

"That's what they call a hanger," he said. "You get 4 points for one of those if it's still standing at the end of the round."

"Gee, I wonder how long it's going stay there," I said sarcastically.

"Not long," he said while sliding a disk that knocked my 4 pointer off.

At the end of the round, he had 5 points and I had 0.

"Do you have any idea what percentage of the Hispanic kids at LBH High are illegal?" I figured the topic could get a conversation going and help me relax.

"I assume quite a few but I don't really care. Why would I want to seek out this kind of information anyway?"

"You know with budget cuts in education across the board, a lot of people are upset about illegals in the schools."

"Let them be upset," he said abruptly. "Californians don't pay that much per student anyway compared to a lot of other states. The cost to the general public to fund the schooling of these children is negligible. Whenever money is tight, blame the immigrants. This kind of xenophobia has been around forever. It's an American tradition, you know."

He took a large gulp of beer before he continued.

"One of the first lessons I teach my kids in my American Government class is about the Plyler vs. Doe case."

"Never heard of it," I said.

"That's okay. Most people haven't. Plyler vs. Doe was a class action suit filed in the early eighties on behalf of Mexican illegal aliens against the State of Texas and several Texas school districts. The Supreme Court ruled that the children of undocumented workers had just as much of a right to a public education as anybody else. And just like any other children, they are required to attend school. I think that's a good thing."

I took a drink of beer and took it in. I couldn't help but be amazed by the polarization of this man's mind. Did the ideas of Bobby Bernard and Jake Duckworth share the same gray matter or were they in distinct and separate areas of the cerebral tissue? I hadn't a clue. All I knew was that this was one messed-up dude.

I went to the bathroom and called Randy on my cell. He was still in my office arranging for the equipment to be removed. I told him to call me at 9:30 sharp. That would be my signal to end the night with Jake.

When I got back to the bar, Jake was still standing in the front of the shuffleboard.

"Your turn," he said.

Maybe I was imagining it but there was something not quite right about the way he looked at me. My gun was in my coat pocket that was hanging over one of the unoccupied stools at our

187

table. I glanced at it and made a mental note of which side my gun pocket was hanging.

"I think I agree with you Jake," I said after sliding a disk a little too hard across the board.

"About what?"

"About the rights of undocumented children to an education. I mean if they are already in the country what's the point of keeping them stupid?"

"Don't assume they are stupid," he shot back.

"I meant to say uneducated. You know what I mean."

"Do I?" he asked arrogantly. "A lot of people think of themselves as not being racist but when trapped in a corner show their real colors. Remember that guy who played Kramer on Seinfeld? What was his name? Oh yeah, Michael Richards I think. Remember how he lost it when those black guys heckled him at a comedy show? I bet he didn't know he had all that racism bottled up inside of him. That's how it is man. Be careful of who you think you are."

"I hear you. I guess there are a lot of things we don't understand about the depths of our minds," I said hoping my alcohol induced sardonicism would be lost on him.

I started this conversation to help me relax but it only seemed to make me more nervous. I peeked at my watch. It was 9:15. I'd have fifteen more minutes of acting to do. I glanced around the bar. The lonely-looking guy in the corner was still nursing a beer. The group of men who were having a debate about satellite TV was now arguing over whether the Giant's move to acquire Barry Zito was wise. I looked at the TV monitor just in time to see Golden State Warrior Baron Davis miss a three pointer.

I had to keep the night moving even though I no longer felt like conversing with him. Just keep playing shuffleboard, I thought to myself. It won't be long until Randy calls. Focus on sliding the disks gently across the board. Use just the right touch and you could beat this guy. Stay focused on details and try not to take in the whole uncomfortable picture. The thought that Concerta would have been useful in a situation like this entered my mind. I picked up my disk and slid it gently across the board knocking his one remaining hanger in the gutter. I had won the round. He toasted me for a nice shot and that's when my cell phone rang. Perfect timing. I could tell from my caller ID that it was from Randy.

188

"Hi, this is Harley." I began my act. "Oh, I see. That's too bad. Don't worry. Just put some pressure on it. I'll be right there."

"Sorry Jake but I'm going to have to run. My girlfriend's son just fell off the washing machine and split his chin open. I'm going to have to take him to the hospital."

"Sorry to hear that. If you need any help, let me know."

"Thanks but that won't be necessary. See you on Monday. Are you going to hang out here a little while longer?"

"Probably not – just long enough to finish this here beer."

As I was exiting from the bar through the pool room he called my name.

"What is it Jake?" I asked.

"You're an okay guy, I think."

I forced a half smile and continued walking quickly out the back door. What struck me from what he had just said was not the words but his tone of voice. I could have been imagining it but it appeared to be the same voice he used when he became Bobby Bernard under hypnosis. The thought caused the hair on my arms to rise.

I drove straight back to my office and parked on a side street. Walking briskly through the front doors, I peeked into Helen's room. It was already debugged and Randy and his men were just finishing up disconnecting the equipment from my office. A man walked in carrying a tray with two coffees from Starbucks. He handed one to Randy and the other to me. I usually don't drink coffee after 8 p.m. but this was going to be a long night. There was a lot of planning to do for Duckworth's upcoming arrest. We'd have to get a warrant to search his house. The video of the hypnosis session should be enough to get that. We'd need to gather as much evidence as possible. We'd need to determine when and where to arrest him. Given the fact that the Bobby Bernard persona was already suspicious of me meant that the arrest should be made sooner rather than later.

CHAPTER 12

"We need to apprehend this guy ASAP before he hurts anyone else," said Randy as he sipped his coffee. "I'd say by noon tomorrow he should be sitting in a cell down at headquarters."

"I understand what you are saying Randy but I think we should wait until Monday."

"Why on earth would we want to do that? The logistics of a school arrest are much more complicated, never mind the danger to the students. You know that."

"Of course I do Randy. I know it would be much easier to arrest him at home but the friends of Alma deserve some sort of closure and I want them to be a part of this."

"What the hell are you talking about Harley? If something goes wrong, our asses will be sued."

"Calm down buddy. Let me explain. First of all, this is clearly a case of mental illness. As long as this guy takes his Blocodine, he will be Jake Duckworth at school and there will be nothing to worry about. I imagine he will cooperate fully when arrested. As far as I'm concerned, the danger for the students is all but nil. I want to meet with them in the morning and prepare them for this. Mr. Duckworth is probably the most respected teacher at LBJ High. The students look up to him and he motivates them to do their best. This is going to be very confusing for them. I want to be the one to break the news. Heck Randy, I've spent all these months at LBH High. Allow me to end this thing on my terms."

"I'll see what I can do Harley. You know this case is going to be all over the news, once the arrest is made. You've got to be ready to answer the tough questions."

We spent the next couple of hours making plans for Sunday. He would take care of getting the warrant and I would try to meet with Mr. Ramos. I got home that night about 11:30. Still wired from the coffee, I knew it would take time to get to sleep. There would be a lot of planning to do tomorrow and I needed to do something to get my mind off it. I thought it would be a good time to read the last passage of Alma's diary again.

August 20, 2007

Another school year is about to begin. The memories of Mexico are beginning to fade and new memories are being created every day. My love for Ricardo gets stronger as each day passes. I spent a lot of the summer taking an AP Calculus course online so I could qualify for the AP Calculus BC class in my senior year, a class that will give me college credit. According to Mr. Ramos, it's very possible that I will qualify for a scholarship to attend Stanford University. There are a lot of obstacles to overcome until that becomes a reality so I will just keep doing my best. The summer has given me some time to reflect. I met with Mr. Franco from Destinos Latinos about the problems I was having getting real positive change at LBJ High. He gave me some good, practical advice. When I was about to leave his office he mentioned a famous quote: "Accept things you cannot change; have the courage to change the things you can and have the wisdom to know the difference." I had heard that quote before when I was a child and accepted it as good advice. Now, as a 17 year old I have a problem with the first part of the expression perhaps because at such a young age I lack wisdom. How could you know what things you can't change until you've at least made an honest attempt? So I will continue to fight to improve the conditions at LBJ High and prepare myself for college. Speaking of LBJ High, I met with Mr. Ramos yesterday at school. I had arranged to meet him early because once school starts he gets so busy. I reminded him of the problems that still existed at the school. He brought me some cold lemonade and talked about the school from his perspective, something he said he had never done with a student before. He said he wished he had the power to meet our demands but his hands were tied by budget constraints and all the bureaucracy surrounding the "No Child Left Behind" legislation. He has to spend 95% of his time making sure our teachers teach to the standardized tests and if the scores don't improve by a certain amount, he and all the teachers could be fired. The punishment for being the leader of a poor school is losing your job or having your school's funding taken away. After our little talk, I came to the conclusion that he wanted the best for us but his hands were tied. I can even appreciate why he was so annoyed with me. I simply reminded him of the problems that he knew existed. Now I know he would have made the changes we requested in a

191

heartbeat if he could have. There was no need to have thrown salt in his wounds. He was trying.

That is why I will begin my senior year on a positive note. The first thing I need to do is convince the school reform group that we should be a little more sophisticated in our approach to solving the problems at LBJ High. I think we can get Mr. Ramos's support if we focus on the source of the problems instead of just whining about what was obvious. We need to look at how schools are funded and this so-called "No Child Left Behind" cloud hovering over our school. The truth is I probably will not see any real changes during my time as a student. After all, this will be my last year of high school. Sometimes a person just needs to do what is right to shine a light for the people coming up behind them.

That last sentence really touched me. She had no way of knowing how bright that light would become for the people she had left behind. I took a deep breath and tried to contemplate the enormity of the loss and the profound and lasting influence the girl named Alma Vargas had on the people around her. It seems it was her destiny to become a martyr to motivate the disadvantaged youth of the Iron Triangle. I've heard that when someone dies they can live on in the people around them. If that's true, Alma was far from dead. Students at LBJ High were doing positive things that they wouldn't be doing at all if Alma hadn't entered their lives. The action these students were taking would affect other lives and so on and so on. Most people five times her age couldn't claim that much positive influence.

As I rested my head on my pillow, I couldn't help thinking of the things Alma had told me in my dreams. I could just remember the fragments: A person of trust was responsible – Don't be too quick to judge –I would not be complete until I could appreciate the shadow cast by a distant, unseen flower. Aren't dreams just a projection of what's going on in the unconscious mind? Perhaps the dreams in which Alma appeared were more vivid than usual simply because of the withdrawal effects of Concerta.

I rolled over on my side and began to think about tomorrow and Monday. How would I explain to the students that the teacher they loved was responsible for her death? It would be easy if the killer had been Superintendent LeCroc or Principal Ramos. They sure had motive as Alma was making their lives very difficult. It would have made logical sense. But no, it was their favorite teacher and Alma's number one mentor, Mr. Duckworth.

In the morning, I called Ramos at his home. He had already been contacted by Randy and was expecting my call. Needless to say, he was shocked to find out that I was a detective working undercover. He apologized for the hard time he had given me about the mice and asked me if I wanted to stay on until the end of the school year. I politely declined. We made arrangements to meet at LBJ High at noon to plan how the arrest would go down.

I ran down to my office to check on Rosanna. I had her working on an insurance fraud case and she had some questions about surveillance techniques. On the way in, I ran into Helen in the hallway.

"Thanks for all that you did for me. I hope you weren't traumatized by the whole experience," I said.

"It was frightening alright. I hardly slept a wink last night. Anyway, I hope that guy gets the help he needs."

"I imagine his lawyer will use the guilty by reason of insanity defense but regardless, he will probably never be a free man again. Juries don't take too kindly to kids being killed and have little sympathy for mental health issues."

"I wished they wouldn't be so quick to judge. I could see there is a healthy side to this man that is worth saving."

"Don't be too quick too judge," I repeated. "Yeah, I've heard that before. I wish I could be so enlightened."

"You know Harley, if we only understood more about MPD, perhaps people like Jake could be completely cured."

"I guess that depends on if we are evolving or devolving as a society. Today, people will want him locked up. There's no doubt about that. Listen Helen, I've got to run but do you mind if I ask you one question about your practice?"

"Not at all. Spit it out."

"Why do you have your clients ejaculate during therapy sessions?" I asked point blank.

"That's simple. Once the sexual tension variable is removed, it makes it much easier to explore the mind. Trust me, it works. The walls blocking the subconscious just crumble to the ground. Therapists like my sister would never have the guts to try something so obvious. Maybe a new generation coming up in the field of psychotherapy will catch on. I don't know. I guess that

193

depends on if we evolve or devolve as a society." She laughed. "Anyway, Harley I got to get going. I've got souls to heal, you know. Have a good day." With that, the unlicensed but brilliant therapist entered her office and shut the door.

I spent the next 20 minutes with Rosanna showing her how to set up surveillance equipment and then headed down to LBJ High for my noon meeting with Mr. Ramos. When I arrived, Randy and another cop I hadn't met before were sitting in his office.

"Mr. Butler, you sure had everybody fooled," said Mr. Ramos smiling as I entered. "Have a seat."

"I used to be a teacher, you know. That means you made no mistake in hiring me. I've got credentials."

"I know you do. That's why I hired you. Anyway, I'd like to apologize for the tough time I gave you the other day. I thought you were going to turn out to be one of those trouble-maker teachers and I wanted to nip it in the bud before it got out of control. I'm still having a hard time digesting the fact that you were here undercover. This is a first for me as an administrator."

"It was for a good cause and I'm sorry to say that you will need to replace two teachers as soon as possible. Has Randy explained to you about Mr. Duckworth's mental illness?"

"Just a little. Frankly, I am in shock. Mr. Duckworth was a pain in the ass but he seemed like the last person in the world who would harm a student, especially Alma. She was almost like his protégé. Are you absolutely sure he did it?"

"Let's just say we have enough strong evidence to arrest him."

"That's too bad. He was a great teacher," he said with a hint of insincerity.

For the next two hours, we went over the logistics on how and when the arrest would take place. We decided it would happen during period 3. That's when Duckworth would have his prep period and should be alone in his classroom. During the passing break between 2nd and 3rd period all units would get into place. The arrest would be made swiftly and hopefully with few or no onlookers. Police cars on campus were not unusual so there should be little or no distraction to students.

I apologized to Mr. Ramos for defying his request that we disband the Alma Vargas Memorial Club and explained that the club was crucial in gathering information for the investigation. I wanted to meet with the club during period 4 on the day of the arrest and asked his help in gathering all the members to a special meeting room in the library. He agreed.

I would need a substitute for the day and Duckworth would need one from period 4 on. Mr. Ramos said he would sub Duckworth's classes for the rest of the day and would get right to work on finding two new permanent replacements.

"It won't be the first time that we've lost teachers in the middle of a school year," he explained. "Are you sure you don't want to stay on a little longer?"

"You know your offer is tempting but no thank you. I will no doubt miss these kids but I want tomorrow's meeting with them to be the last. I'm sure they will be surprised and may even feel deceived. I can only pray that the positive seeds Alma planted in their minds will continue to grow. They will need a lot of support," I said looking straight at Mr. Ramos. "My biggest fear is that when they find out Duckworth killed Alma they will become apathetic and cynical about the future." I still haven't figured out exactly how I will break the news to them but I've got to prepare one hell of a lesson plan tonight."

When I got back home that afternoon, I sat down at my kitchen table, pulled out a notebook and tried to figure out what I would say to the students. I even made a checklist:

✓ Explain to the best of my ability what MPD is and why the Mr. Duckworth they know and the Mr. Duckworth who killed Alma were two different entities.

✓ Tell them about my past as a teacher, how I became I detective and why I went undercover at LBJ High.

✓ Get the message across that in spite of the world not being fair, they can make the best of the cards they were dealt - just like Alma was doing.

✓ You will have good and bad teachers. Use the good ones as a precious resource. Try to inspire the bad ones to do better.

✓ The world doesn't owe you anything. You owe the world something.

✓ Set goals and use every piece of life energy you have to reach those goals.

✓ There is an Alma Vargas living in every single one of you.

That was enough for the time being. If I planned too much it would seem contrived and insincere. The best thing I could do now was relax and go in tomorrow with a positive mind. I opened a bottle of Portuguese vinho verde and poured a glass. I did some household chores and went to bed early.

As I lay there, I thought about Alma's parents. After the Duckworth arrest, I wanted to visit them if possible. They deserved to know everything. Yes, tomorrow would be a busy day but I felt calm and confident about it. Sleep came easily and the night was filled with pleasant dreams.

In the morning, I had my usual boiled egg and cup of coffee. After skimming the newspaper, I jumped in my Corvette and drove directly to LBJ High. As I walked through the staff parking lot, it hit me that the routine that I had become so accustomed to over the past few months was indeed coming to an end. As I approached the graffiti covered statue of LBJ, I stopped and looked at the exterior of the school. Gray and windowless, it really was an unsightly campus. In contrast, outside it was shaping up to be another one of those beautiful, Indian summer days. I inhaled the crisp and refreshing air. For some unknown reason the memory of my own high school days came to mind. This would have been a great day to cut a couple of classes, I imagined.

It was 7:30 and not too many teachers had arrived yet. I went directly to Mr. Ramos's office to rehearse the schedule. He had arranged a private room in the back of the office for Randy and I to set up communications with the field officers. I was surprised to see Mr. Prince in the room with Randy.

"Mr. Ramos told me everything," he said with a big grin on his face.

I wondered how many other people Ramos had told. This could compromise the arrest, I thought. Hopefully, he was wise enough not to tell anyone who could possibly tip-off Duckworth. We decided to use Mr. Prince in place of an undercover officer near the 900 buildings during period 3 since he would be a familiar sight for students. Looking at a poster on the wall of Jackie Robinson, Randy decided that he would radio us with that name to confirm that Duckworth was alone in his room.

For the next couple of hours, Randy and I engaged in small talk while occasionally radioing field officers to confirm their locations. At 10:15, Mr. Prince's voice could suddenly be heard through the walkie-talkie speakers.

"Did you know that Jackie Robinson was traded to the New York Giants in 1956 but retired before the deal could go through?"

"You learn something new every day," answered back Randy.

We radioed the field officers to give them the green light. If things went according to plan, Duckworth and his Bernard alter ego would be handcuffed and in the back of a cop car in less than 15 minutes. I wondered if he would understand why he was being arrested.

The simple truth was that I was still confused about a lot of things with this case. Were the evil deeds of Bobby Bernard completely hidden from the Duckworth psyche? He was taking Blocodine so we know he was aware of his illness but during the course of a normal day did Bobby Bernard make uninvited appearances? What triggered the change from one psyche to the next? It was all new territory for me. Maybe Helen could give me some insight later.

We got a call from one of the field officers reporting that the arrest went according to plan except that a few students saw and waved to Duckworth as he was whisked away in a police van. That meant it wouldn't be long until the whole campus would know something was up. It also wouldn't be long until the press showed up with their cameras asking questions.

I bid farewell to Randy and walked over to the room next to the library that Mr. Ramos had arranged for my meeting with the Alma Vargas Memorial Club. It had one long table and just enough chairs for the group. Fiddling with my thumbs nervously, I looked at the notes that I had prepared the night before. I knew they'd be useless once the students arrived. All I could do was be myself, tell them the truth and hope for the best.

The passing bell between period 3 and 4 rang. The first one to arrive was Caleb.

"What the hell is going on? I heard Duckworth got arrested," he said with a tint of anger.

"That's what we're here to talk about," I responded.

197

He looked at me with an expression of tense curiosity and sat down. Within a minute, all the members had arrived. I walked slowly around the table making eye contact with each and every one of them and then walked back to the front. Their faces looked hyper-attentive as if they were waiting for survival instructions in an evacuation zone. Ricardo and Ruth were in the seats nearest the front gazing at me nervously. I took a deep breath and spoke.

"What I'm about to tell you may come as a shock but before I begin I want to ask a favor of you." I paused for about 10 seconds before speaking again, nervously looking around from face to face. "Please allow me to finish what I have to say before asking questions or interrupting. The rumor that you may or may not have heard yet today is true. Mr. Duckworth was in fact arrested during period 3."

"What was he arrested for?" blurted out Carnell.

"I'll get to that but again I ask you kindly to let me finish before asking more questions. When I'm done, you can ask all the questions you like. First of all, I am not who you think I am. Let me rephrase that. I am not completely who you think I am. I am a certified teacher and do care about you as students. Several years ago I switched professions and became a private detective. Although I work independently, occasionally local police departments seek my help in solving difficult cases. I was contracted by the Richmond Police Department to go undercover to help solve the Alma Vargas murder. No one on this campus including Mr. Ramos knew that I was undercover."

Their mouths hung open and their eyes looked at me with disbelief. Ricardo's eyes were bulging like they were about to pop out of their sockets. I continued on.

"I interviewed for the job and was hired just like any other teacher would have been. I took the teaching job seriously but at the same time I searched for clues to solve the Alma Vargas case. Although I can't tell you exactly how the case was solved, I think you have already guessed that it has something to do with Mr. Duckworth. I want you to know that Mr. Duckworth is not well. He suffers from a mental illness called Multiple Personality Disorder or Dissociative Identity Disorder. Yeah, I know what you are thinking. What the hell is that? Basically, it means that there is more than one personality living in his brain and one personality may not know what the other personality is doing or thinking. The Mr. Duckworth

198

you know here at LBJ High would never have killed Alma. We know now that there is another personality living within Duckworth and this personality is dark, evil, and dangerous. Duckworth was aware of his illness and was seeking treatment to keep his symptoms at bay. Obviously, the treatment didn't always work."

Ricardo began waving his hand wildly.

"What is it Ricardo?"

"Duckworth didn't kill Alma. He was framed by somebody. I know it. I bet you it was Ramos."

"Try to be calm please as difficult as it is. I know it's hard, maybe even impossible to believe at the moment but I can tell you with absolute certainty that there is a side to Duckworth that you don't know. I've seen the evidence against him and it's very strong. I wished it weren't the case but it is. You need to trust me on this one. Over time, more information will become available to you. Do you guys have any questions?"

"Why would Duckworth kill Alma?" asked Ruth in a quiet voice.

"Ruth, The other personality living within him is evil and that part of Duckworth killed Alma."

She gave me a look of total incomprehension so I tried my luck with Spanish.

"Tiene multiples personalidades, y una de ellas es malvada."

She nodded to show she understood.

"Alma simply had the misfortune of becoming the target of Duckworth's alternative personality. I'm not sure what causes something like this but I do know that Duckworth had a very rough childhood. That may or may not have been the cause. Recently, I've read up on the disorder and it appears that it may be caused by a genetic factor. Anyway, learning more about it will not bring Alma back."

"That's fucked up," said Pedro. "I have a question for you Mr. Butler. Are you going to stick around for the rest of the school year?"

"Unfortunately, I have a lot of catching up to do with my detective work. I had to put a lot of things on the back-burner to take this case. Sadly, today will be my last day. I'm going to miss you guys though. If you ever need a detective, you know who to call."

199

"I want to thank you again for standing up for me the other day. Nobody ever did that before. We're going to miss you too Mr. Butler."

"How can we contact you if we need to," asked Ricardo.

I pulled out a stack of Tantei Man business cards from my wallet and passed them out. They looked them over with curiosity.

"Hey, you have the same address as my therapist," noted Caleb. "That's why I saw you on Solano the other night, isn't it?"

"Yeah, you almost blew my cover," I said smiling.

"What a trip!" he said slapping his palm on the table.

"There's one more thing I want to talk about before I go. I want you guys to make this club even stronger. Not only did you lose Alma but your most inspirational teacher turned out to be her killer. That's an awful lot for anyone to digest. It doesn't mean you should lose hope though. From what I know of Alma, she sure wouldn't have lost hope. You know her spirit is alive in each and every one of you. Just like she did, I'm expecting you to set high goals for yourself and then do everything in your being to reach those goals. I'll be checking on you every now and then to make sure you're keeping up the good fight. I love you guys and mean it from the bottom of my heart."

We exchanged embraces and promised to keep in touch. When I was about to walk out the door, Mr. Ramos's voice came piping through the intercom.

"Good morning everyone and sorry for the interruption. This is your Principal Mr. Ramos speaking. I want all students to know that we will have extra counselors in the main office all week for anyone who feels a need to talk about today's events."

"We have each other to talk to," said Miriam in defiance. With that all 13 members stood up and got into a huddle. I walked over from the door and joined them. We just stood there for five minutes. There was not a dry eye in the circle including mine. Ruth was sobbing uncontrollably. Finally, Ricardo spoke.

"Alma, I know you are here with us. We thank you for your gift of love and compassion. You knew how to live and make the best of each and every single day. It was not fair that your life was taken away, especially by someone you trusted but we take comfort in knowing that a spirit so bright does not end so abruptly. Your light will shine on us for the rest of our lives and we will live our lives respectfully in honor of your memory."

With tears still in my eyes, I waved to them one last time through the window as I exited the library. I took a deep breath and exhaled. My life at LBJ High was over. What an experience! As much as I'd miss the kids, I wouldn't miss the routine.

I headed to the exit quickly. The last thing I wanted to do was to have to explain to teachers who I really was and what I had been doing there. That would be Ramos's job.

I paused in front of the graffiti covered statue of LBJ and read the excerpt from the Great Society Speech on the tablet one more time. *We have the power to shape the civilization that we want. But we need your will, your labor, your hearts, if we are to build that kind of society.* As I stood there, my train of thought was broken by loud rap music coming from a car that was passing by. It was so loud it caused the sidewalk to vibrate. As the car and its occupants continued down the road, the sound slowly faded and my mind drifted far away. I found myself in an urban alleyway in the Omotesando district of Tokyo. It was late afternoon in autumn and I was killing time waiting for the evening to arrive. I had made plans to meet a girl in front of the Laforet department store in nearby Harajuku but that would be hours later. I remembered finding a bench to sit on across from a bakery. A large pot with a lone chrysanthemum set against the wall on the other side of the alley caught my eye. I just sat there and watched as the long shadow it cast changed shapes gradually as the sun slowly set. I remember thinking that this was my moment. Nobody in the world would appreciate that shadow like I am. Most people would just pass on by without noticing and even if they did, they wouldn't contemplate it in the way I was. That shadow meant something to me. It had to. Here I am a decade later standing in front of a statue of LBJ thinking about those brief fleeting moments and that's when it struck me. I think I understood now the strange connection I had between day to day life and daydreams. The shadows cast in those quiet moments were the glue that held my soul together. Without them, I wouldn't be an individual. I paused and thought again about the tragedy of Alma Vargas. I felt comfort knowing that the shadows that Alma cast would be around for a very long time.

Steven Mark Pinto is a San Francisco Bay Area native. His work has been published in the USA and Japan. He currently resides in the East Bay.

www.ingramcontent.com/pod-product-compliance
Lightning Source LLC
Chambersburg PA
CBHW020952180626
46814CB00003B/1057